Beyond Image

Lanny May Freedman

Copyright © 2013 Lanny May Freedman
All rights reserved.
ISBN-10: 1482624338
ISBN-13:978-1482624335

'There always emerges and has always emerged in the long run something for the sake of which it is worthwhile to live on earth, for example virtue, art, music, dance, reason, spirituality – something transfiguring, refined, mad and divine'. Friedrich Nietzsche *'Beyond Good and Evil'*.

'If I create from the heart, nearly everything works; if from the head, almost nothing'. Marc Chagall.

CHAPTER ONE

The new Du Pre gallery is in Holland Park. Michael accompanies his wife, Alice, to the private view of William's first show because he thinks he ought to. She is, after all, one of the exhibitors, albeit a minor one. They arrive at six-thirty. The place is already buzzing. A crowd of press people have turned up, mainly because Josie Wishart and Tom Gerhardt are exhibiting some of their latest works. Cameras keep flashing on and off. The atmosphere is highly charged. William, the owner of the new gallery, looks to be on a high. He's evidently sniffing success. He comes over to Alice, red-faced and beaming. She introduces Michael, but he pays scant attention to him. Shakes his hand briefly, then starts whispering to Alice in an excited, conspiratorial fashion about some *important collectors*.

'Over there, d'you see?' He indicates a couple of men and a woman who are scrutinising a Josie Wishart work – one of her calico stuffed objects series: it occupies pride of place in the centre of the room.

'Definitely *very interested!*' William's hands are trembling with emotion.

He moves away in the direction of the dealers.

Alice well remembers the first time she encountered Josie Wishart's work. It was six months ago, at William's old place.

The gallery was in Piccadilly. One of a multitude, row upon row, that line the maze of narrow back streets behind Old Bond Street, between Berkeley Street and Cork Street. It looked to Alice when she arrived like a prosperous nineteenth century merchant's premises, selling perhaps officers' made to measure uniforms, or Chinese porcelain. The dimly lit window displayed gloomy eighteenth-century paintings of ships at sea, and pale English landscapes framed in heavily ornamented wood and gold.

She had approached the lofty black door with some apprehension, touched its shiny brass handle. Though unsurprised by its forbidding frontage – she'd known what to expect – Alice felt her enthusiasm ebbing away as she walked tentatively through the door.

A rigid-haired blonde sat behind a mahogany desk to the right of the entrance. She raised her head briefly to stare wordlessly at Alice. Her look was unsmiling, accusatory. Her mouth was painted the colour of ripe damsons. Alice smiled, but the woman made no response. She simply lowered her eyes to her desk and returned to her scribbling and paper-shuffling.

Alice cleared her throat, approached the desk. The air was thick with the scent of musk and sandalwood. It smelt expensive. The receptionist underlined some words in the top sheet of the pile, slashing her pen across the page viciously.

'I have an appointment with Mr Du-Pre...?' Alice began. The woman looked up abruptly. 'Mr *Hoskin*-Du Pre?' she hissed.

Alice nodded.

'Alice Wakefield. Two-thirty.'

She proffered another hopeful smile. No use.

'I'll let Mr Hoskin-Du Pre know.'

The reply was forced through clenched teeth.

Alice looked at her watch. Twenty-past. She walked slowly towards the further room of the gallery and eyed the works on display. She noted a remarkable contrast between the two rooms. The first felt oppressive and dispiriting. Overburdened with gloomy wooden panelling and faded green carpeting, it offered a selection of uniformly dull canvases and prints of the same period as those displayed in the window. Ancient lives, corpses. The smell of a finished life was inescapable, like the inside of a wardrobe with the dead person's clothes still hanging inside.

The second room was separated from the first by an archway and short corridor. Alice entered into a different world. It was brightly lit, its walls painted white, the floor bare wood. The works were a contemporary mix. The feel was uncluttered, minimalist, a relatively small number of works on display. The paintings were, in the main, abstracts. There were also a few quasi-expressionist ones. Alice looked at the names. None were known to her, except one: Tom

Gerhardt. She remembered seeing some of his work earlier that year in a small gallery in Chelsea. She had quite liked it. She liked this one too.

Her attention was drawn not so much to the paintings as to other things on display. One in particular fascinated her: a pale small object, about the size of an outstretched kitten. It lay upon a concrete pillar enclosed inside a glass case. She approached it to observe it more closely. It seemed to be made of calico stuffed with horsehair, some of which stuck out of gaps in the seams. It reminded her of a rag doll, stained with age, its limbs parting company with the torso. The doll figure was naked, hairless and sexless. The face was empty of features. It conveyed a sense of desolation. Its title was *'Absence'*.

'Alice Wakefield?'
Startled, she span round.
'Sorry! William Hoskin-Du Pre'.
He stretched out his hand. He also looked at the work in its glass case.
'Interesting, isn't it? Josie Wishart. You may have heard of her?'
Alice shook her head.
'Starting to make a bit of a name for herself. A growing market probably. Well, no, not probably, *certainly*,' he added emphatically.

He smiled. His handshake was firm. He was tall, dark-suited, tinted glasses. His fair hair slicked back, no parting. Gleaming with oil.

'Sorry to have kept you. Come and sit down.'

He led her into a small office, most of which was taken up by a desk, its top invisible beneath a clutter of papers, books, boxes of slides and CDs, photographs and pens. The room reeked of garlic overlaid with citrus.

She watched as he sorted through the transparencies she'd sent him.

'I think we might consider showing some of your work,' he said, peering at them in turn as he held them up to the light.

'This is quite nice.'
He squinted, as he attempted to decipher the title.

'Yee-ess... What is it? Oh yes. *'Untitled'*. Mmmm. Right. And this. This is a nice one.'
He put the slides carefully back onto the desk. Sat back in his chair.

She waited in silence.

'So... I should say, Alice, right from the start. I mean, so we all know where we stand, so to speak...Your stuff...'

He paused, twisted his mouth, glanced up at the ceiling, searching for the right words.

'I mean... your work, well, it's not *exactly* what I'm looking for, to be honest. Look. Let me explain.'

He clasped his hands together and looked again at the ceiling.

'Fact is... We're on the verge now. On the brink. A radical sea-change. Radical. Absolutely!'

He looked fixedly at her, his eyes gleamed, widened behind his glasses, his enthusiasm ignited.

'It's finished, you see. All this.'

He waved his arm in a loose circle around the room, which was also meant to extend to the first room, through which you passed to get to the second, the future.

'All finished. Done with. We've got to move on.'

Alice listened quietly while he explained that when the lease ran out later that year, he was not intending to renew it. He wanted to move lock stock and barrel to new premises, in a different part of London. Start again. New place. New art.

'Simple as that!' he declared joyfully. 'Anyway. To come to the point.' He picked up one of her slides again. 'Your work. Not what you'd describe as *cutting edge* exactly... but never mind. I think it'll find its place. Quite nice. I have to say. Pleasing. The kind of stuff... I mean, you know, would appeal to the sort of collector, well, who maybe isn't quite ready to take on people like Josie yet. Still tottering a bit on the edge? You know? Not that it'll take that long of course. We can't afford to forget him though, can we? Still a market there...'

Alice was not sure how to react. She felt annoyed at his disparaging 'not *cutting edge* exactly' but before she could speak, he was offering her terms and conditions.

'Thirty-five per cent commission. Everything unsold within – say six months, going into stock for a further period, to be agreed, of course. Or returned. Subject to agreement. OK? Agreed? Any questions? Right then. We'll be in touch.'

Thus was Alice's first encounter with William. When she left the gallery, she walked along Piccadilly towards Green Park. She felt oddly flat, unmoved. The prospect of exhibiting her work in the heart of London, once again after nearly twenty years, previously so ardently desired, was now a matter of indifference to her. Why? William had talked enthusiastically of the exhibition he was planning in the spring to launch his new gallery. He wanted to include several of her pieces, he said. So why was she not feeling gratified and delighted, jubilant, even?

It was a bright still day. Unseasonably warm for October. She sauntered slowly, aimlessly, accompanied by an unmodulated rumble of buses and cars which she barely noticed. Her mind was a blank. She had no other appointments that day. Nothing to do, nowhere to go. She moved in auto-pilot. Her steps led her into Green Park. She wandered along the tree-lined paths till she came to the Mall, then crossed into St. James' Park and stopped to sit down by the lake. For a while she watched the ducks as they glided about in search of bugs or crumbs, now and again upturning themselves into the water with their backsides pointing to the sky. Then she headed back to the Mall where she caught a bus. She alighted at Trafalgar Square, with still no clear idea of why she had or where to go.

The National Gallery extended a mixture of promises to the stream of bodies that flowed unceasingly through its portals, speaking a multitude of tongues. For ten minutes or so Alice stood and watched them. What were they seeking? A cultural experience? A box to be ticked on the tourist circuit? A cheap way of passing an hour or two between appointments or trains? Or something that ran deeper – the fumble for meaning, something timeless?

The current swept them into the cavernous interior, they did not look back, passive and trusting, then an hour or two later, the whale would regurgitate them from its belly, whole, unharmed, unchanged for the most part. Yet something might have happened to one or two in the intervening time. Some turning of a corner. Perhaps, even, flung headlong into a dream with no turning back.

Years ago, it had happened to her. She was no more than ten or eleven. A school trip. Escape for a day from lessons and the dreariness of school. But the giggles and fun faded to a barely audible hum. It was Piero Della Francesca that did it. Definitely no turning back then.

How many minds and hearts would be changed today? How many hundreds more would remain untouched, feathers unruffled, memories already emptied as they streamed towards dinner or tea?

She trod familiar passages, moving first through grand, dry, nineteenth century rooms. The brittle scent of antique wood, creaking floor, seats of black leather worn dry by generations of bottoms. Then on to the new wing, a century younger, which, paradoxically, houses the oldest paintings. She greeted old friends: pictures whose every detail she had studied, like the lines on a face, the set of a mouth, the sound of a voice. Family. Lovers. Their dignity undiminished by time or familiarity. Hours she had spent in contemplation of these images over the years. A lifetime of looking and loving. And each time the discovery of something new.

She would contemplate, wonder, question, endlessly copy, mentally and emotionally devouring the paintings. She grew so close to them that her consciousness must surely have been moulded, in part, by these artists and the images generated from their minds.

She stopped before Piero Della Francesca's *Baptism of Christ*. She invariably found herself drawn to the early Italians. This one in particular encapsulated for her the spirituality and stillness of the early Renaissance. She stood in awe before the pale, delicate tones, ethereal blues, creaminess of flesh and earth and the central vertical of the tree echoing the upright Christ. The merest shading of umbers and siennas giving substance to the pale forms. Contrasting touches of rose madder and indigo blue describe the clothes of the angels who watch and wait in the left foreground, the colours echoed in the smaller figures on the right. The perfect balance of the painting was for Alice what art was all about: wherever, whenever; fifteenth century or twenty-first, or five hundredth.

Erasmus, her mentor, used to say that art was like a tree, sprouting branches in every direction, its aim to reach ever higher into air and light. Every branch is different but all point to the same end.

All honest art aspires to the condition of the tree. To reach higher, always higher to somewhere beyond itself. But that place can take an infinite variety of forms. Whatever you think art is for, however cogently you argue your case, you will always find another argument which aims to prove the contrary and is equally convincing. The simple fact is that both are right. All are right. Honesty is the only 'ought' in art, as in life. Whatever you do, just be sure you do it for the right reasons. How do you know? Listen to your heart.

Leaving the Piero *Christ*, Alice moved on till she came to another work which had always intrigued her. Something of a curiosity. By Piero di Cosimo it is entitled simply: *A Mythological Subject*. There is no further clue to its meaning. It is painted on an unusually-shaped panel: long and narrow, a horizontal rectangle. Virtually the whole of the picture is given up to three figures on a grassy bank covered in flowers. A young girl lies outstretched on the ground on her side, facing the spectator. She seems to be dying. Blood flows from wounds on her throat and arm. She is almost naked except for drapery covering her nether regions and thighs. Her feet are clad in sandals. At her head, bending over her with his face and body exuding immense tenderness, kneels a faun. His left hand rests on her shoulder, the other gently touches her forehead. At the girl's feet sits a large brown dog: its head turns towards the girl with an inscrutable expression in its eyes, whether of grief or indifference is impossible to say. In the middle and far distance two other dogs and a cat play on the shore of an inlet on which tiny waterfowl and boats can be seen against a background of blue hills.

Alice did not know what mythological tale was represented. She never managed to find out, but she always found it curiously moving. It seemed to speak of so many things. A poem or a song about love and loss; the pleasures and beauty of the earth; time, death and leaving.

As she gazed and pondered, she became aware of a small boy standing next to her. He was also contemplating the painting. He kept fidgeting from one foot to the other, every so often looking back towards the entrance to the room.

'Are you on a school trip?' Alice heard herself inquire, surprising herself, since she was normally reluctant to engage in conversation with strangers, particularly children.

The boy glanced up at her grumpily.

'I'm with my mum and my sister. They're back there looking at some boring stuff.'

Alice started to move on, thinking the conversation was at an end. But then he began to express comments on the painting.

'It's stupid... The man's got furry legs and dog's feet and funny ears. What's wrong with him?'

'He isn't a man. He's a faun,' Alice told him.

'A what?'

'A faun. The Romans told stories about them. Creatures that were half-man half-goat...'

'Ppfff!' The boy exclaimed derisively.

He grinned and shook his head in disbelief. 'That's stupid!'

Alice went on:

'The Greeks thought of them first. They were supposed to be gods that wandered round the countryside. They were called *satyrs* by the Greeks.'

The boy shrugged.

'Well I think that's stupid,' he repeated. 'Nobody could believe in stuff like that.'

A pause ensued.

'Do you believe in aliens?' Alice asked.

He pondered this for a moment.

'Well…I don't really… I mean, I don't know… I don't completely *not* believe in them. They could exist, couldn't they?'

Alice nodded with satisfaction. 'Well, there you are, then! It was the same with fauns and satyrs. People imagined what they looked like and made pictures of them, like this. You like books with pictures, don't you?' she continued.

He shrugged again.

'S'pose so… Anyway, I still think it's a stupid painting…'

He moved closer to it, peering at it and frowning.

'And why is she a normal lady? Why isn't she a faun as well?'

He span round to confront her, demanding an answer.

'They didn't have lady fauns.'

'Why not?'

'That's how it was.'

He shook his head in exasperation.

'Well that's just weird. Don't make sense.'

Alice could see how ridiculous it must seem. Why go to all that trouble to produce a picture like this? Something that obviously could never really exist. Finding a way of making him see… For some reason this had suddenly become very important. She said:

'Pictures like this… They're supposed to make you think about other things. You know, reminding you of something else…'

She could see he didn't understand. He frowned, looked blank. She was making a mess of this. Hopeless. Try again.

'What do you think the faun is feeling?'

He said nothing for a few moments. He inclined his head and looked searchingly at the painting.

'Sad,' he declared finally.

'Why do you think that is?'

'Because she's his friend. She's hurt. That makes him sad…'

Alice nodded.

'Yes, that's right. So this painting…It's really about being friends, when you care about someone…'

He looked at it for a while.

'I felt like that when my rabbit died.'

Suddenly he caught sight of his mother and sister and ran off to join them without a backward glance.

Late afternoon. The sun was still warm. It streamed through the glass, almost burning Alice's cheek and neck. The bus lumbered haltingly through the rush-hour traffic. It felt like an island of tranquillity. Her shoulder was pressed to the window. She was cocooned in invisibility. Like Baudelaire's *flaneur*, she was the unseen observer. The sunlit swards of Hyde Park lay tender and serene, inviting daydreams.

The bus jarred suddenly and spluttered to a halt like an expiring buffalo. Her eye was caught by a heap of tattered grey clothing dumped on the pavement. It was piled against the railings of the park. On top of the pile perched a rust-coloured cylindrical hat, like a woollen fez. Her torpor vanished instantly as she noticed a black hand protruding from one of the ragged sleeves.

The hand was the only visible sign of the presence of a human being. No face. No movement. Then suddenly there was a barely perceptible shift in the hat's position. A man lay asleep: his head was slumped forward, completely concealed beneath the hat. On his right: another, smaller, heap. It consisted mainly of cardboard boxes, cereal packets, washing powder cartons. They clung precariously together to form a makeshift shelter, partly covered by sections of blue and white striped PVC. Propped up in front of his left sleeve was a brightly coloured cereal packet. On the front a prize draw announced itself. Bold black digits screamed against vivid yellow : *£100,000!!! **Everything to play for!!!***

She watched people as they hurried past. Indifferent. Nothing but a heap of rubbish.

The bus eventually heaved into life. Moving on. Like the passers-by, indifferent. Not one of them stopped even to see whether the hand protruding from the rotting coat was alive or dead.

It made you feel good: posting off your cheque to the *Save Africa Fund*; pressing a coin, with a beam on your face, faking solicitude, into the hand of the *Big Issue* boy (*'please keep the change!'*).

She saw nothing but his hand, but already she was picturing his life. The child he had been, growing up, loved by somebody – a mother. Probably. Or somebody else. Everybody surely was loved at least once, by at least one other soul. Friends. He must have had at least one friend. Dreams. What were his dreams? He must have had plans, hopes once, expectations. Had he lived in warmth surrounded by children? His children? A wife? Did he come home at night after work, his weariness melting away in a woman's embrace? Had his life begun somewhere miles away from here, on the other side of the world? What conjunction of events had conspired to steal the future away, to reduce a human being to a heap of ragged clothing and cardboard boxes dumped onto a London pavement? He was like the dogs and cats that roam wild around the city, searching for warmth and food, a place to sleep. Nothing left of his mind but a jumble of bleary images. Perhaps he could no longer tell which of them were memories and which just dreams of things that perhaps never even existed.

She saw this desolate wreck and thought of the boy in the gallery. She, rabbiting on about *caring*, he, listening in silence, his fidgeting finally stilled. But it was a lie. She felt shame suddenly. The betrayal of a child's trust. Despicable. *How could I, of all people, stand before him preaching about caring?*

A private world of perfect balance. To create and experience this was the ultimate aim. Let's be completely honest. *Caring?* That's rubbish! It didn't matter whether it was her own or others': caring just got in the way.

But she couldn't very well tell him that, could she? Better to have said nothing at all.

It was already dark when she got home. Michael's car was in the garage. She was hungry and tired. She couldn't be bothered with the garage doors and left her car in the drive.

'You're late,' he said, putting his arm round her shoulders. 'Was getting worried. Drink?'

'Definitely!'

While the pizza heated up, she told him about the pitiable sight she had seen from the bus.

His response was predictable.

'People like that – they get what they deserve. Nobody has to end up that way.'

He walked to the drinks cabinet and poured himself another whisky. 'But you don't know what happened in his life.

Some awful tragedy maybe. So he lost the will to go on. Things happen. You've no idea…'

'Nobody has to give up. You can always overcome. It's up to you. Make the best of things.'

'You're too harsh,' she protested. 'It's easy for you to say that…'

He laughed.

'What? Every day I listen to people spinning me their hard-luck stories. People who tell me they didn't deserve what happened to them. If I started feeling sorry for them I couldn't do my job. I have to sort things out. I just look at the facts. Believe me, in nine cases out of ten, what happens to people is their own fault. One way or another.'

No. He's not unfeeling. Of course not. Just realistic.

Alice's eye is caught by a group of reporters forming a rowdy circle around a young woman. She is animatedly addressing the cluster of eager faces. She exudes confidence, relishing the attention. Alice is too far away to hear the reporters' questions, but Josie Wishart's shrill, slightly nasal tones are clearly audible above the general chatter.

Josie wears black velvet leggings that cling to her slim hips and legs. With tall, thick-wedged black shoes. A canary-yellow vest reveals her thin frame and small breasts.

Emblazoned across the front: the message 'CAN U C ME?'; at the back: 'I CAN C U'. She has cropped hair like a boy's. It is coloured in different shades of violet and vermilion, starting in fuschia tones at the nape of the neck, warming to orangey red at the crown, then creeping back to cool lilac at forehead and temples.

Alice, intrigued by the girl, watches and listens.

'It's only life, yer see…Nothin' else. Just the fuckin' EXPERIENCE!' She waves her arms around wildly as she holds forth. The reporters scribble furiously, intent on not missing a single word.

'It's a fuckin' tragedy,' she says in response to a question, ' life. Whichever way you look at it. EXPERIENCE. That's all. Nothin' else…' She stops in mid-flow. The reporters wait in rapt silence, pens poised. She stares at them, blinking, dazzled. A woman reporter breaks the spell prompting her with a question about her calico and solid space series. Instantly Josie is off again, flinging out pithy phrases that fall like hailstones onto the heads of her audience.

'If you wanna know about *relevance*,' now she's almost screeching, 'well just look around you. Yeah… It's not the kinda shit that people go on about… Creepy shit, comin' out of their 'eads… Yeah? Nothin' about *life*… Me, I take stuff that's lyin' around. Stuff you see every day. Stuff you chuck away. Don't matter. What's the point?'

Alice catches one questioner shouting defiantly from the back: 'Does this mean your art is disposable? If so, is it art?' Josie's black-ringed eyes narrow and harden. She directs them fixedly at him for a few moments, then abruptly appears to lose interest. With indifference she looks over them all, waving at someone on the other side of the room. The reporters twist their heads in unison but can pinpoint nobody in particular.

As her final shot: 'If someone gives you a present for yer birthday or somethin', it's your business what yer do with it, innit? It's not the thing, is it? It's you. Yeah.'

She nods emphatically and someone offers her a cigarette. She puts it to her lips, accepts a light, takes a drag and walks away. The reporters take the hint, they make no attempt to follow her.

Alice scans the room for Michael. Maybe he's gone in search of her paintings, displayed in the second, smaller room. She feels not the slightest desire to view her own work. She reflects on relevance. Is it just being connected with life? But what life? Any old life. Any old experience, no matter how trivial? Where's the relevance in that? It's the *something more...* Otherwise, what's the point?

She moves reluctantly towards the second room. Walks in. It's much quieter here. Almost empty. Just a handful of people speaking in low, serious voices. Michael, standing alone before one of her paintings. He looks uncomfortable, wishing he were somewhere else. Her work, exposed to the public gaze, now seems flawed and inadequate.

She feels like the alchemists. On a quest for something that permanently eludes her. Yet she is compelled to continue with the process, pushing ever further and deeper. But the same thing always happens: the alchemy stops just as the object starts to exist, to be: an immutable thing in the world. It is the ponderous *thing-ness* of a painting, its weight, its inescapable actuality. That's the problem. If it could only somehow retain within itself the lightness, the airy mutability which surrounds it while it evolves.

Music is different: insubstantial, flowing, always on the move. Music retains spirit. More than anything she desires to emulate the flux of music. So she purposely leaves ambiguities remaining. She wants people to see her paintings changing as they look at them, discovering something new each time they return.

And yet, despite her efforts, it never works out as planned. The initial elation at finishing is almost instantly obliterated by a sense of failure and shame. And here they now hang, defenceless. No comforting dark cupboard in which to lock them away. No escape.

She is about to join Michael, when she hears William's voice behind her, urgently calling her. 'Alice! Alice! Wait a moment!' She turns to see him careering towards her, almost tripping over, waving to grab her attention, even shoving people aside in his excitement. Finally getting to her side, he informs her in a pregnant whisper: 'I want to introduce you to *someone*.' He seizes her arm and gripping it tightly steers her back into the main room. Before she has a chance to protest or ask him what he's doing, he starts waving enthusiastically to a woman who stands by the door, putting on her coat. She is short and stout, her greying hair cropped into an austere masculine style.

William calls to her: 'Gitte! Before you go!' he smiles engagingly. 'Let me introduce you...' He pushes Alice forward. 'This is Alice Wakefield.'

He keeps his grip on her arm until they are standing alongside the woman.

She shakes Alice's hand firmly and warmly. 'My dear!' she exclaims. 'I am *so* pleased to *meet* you! *Where* has William been *hiding* you?' The tones and emphases of her speech reveal her Scandinavian origin.

'Alice, may I introduce Mrs Gitte Blomberg!' William is practically bursting with glee. His effusiveness makes Alice feel uncomfortable. Was he actually bowing a moment ago?

Gitte Blomberg seizes Alice's hand again. 'Your paintings are so...' pausing to lift her eyes for inspiration, 'so terribly... *expressive*! So abso-*lute*-ly *full* of *e*-nergy! And *colour*! Wonderful! I really love them!' William is beaming till his face could crack.

Alice is confused. Unsure how to reply. William stands, a picture of tension, behind Gitte Blomberg, his mouth has started twitching at frequent intervals. He looks like a nervous parent watching his child perform for the first time on a public stage and praying she doesn't make a mess of it.

William transparently sees himself as impresario, magician and puppet-master rolled into one. Having set up the elaborate staging, he is desperately aware that everything now depends on how well the trick can be pulled off. Everything hangs on the success or failure of the performance. So he watches in agonised suspense the unfolding of the show as it approaches its end.

Gitte Blomberg is far and away the wealthiest of William's collectors, and also the most unpredictable. Her eclectic taste defies categories. There is no way of knowing where her magpie eye will alight. Even so, the fact that Alice's work is turning out to be the surprise hit of the evening is as unexpected to William as it is to Alice.

'I suspected Josie would be too far-out for her,' he confides to Alice when Gitte has gone, 'but I thought she might go for Tom...' Tom Gerhardt with his brash, sweeping abstracts he suspected might capture her interest. 'Have to confess – sorry, Alice – but I never imagined she'd go for your stuff. She says she wants at least two of your paintings. Good news for you, Alice! Good news for us.'

CHAPTER TWO

Alice, from the outside, is exactly like the other guests who sit small-talking round the table. Obediently, she waits, like a child, on the chair allotted to her by Emily, her spine pressed uncomfortably against its hard wooden back. The dining table is polished oak. A single crescent-shaped scratch to the left of the flower-bowl in the centre mars its otherwise flawless gloss. Alice remembers it from previous dinners at Ralph and Emily's.

She sits in her customary place, next to Emily, at the end furthest away from Ralph, who stands at the head of the table, clutching a bottle of Chablis and bellowing in his usual fashion. She also recognises the Wedgewood dinner service and silver cutlery, which Emily has, with mathematical precision, disposed before each of her guests. Hand-painted illustrations of tangerine fruit and gherkin foliage smother Alice's plate. They are partially obscured by a translucent fan of smoked venison slithers, flanked by two sprigs of lettuce, one of palest green, the other pink and crimped, opposite which a baby plum tomato, sliced neatly in two, nestles beside a glistening sphere of scarlet jelly.

Alice observes the geometrical exactitude with which this arrangement has been replicated on every plate. Ralph has abandoned his position now to walk round the table serving wine. He continues to bellow all the while. Something about the '*state of farming today*'. Every utterance is punctuated by a humorous aside and a raucous laugh.

'Chablis, darling?' While he fills her glass, he passes his left arm familiarly around her shoulders. She observes that he does not repeat this gesture when filling the glasses of Anna and Jane.

Back in his place, with a flourish he shouts 'Start away!', though Emily is still not seated. She hovers uncertainly within the arched frame of the hallway, peering worriedly at her guests. She is close on six feet tall, a good three inches taller than Ralph, and brittle thin. Her long limbs appear emaciated. A human stick insect. She wears a short skirt of some clingy fabric, beneath which her calves arch away from one another in the Asiatic manner. Even when she stands with her large feet closely pressed together, her knees refuse to meet. Her body teeters permanently on the verge of uncontrol.

The light from the hall behind her highlights wisps of fine blonde hair, floating about her head like an aureole. Her pale skin is flushed. Satisfied that nothing on the table requires replenishing or adjusting, she moves to her place at the table, opposite Ralph, and pulls out her chair. As she bends to sit, her knee knocks against a table leg. Several hands fly to steady wine-glasses to prevent them keeling over. Emily flushes a shade deeper.

Her smile remains pinned to her face, even while she eats. It occurs to Alice that she has rarely, if ever, seen Emily unsmiling. The design of her mouth makes it impossible for her to stretch it laterally without the upper lip curling back to expose the majority of her top teeth and a large expanse of gum. Evidently, her lips, like her knees, meet only with effort.

Does she carry her grinning mask even into sleep?

The first course passes seamlessly into the second. Plates piled with meat shrouded in a thick puce-coloured sauce appear, and dishes of vegetables of various kinds and colours are shifted around the table.

'What's this we're eating, Emily?' Nigel shouts, his mouth exposing its cargo of half-chewed food. 'Bloody marvellous!'

Emily's grin widens. 'Only pheasant in wine and cream. Nothing exotic!' She speaks in a shrill voice, permanently overlaid with relentless enthusiasm. Everything is always *such fun!!* She turns to Alice, who sits on her right.

'Isn't it exciting!' she enthuses. 'About the new store in the village?' She waits expectantly.

'so fabulous! 'such fun! 'so exciting!'

Alice takes a sip of wine.

'New store? Which one?' she inquires innocently.

Emily's smile barely flickers.

'Haven't you heard, *darling*? D and G, of course! Fabulous clothes! You could only get them in London before. Now it's going to be on our *doorstep*! Isn't it *exciting*?'
Alice smiles non-committally. Emily turns away and starts talking to Tom, who sits on her left.

'What's the point?' Alice hears from her right. Nigel stares at her quizzically. She gives him a blank look. 'The point? Sorry. I was miles away.'
He raises an eyebrow. With faint irritation, he repeats:

'The minimum wage. Going up again. Ridiculous! Don't you agree?'

Agree? Hardly.
She says:

'Well, I suppose it makes sense to some people.'
He tuts impatiently.

'It's insane. Government's completely off its rocker. It'll ruin small businesses. What a shambles!'
Alice puts her knife and fork together. Her plate is half-full. Ralph calls from across the table:

'All fine? Seconds anyone? Loads more. Help yourselves.'
He gestures to the dishes still piled high with variegated vegetables: shades of glistening green, orange and burnished gold.
Now he stands behind Alice, again offering wine, this time a red Burgundy. He waits for a split second before filling her

glass. Staring with effrontery into her eyes. The insolence shocks her, though it is not unfamiliar. Smirking complicity distorts his features. All part of Ralph's well-rehearsed strategy for female conquest.

Not a chance!

She looks across at Anna, who has turned to her right and is telling Tom he is immoral because he works in advertising.

'Can you sleep at night?'

'Oh, absolutely! Why shouldn't I?'

Tom carries on forking food into his mouth. He stops for a second looking to see who is listening. He meets Alice's eye and winks.

'All that lying!' Anna needles tenaciously.

Tom, who works for a London agency, epitomises everything Anna most despises. Urban values, in thrall to the market, the unquestioned pursuit of profit.

Escaping from the City ten years ago to open a small market garden selling organic produce was Anna's salvation from all that. Only Ralph, with his unique combination of cruelty and mischief, could have thought of orchestrating this verbal cock-fight by deliberately placing Tom and Anna together. From the corner of her eye Alice witnesses his delight.

'Why so intense?' Tom queries, irritation beginning to surface. 'Calm down, Anna. It's only window-dressing for God's sake.'

Ralph stokes it up:

'What? Wasn't it your lot that dreamed up that recent load of bollocks on the box? The one about the *'miracle cream'* (he makes quotation marks with his fingers) 'that guarantees a sixteen-year-old skin to ladies on the wrong side of fifty? No need for Botox or the surgeon's knife any more. You know the one?'

Tom shrugs carelessly.

'Well, if you're thick enough to believe that…'

Anna, exasperated: 'That's not the point though, is it? It's not about being believed. It's about what you say. Telling the truth…'

She tails off. Alice fleetingly pities her.

Can't you tell when you're being set up?

She stares at Ralph, willing him to move on. But he hasn't had enough yet. He changes tack.

'You should know all about truth and lies, Mike,' he says.

Alice is relieved. Her husband can always be depended on to calm things down.

Michael sits on Anna's left, between her and Ralph. With a half-wink at Alice he keeps everyone waiting till he's finished chewing and swallowing his mouthful of food, then starts to speak, in his comforting, careful lawyer's tone:

'Truth? Yes. An interesting concept. Different things to different people, of course. Nothing absolute about it. You learn that in my job. Everyone has their own story, you see. That's what I do. Just tell people's stories for them. Their story, their truth. Simple as that.'

He placed another forkful into his mouth.

Ralph not content, wants to push it further.

'I see. So that's how you lawyers get away with bending the truth is it, Mike?'

He chortles and looks around him for support. Tom stares at his plate. Anna nods vigorously. Alice is untroubled, the challenge a commonplace, Michael a consummate manipulator of argument.

Pausing to put down his knife and fork, Michael says:

'First and foremost, I'm a listener. I listen to a story. Then I tell it back. I say "is that what you mean?" I lay their chances on the table. The decision to go further is theirs. If they do, my job is: tell their story as convincingly as I can. That's all it amounts to. No question of bending anything. We never invent, you know.'

He stretches his lips into the winning position.

Un point, c'est tout!

Alice pushes soggy bits of summer pudding around her green and orange plate. The momentary silence shifts to a hum of fragmented talk. Emily catches Alice's eye. Leaning close, she says:

'Haven't seen you for ages, Alice. Ridiculous isn't it? Living so close… How are things?'

Alice says things are fine.

'Girls OK? Let's see… how old are they now?'
Alice tells her.

'Yes of course. Just a bit younger than our boys. John's off to Cambridge next year, you know!'
She pauses for effect. Her large, round eyes gleam with pride. Alice nods.

'And how about you? How's the painting going?'
Alice is about to reply but Emily has already lost interest. Her body still bends towards Alice, her mouth smiles, but her eyes are elsewhere. She follows an exchange of pleasantries, laughs, then rises once more to collect plates and heads back through the archway to the kitchen.

Alice glances at Michael. He smiles back. Ralph is commandeering the proceedings again. Someone brings up organic farming. Probably Anna.

'I'm all in favour of it!' he proclaims, 'but not for the same reasons as some people.'
He looks pointedly at Anna, who purses her lips and frowns. Uncorking another bottle, he walks round the table, refilling glasses.

'It's a religion, you know. Nature! Natural things!'
He puts the bottle down and places his hands together prayer-fashion. Rolling his eyes towards the ceiling, he goes on:

'Pure, unadulterated! Pure, clean soil uncontaminated by all those nasty chemicals. Pure, clean carrots and cabbages, crawling with pure, clean slugs and bugs!'

Muffled titters from around the table greet this utterance.

'It's all the same to me. If them up there,' he jerks his thumb upwards, 'that decide our futures see fit to pay us twice as much to grow cabbage whites and weeds than wheat and barley, who am I to complain?'

He empties the remains of the bottle into his glass and beams.

Anna cannot contain her irritation and insists on pursuing the argument, though it is plain to all that Ralph is relentlessly playing with her.

Alice switches into disconnect mode. Her mind, like a balloon detached from its moorings, drifts into a solitary world, free from voices, time or boundaries. She visualizes the painting that stands on her easel at home. Strokes of thick green and umber. She has been dragging the paint around the canvas, exploring. A new one. Just a few days old.

The paintings she makes are like doors opening onto a separate reality. Not pictures. Anything but pictures. Yet sometimes they seem to show glimpses of things you know. The sea. Shining pools. Patches of light in the midst of shadows. Rocks or dense vegetation. Foliage with sunlight beckoning through a forest. Her intention is not to represent nor even resemble. She wants them to grow and exist by themselves, like natural things. Eliminating control. Her own part in the generation of her works limited to watching and selecting. The painting, on the whole, paints itself, grows into itself.

She had to drag herself away from it to come here. She detests dinner parties. Is sitting here enduring it, longing for its end, only because of Michael. For him this ritual is more than mere enjoyment. The presence of others is so essential to him. He has a need to communicate, no matter how flippantly. He abhors solitude. Needs to sense the proximity of his fellow-creatures, sounds of voices, passing traffic, the mingled signs of other lives evolving around him. He finds it reassuring.

Alice is the opposite. Her ideal, as portrayed jokingly by Michael, is to live alone in an abandoned monastery with sound-proof rooms on a desert island.

The dining-table, arrayed with half-empty dishes and glasses and the flickering dregs of candles, stands abandoned. Everyone has moved into more intimate surroundings, a dimly-lit room with beamed ceilings and walls, an open fireplace and striped pink and grey furniture.

Brandy and port now make the rounds. The talk reflects the alcohol already consumed and has begun to degenerate from polite to coarse. Ralph is describing someone's sex life – his own perhaps – as 'genitals occasionally meeting'. It is late. The time for embarrassment has passed. A kind of sloppy conviviality washes over them.

As people start leaving at last, Alice climbs up the stairs unsteadily to the bathroom. When she emerges, Ralph is standing by the door. She moves aside to let him pass. He grabs her deftly by the waist and holds her fast. His breath reeks of alcohol and meat. She feels his mouth, soft, wet and hot on her neck. She twists away. She is repelled yet, at the same time, curiously excited. She pulls away and he releases her. He watches her and grins as she stumbles down the stairs, gripping the banisters to save herself from falling.

She lies beside Michael as still as a stone, willing him not to touch her. His foot brushes against hers and instantly, depressingly, he is awake. She braces herself for the routine. Stroking followed by squeezing followed by the slow, creeping descent down her body, mouth and tongue coming into play. As his excitement heightens, he proceeds to probe her interior places, as if testing the waters.

And so on.

Sometimes, she amuses herself by glancing at the luminous digits of her clock, mildly interested in timing the operation. Its brevity always a surprise. Finally, the clambering denouement. A series of thrusts, a final surge, a few grunts and swallows.

All over.

Impassively, she watches the sequence of events unfolding. She sees them both as they silently engage in this wordless absurdity. This has nothing to do with her. She herself is miles away. Swimming along in dark rivers. Flying through bright white space with gulls that swoop and scream. Running up and down the hills and valleys of an exquisite melody. Something played by John Coltrane or Charlie Parker or sung by Billie Holiday.

The abdication of desire. Ralph's words 'genitals occasionally meeting' and the sniggering that ensued echo in her mind.

It wasn't always so. Long before Michael. Once there was Justin. Times when her body was suffused with longing. Desire that drew every part of her on to its inevitable extinction, yet complete in itself. Different in nature to the act of consummation and greater, even, in intensity.

The orgasm itself she compares to ice-cream. Too easy. Too available. But almost never living up to its promise. Fated now, it seems, to be given endless ice-creams without ever really wanting them. At forty-three, can she really expect more?

One cold autumn day, Alice was in Anna's kitchen, drinking coffee. Anna, in a rare moment of intimacy, began without warning to describe to Alice the way she and Nigel had come to terms with, as she put it, the 'fading out of passion'.

'We had sex one night. And we just decided then and there, both of us at the same time, to stop, you know, *pretending*.' She grabbed a bunch of her long, straight fair hair and began smoothing it over and over in the cleft between her thumb and forefinger.

'We didn't want to split up. Not over that. I mean, we do get on, and everything. We simply couldn't imagine going off and living apart. I mean – it's been so long… So we decided to have this… arrangement.'

She nodded several times.

'We both enjoy sex, you see. But not with one another. Unfortunately,' she added, with a short laugh. Then, gently probing, she continued:

'But you and Michael… You seem to have something special you two…'

There was a questioning pause. Alice said nothing.

'You're lucky.'

Alice was taken aback by Anna's confession. Usually they nattered on about children, cooking, shopping. The prospect of colluding in this distasteful tete-a-tete filled her with nausea. But there was no stopping Anna now. She seemed compelled to recount more and more about the *Arrangement*. She brimmed over with delight and pride. How contemporary, how sophisticated. She even started to list the names of men she had bedded, some of whom were known to Alice.

'Ralph. Of course. Who hasn't slept with Ralph? And Tony – you know, that builder from down the road. And Jamie Bannen. D'you remember? The BBC man. You met him here once.'

Alice looked pointedly at her watch. She made an excuse and hurriedly departed.

The day was flooded with sun. Alice sped thankfully out of Anna's drive in the direction of Eastminster, where Jennifer lived. She drove through a riotous medley of colour. Lemon yellows, mild shades of green, ochres, rust-reds and amber gold. Showers of leaves, caught by the wind, whirled and cavorted through blue and white space, resplendent in death.

Trees and their branches combining with telegraph poles and their wires, cast shadows along the roadway, creating an intricate filigree. The linear dance ornamenting the blank grey surface. Leaves bounced, leapt and chased each other in wild hilarity making a playful counterpoint to the flat, formal curlicues.

A recording of Clifford Brown playing *'Body and Soul'* lifted her heart as she drove. She hummed rapturously. Her senses were replete. For a moment she forgot where she was going. She sped past the turning that led to Jennifer's house and had to stop in the next village and back track.

She was late. Ten minutes or so. As she parked outside the Morgans' gate, she noticed Jennifer's father standing at the front window. He lifted his wrist to examine his watch pointedly. She apologised, offering some excuse. Could hardly say that Clifford Brown's trumpet-playing, the golden dance of the leaves and the shadow tracery on the road were to blame.

Jennifer was ginger-haired, eleven, small for her age. She wore her hair in a thin plait that snaked down her back. Train-track braces concealed both rows of teeth and caused her to speak with a lisp. When Alice entered the living-room she saw Jennifer sitting glumly at a table in a dark corner by the fireplace. For a month now, Alice had been trying very hard to raise Jennifer's standard in French to the entrance requirements of a nearby independent school. Her parents were determined she would get in, by hook or by crook.

Alice pretended not to hear the father tut-tutting behind her back. She resisted the urge to wheel round and tell him he was a nasty little weasel who understood nothing about the meaning of education or a child's mind or creativity or beauty or Life, at all. She asked herself why on earth she'd agreed to take Jennifer on when she'd decided long ago to give up teaching. But seeing Jennifer's face light up with one of her infrequent timid half-smiles, she remembered why.

The Morgans, in search of private tutors, had contacted the teaching agency she ran some months ago, but not content with telephone booking, had visited in person, dragging Jennifer along. Though she managed to find tutors for maths, English and science, no French tutor was available on her books at the time. Taking pity on the waif-like creature sitting dismally between the Weasel and the Walrus, Alice impulsively agreed to do it herself, not entirely knowing why.

When she herself was about ten or eleven, there had been a timid girl in her class, who had no friends. Her name was Veronica. She too had ginger hair, with a curiously aged face and she walked with a limp. Every playtime a group of girls would approach the wretched girl, pulling her hair and taunting her until she dissolved into tears. Alice and her best friend, Imogen, tried to protect her in the only way possible, by annexing her to their twosome, at the risk of derision and opprobrium from the rest of the class. More agonising to Alice was the fragmentation of the cherished Alice-Imogen partnership. Friendship was sacrificed at the altar of altruism. Though Veronica left the school that year, Imogen and Alice never recovered what they had before. Something had gone.

At the time, neither understood the reason for their drifting apart. Each gradually gravitated to separate groups of friends and after the passage of just a few months, they hardly had a word to say to one another any more. After their early school years, so close they were like the two sides of a coin, their estrangement happened with what seemed to Alice at the time inexplicable rapidity. When reflecting on it in later years, she concluded that Veronica had engaged the friends' pity to such an extent that they had concentrated the whole of their combined energies on protecting her from the assaults of others less sensitive and, in so doing, Veronica, the victim, had unwittingly become the lynchpin of their union. Once this had disappeared, there was nothing to hold them together. Rather like a marriage that falls apart once the children have left.

The French lessons were held on Saturday, which meant that the Weasel was invariably at home. As soon as Alice arrived, he would install himself in the bay window seat opposite the corner table. He stayed for exactly ten minutes, loudly rustling the pages of his newspaper. His presence, laden with disapprobation, stifled spontaneity. He eventually closed the newspaper, folding it slowly and carefully and laying it down on the gleaming walnut table by the window, before finally leaving the room. Instantly, there seemed to be an influx of light and oxygen. Purple-black clouds gathering for a storm had suddenly been dispersed.

His departure signalled that the lesson could now be turned on its head. Throwing aside the painful process of wading through the quagmire of past tenses, irregular verbs, number, gender and so on, Alice led Jennifer into a realm of play. The Weasel had advocated 'Repetition! Repetition! Repetition! Hammer it home! Once ingrained, never forgotten!' but Alice knew Jennifer would never move an inch along that route. Alice stressed this to him repeatedly, but he was immoveable. He was the kind of man whose conviction that whatever he believed was right never wavered for a single instant, even should he be confronted by monumental evidence to the contrary.

'Let's imagine...' Alice began. And instantly, Jennifer's willow-green eyes brightened and her mouth, struggling through the burden of wire and metal, softened into a wide grin.

'Let's imagine we're in the middle of a forest. *La forêt.* We're lost. *Perdues.* There are lots of animals about, but no people. Some of them are friendly, but not all of them. Luckily, they can all speak, but they only speak French.'

They played alternate roles. Lost children, or animals. And as Jennifer's absorption in the game intensified, she began to use the language naturally, no longer frozen into silence by the terror of making a mistake. Alice gently cued and corrected without seeming to be doing other than playing her part.

'*Regarde! Voila le chemin. Tu vois? Le petit chemin par la. Depeche-toi. Il est déjà tard. Quelle heure est-il? Bientot il fera nuit. Ou allez-vous? On est parti ce matin a huit heures. On est tres fatigue.*'

Alice covered sheets of paper with drawings as they played: animals, trees, pathways, figures. She wrote words and phrases to accompany the drawings. Finally, as the lesson drew to its end, she wrote down some exercises.

'Think about these,' she told Jennifer, 'and write a story about what happens when they find their way out of the forest. Pretend you're one of the animals and you want to go with them. Tell me next time.'

Alice recognised in Jennifer a creative imagination which gave limitless scope for role-play. She loved teaching this way, but it could only work with people like Jennifer, who were born with some potential for rhapsody. For the rest, only the grammar-based method would work. She feared that John Morgan would put his foot down and insist they return to the only style of instruction he understood. Already he was starting to hover around at the close, casting a suspicious eye over Alice's drawings. He was unimpressed by Jennifer's enjoyment, being of the view that pleasure and education should not mix. Poor Jennifer. In the face of odds like these, how would she ever manage to keep her creative spirit alive?

As a child, Alice had loved books. Some she read and re-read with undimmed delight. One of her favourites told the story of two children's adventures in a place called *'Eiderdown Country'*. The only way into this land was to stare in a special way at the eiderdown on your bed. Your eyes had to bore into it till they almost popped out of their sockets. Then, miraculously, the quilt would disappear. And there you were, right in the middle of Eiderdown Country. She read it so many times she could recite it almost word for word. And each time, she felt as if she had slipped seamlessly from one world into another.

Rivers of incandescent silk snake downward through deep reds and purples, plump and soft. Swathes of black velvet flecked with vermilion. I follow pathways along hills of warm ochres. Umbrageous forests enclose me in their embrace. Birds of many kinds and shapes with multitudes of coloured feathers flap their wings and draw me into their flight.

High above land, I see that everything has boundaries. Hills, forests, rivers and seas, stone walls, rocky cliffs. Wooden and steel fences are knives that slash this land. I fly on, longer and further. The wounded land disappears. I fly through mists of blended water and light, evanescent in violet-greys, forever nearing blue, but never quite.

I am without beginning or end. I am.

Growing up in London in the late nineteen fifties, Alice had been lucky, very lucky. A secure, unthreatening, comforting world. Walks in Regent's Park, Marmite sandwiches, lemon squash, boiled eggs for tea, *'Children's Hour'* on the radio. Not even a hint of the so-called post-war austerity she first heard about only years later. She read about it with astonishment in a newspaper article.

Austerity? What austerity?

Her life began in a tall shambling house on the borders of Bayswater and Kensington. One of a quiet square of similar houses overlooking a private garden, thick with well-tended flower-beds, lawns and ancient chestnut trees. The whole of her childhood was spent in this house with her parents, her father's parents and David, her brother.

Julius, her father, was a musician and her mother, Estelle, a stage actress, who became a theatrical agent soon after Alice was born. The house resounded constantly with music. Recordings of big bands, Benny Goodman, Count Basie, Duke Ellington. Julius playing gypsy music on his violin, or practising Heifetz, or going over the latest orchestral bits and pieces for his next gig on violin or tenor sax. He supplemented his income with session work at recording studios. He wasn't particular.

'I'm just a jobbing musician,' was his stock response when Estelle complained about him wasting his talent. 'Who cares? It's all music. Anyway, I play from the heart. That's all that matters.'

Alice understood why he truly harboured no regrets. He might have been a concert violinist and enjoyed a glittering classical career, but fame didn't matter to him. He had a philosophical, easy-going nature. He could find something good in the very worst of circumstances.

'So what do you expect? I'm a Jew, after all.'

He used to repeat this frequently and always accompanied it with a stereotypical lifting of the shoulders accompanied by a clownish rolling of the eyes heavenwards.

He carried his Jewishness casually, with a humorous irreverence that annoyed his mother, Edda, but amused everybody else. He had no time for Jewish orthodoxy or outdated rituals. In the early years, in Prague, before the war, he had been sent to *cheder* with the other children, learnt Hebrew, attended synagogue. But that was so long ago, he hardly remembered any of it. He found it absurd that having lived in England for over twenty-five years, his mother still refused to eat pork, or have meat or milk at the same meal, or travel anywhere on wheels on a Saturday, or continued obdurately to light the candles every Friday evening for the Sabbath.

Everything about the Jewish experience for Julius exemplified varying degrees of absurdity. Everything, apart from Jewishness itself, that is. Something, somehow, remained after every particle of the religion and its practices had been thrown by the wayside. Something about what you were. Something indefinable, but whatever it was, it ran deep.

Alice absorbed the Jewishness of her ancestry unquestioningly, almost indifferently, neither valuing nor regretting. It was just one of all the different pieces that came together to make up her identity, part of the list – being a girl, having brown eyes, coming into the world at a certain specific time, in a certain specific place – something intrinsic. It was not a matter of choice. It rarely entered into her consciousness, yet it formed the bedrock of her life, an almost inaudible whisper somewhere in the furthest regions of her mind.

When Julius first announced he was going to marry Estelle, the daughter of French Catholics, his mother turned white. For a moment he thought she was about to faint, but it was rage that was draining the colour from her face. She told him he might as well pack his bags *now*. She would *never*, she shrilled, *never* have a *shickse* living in the same house. He said he didn't want to stay there anyway. He was sick and tired of her tantrums and her stupid ways that had no place in the modern world. She ranted and screamed.

'Well and good! You break off your engagement or I never speak to you again!' and she stomped out of the house, slamming the front door behind her.

It was Josef, Alice's grandfather, who defused the crisis. As he always did in the end. Every time. Logic prevailed. It had to. He could see that Julius would not be deflected, however plaintively Edda wailed on about dishonouring the family, dishonouring his race. No matter how strident her vows to disown him, he would not be moved. There was a stubbornness about Julius that would not be broken by anything, including the threat of physical pain. He had been that way all his life.

He was an unshakeable then as the time when, as a small boy, he insisted on bringing back home an emaciated black kitten he had found starving in a back street of Prague. He kept her at home, in the face of the combined opposition of both his parents. Threats of locking him in his bedroom without food, or even beatings had no effect. Mimi stayed. She shared the family's life for the few years that remained before they themselves were forced to leave.

CHAPTER THREE

In an unusual demonstration of beneficence, William decides to throw a party a week after the private view, to celebrate the opening of the Du Pre Gallery. Michael is away on business, so Alice goes alone. William lives in a penthouse in Fulham, near Putney Bridge, with views over the Thames. The party is taking place in a large room which reminds Alice of the reception area in an exclusive contemporary hotel, angular furnishings, pale leather upholstery and a number of large abstracts adorning the walls, everything coloured in neutral shades of white, cream and mushroom, including the abstracts.

A dark-skinned man dressed in black and white catering gear opens the door and takes her coat sullenly. A female version, equally unsmiling, materialises offering a tray of drinks. Alice swiftly grabs a glass of champagne and downs half in one go. Feeling fortified, she proceeds into the fray. There are no more than about thirty people she reckons, but the noise is ear-shattering. Speakers placed high up in every corner pump and throb, the music itself reduced to nothing but the regular thud of its bass-line. Even this is almost drowned out beneath successive layers of shrill chatter, shrieks of laughter and clinking glasses.

Nobody, apart from the taciturn catering staff, appears to have noticed Alice's arrival. She feels a powerful urge to skulk away. She would hardly be missed amongst this dazzling array of semi-celebrities and wannabes. She stands on the fringe, contemplating their posturing, yet at the same time feeling like a lump of over-kneaded, unrisen dough that has somehow found its way into the midst of a cloud of freshly-baked brioches.

Another champagne tray floats past. She helps herself to a second glass. She downs as much as she can of the fizz without choking, then heads purposefully towards William. She's just spotted him deep in conversation with a man she knows from somewhere.

Seeing her approach, William opens his arms wide in welcome. He kisses her on both cheeks.

'Alice, you know Ben Grantley, I think?'

They haven't met, but Alice knows of him, of course. Difficult not to. His works can be seen in a scattering of galleries around the world. Even the Tate has a couple. He narrowly missed being short-listed for the Turner Prize not so long ago. Grantley's work is favoured by critics of a philosophical bent. Even the wider public knows about him because one of his more monumental pieces has been purchased recently by some local council somewhere up north. It stands on a hill in the centre of the town's recreation ground. The acclaim has been mixed.

'I confess I'm not familiar with your work,' he tells Alice, looking down at her from his six feet plus height. 'Do you mainly exhibit in this country? I must have missed you. I'm away such a lot these days…' He has a long, thin face, with a beaky nose and curly hair that was once jet-black but is now mainly grey. He peers down at her through narrow, rimless glasses. There is something raven-like about him.

Alice observes that he averts his eyes each time he comes to the end of a statement. Disconcerting. He gives you the impression that he has no further interest in a subject as soon as he's finished delivering his view. That there is nothing more to be said, that his is – must be without question – the definitive statement about anything. That he can hardly wait to move on straight away to something else.

'Well, to be honest,' Alice replies, addressing the side of his face, 'this is my first important exhibition for years. So you wouldn't probably have heard of me.' She flashes an ironic half-smile in his direction, but he doesn't notice it, since his eyes are darting between diverse groups of chattering drinkers.

A sharp twist of the head and he zooms back.

'I do think it was brilliant of Will to get the mix exactly right for the show, don't you?' he announces, having twisted his head to look intently at her.

Alice assents with a silent nod. A glance at William, enlivened by a smile lasting no longer than a split second, drifts along the arc of his gaze as it returns once more to its natural position, locked into middle distance.

It's a bit like talking to someone with a lazy eye. You have to concentrate on addressing the good one, otherwise you get the feeling you're not being listened to. In Grantley's case, it's twice as disconcerting since neither eye looks at you. Both are too busy roving round the room trying to spot someone else more interesting, more important, or more influential he can alight on to go and expound to.

Alice presses on: 'It was probably wise not to include you, don't you think, Ben? I mean, your work would have looked a bit – well – out of place in the show. Don't you agree?'

His head twists again from profile to full face.

'How so?' he enquires with a note of faint concern.

'Well, I mean… they depend so much on print, don't they?'

'I'm sorry?'

Out of the corner of her eye she notices William fidgeting nervously. William isn't Grantley's dealer. He and Ben have been close friends since Eton. Having, in increasing bafflement, followed the rising acclaim for his work among critics and the art-going public over the years, Alice has long wanted to meet Grantley face to face.

Benedict Grantley is a sculptor specialising in cast-iron, or occasionally bronze, representations of the nude male figure, usually in a rigid upright pose and highly simplified. Like the Ancient Greek *Kouroi* from which they derive, the figures are, to all intents and purposes, almost exact replicas of one another, all appearing to originate from one and the same mould. Unlike the *Kouroi*, however, their heads are virtually faceless, with only the faintest suggestion of features. They seem to have been stifled, mummy-like, beneath layer upon layer of bandages.

'All those acres of print,' she continues, 'you know what I mean, Ben. Lots of people know your name. But how many do you think really know what you're about?' She pauses for an instant, the question hanging ponderously in the air between them. His brow creases slightly as she continues:

'This show – well I doubt any of us is as well-known to the general public as you. Well, I know that. Even Josie. But even though we're all so different, I think there is a common denominator. What I'm trying to say is – well – you know, it seems to me we're all of us trying to make art that speaks for itself, aren't we?'

William buts in hurriedly, sensing trouble.

'Alice,' he says, 'Ben has his own dealer. I'd have been delighted to show his work here, but unfortunately…' He raises his hands and eyebrows in unison regretfully.

But Grantley isn't happy to let Alice's comment pass. Ignoring William's intervention, he presses her further. 'Why do you say that – about art speaking for itself. As if mine didn't? That's plainly what you meant, isn't it? But isn't all art dependent on words, to some extent at least? I mean, the so-called spontaneous gut reaction theory to art – it's all a myth really isn't it? We all know it comes down to association, interpretation… And that means words.' He nods several times to emphasize how strongly he agrees with himself.

'Really? D'you think so?' Alice persists. 'But you remember what Bacon said: "if you can say it, don't paint it!".' She flashes a satisfied smile in his direction.

'Bacon!' he exclaimed, dismissing him with a contemptuous 'pfff!' 'I wonder how many Bacon devotees would have turned into devotees without the help of all those acres of print, as you put it.'

Changing tack, in an innocent tone she begins: 'I've often wondered, looking at your work, whether you feel yourself to be, so to speak, carrying on a sculptural tradition. You know, something that started with the Egyptians and the Greeks and ended up with you? The same sort of simplicity. Do you feel that, actually?' She looks up at him reverentially. He seems taken aback suddenly, just a bit.

'Well…' hesitating. He gazes into the middle distance as if searching for inspiration. 'I suppose… I'd like to think… Well, I'd like to believe that I do share with the Ancients something of their formal simplicity… That wonderfully pared-down quality.' He sighs briefly. 'Purity of line,' he goes on, still not looking at Alice, 'Of course, *my* figures, you know, have – I think you have to say – more of a *universal* significance really... The sculptures of the Ancient World, all serving particular purposes.' He nods again emphatically several times. Alice makes an attempt to speak, but he talks on, ignoring her.

'They represented gods, heroes, famous athletes... They served to mark the graves of men – individuals – who were looked up to in their community.'

Alice thinks *so what else is new?* but remains silent. He's off on his favourite trip. A well-rehearsed and oft-repeated spiel, given that he's one of the contributors to a soon-to-be-published book entitled *Contemporary British Sculptors By Themselves*. Alice knows about it through William. *Can hardly wait to read it...*

Her attention drifts across the room to a couple of men dressed in identical tight jeans and black shirts open to the base of the chest, moving together like entwined serpents to the rhythm of the music.

Meanwhile, Grantley's voice drones on. She picks up the thread a few sentences later. '...the Greeks themselves – they didn't think of their sculptures that way. It's us that have imposed the ideal thing...'

Alice interrupts: 'So is that how you see *your* work then? As a kind of ideal representation?'

Grantley grows keener, seeming to warm to the opportunity she is handing him. Turning to face her for the first time since his exposition began, he begins to hold forth with gusto: 'Well, no. No... Not exactly an ideal. More a kind of universal symbol. I mean, you could describe it as the relation of Man to the world.' He giggles, then swiftly covers his mouth with his hand in mock apology.

'Oops! Sorry. Not supposed to say that these days... Should talk about human beings, shouldn't we?' He nods in her direction, 'Women not excluded. Naturally!' Then with eyes misting over, he turns once again towards the middle distance. Gazing beyond the chattering groups, he seems to have entered into a transcendent world visible only to himself.

'I'm sorry,' Alice interposes in a matter-of-fact voice. He casts a look of annoyance in her direction. 'I mean, it's very thought-provoking and all that, but... well... I don't quite understand. OK, obviously they're meant to be symbols. Like you said. That's clear. After all, they all look exactly the same, more or less. But I don't understand the bit about relating to the world. How does this work? I mean – how do we exactly *see* this in your figures? In *themselves*, that is? With the greatest respect I do think some people might say it wasn't blindingly obvious... Sorry, I don't mean to be rude.'

Alice sees his lips tighten. She notices that a muscle under his right eye has begun to twitch. He raises his hand to the offending place, as if to wipe it away, but the twitch continues. His former sublime expression has vanished from his face like the moon disappearing behind a cloud.

His voice is terse: 'The siting of my figures is all-important. Naturally.' He smiles quickly at Alice, a smile which combines disdain and pity. A look reserved for the poor unfortunates fated to live out their lives in ignorance of the luminous world of Absolute Truth.

She arranges her face to light up with an apparent flash of understanding. 'Aaah yes! I see! So it's their *site* that makes them significant then! Being in a landscape, on top of a hill. Up a tree. Perched on a roof. Or peering over a wall. Even up to their knees in a river perhaps? Yes I see. I get it now. So you're supposed to look at them and imagine *yourself* gazing out – over a valley, or a city… *Relating* to everything. Is that it?'

He responds gruffly: 'Yes. Well, more or less… You're simplifying a bit.'

She is tempted to suggest that if relating is all, it would hardly matter what kind of human facsimile you stuck on top of a hill. Even a shop mannequin would suffice. Why not cast one of those in iron or bronze?

But he is already retreating. His sleeve has been grabbed by a twenty-something nymph in apricot silk. Alice follows his progress across the room as he is dragged willingly away to join a group of similarly nubile devotees of both sexes.

Perhaps because of the quantities of champagne she's imbibed she feels her almost empty stomach churning away dangerously. She can no longer avoid the warning signs. She staggers out in search of the bathroom.

Somebody – she doesn't know who, at some point soon after this, bundles her into a taxi. She wakes up next day at about three in the afternoon in her brother's flat in Islington, with a splitting headache and barely any memory of how she got there. Apparently, as David later told her, her mobile had rung when she was laid out on the floor, blotto. Someone had answered it, but too late to speak. A message was left by Michael, calling from Berlin. William had scrolled through her contacts list and gleefully pounced upon David's number, the obvious solution to the embarrassment of having a semi-comatose female littering his expensively-carpeted floor. David gave him his address and a taxi was summoned post-haste. The last thing William wanted was to have an inebriated woman stumbling about the pristine flat embarrassing everybody, including herself. His relief, David told her, at having found someone to offload her onto, was palpable.

CHAPTER FOUR

For Alice and David: a little memoir
(and also for their children and their children's children and so on)

I think my greatest sorrow was having to leave Mimi, my cat, behind. I minded more about that than leaving anybody or anything else. My grandparents, my aunts and uncles, my cousins. More even than my friends. When I stroked Mimi's silky back for the last time and said goodbye to her, it was a veritable torture for me. I left her with my auntie Hana. She held her in her arms, like a baby. I cried from that moment almost with stopping till we arrived in England. Auntie promised me she would bring Mimi later, when they followed us. I didn't believe her. I knew I would never see her again. Funny, but it never occurred to me that I would never see my auntie again either.

Your grandfather – that is, Alice and David's grandfather, I mean – wasn't a Zionist. Far from it. Josef had no interest in Zionism. Though his family nominally belonged to the Jewish community in Prague, his father had owned a small shop selling hardware and ironmongery goods and cared only for furthering his business and profits. He had no time for politics or ideology or religion, any of those things.

My father and his brother went to German schools right from the start, as most Jews did then, in Czechoslovakia. I did too, before I came to England. Anti-Semitism was not an issue for my father, any more than it was for me. For my mother, it was a different story. Being a rabbi's daughter she had been steeped in Judaic culture from the day she was born.

As early as her mid-teens she became heavily involved with the Zionist movement. She was a fully paid-up member of the Theodor Herzl Association, needless to say. I can remember a book – hard black cover and well-worn, looking shabby even then – it occupied pride of place on top of the bookcase in her room. Its location showed it to be almost as important as the Holy Torah, which stood right next to it. It was Martin Buber's *'Drei Reden uber das Judentum'*, *'Three Speeches on Judaism'*. This was a transcript of three speeches Buber had given in Prague in around 1910. She was too young to have heard the great man herself, but her father had – one of the highlights of his life, by all accounts.

That book, she was regularly dipping into it – virtually every day – it was one of the few books she brought with us when we left. It quickly took its rightful honoured place once again when we settled in England, side by side with the Torah. I'm sure you must remember it too. Dog-eared and faded. I have it still. I'm ashamed to say I have never actually read it myself. But what with all the extracts from it she was continually quoting to me over the years, I didn't really need to. I would never get rid of it: that would be impossible. When I lift it in my hands up close to my face, I can almost smell her. Her life remains captured in those pages just the same as if she had written them herself.

Poor woman, she never did achieve her most profound wish. I don't think she ever actually gave up hope of getting to Palestine. Even many years after Israel came into existence, she still nurtured the hope of ending her days bathed in the radiant light of 'our people's land' (as she saw it, anyway.) But Josef: things could not have been more different for him.

His great mission in his youth was independence for Czechoslovakia. He dedicated himself to that from his earliest days as a student in Prague. Even at the age of fifteen or sixteen, while my mother was growing from childhood to maturity at the opposite end of the city, somewhere on the outskirts of Prague, he was working away diligently, doing everything he could to achieve the nationalist ideal. Always he was a political activist first and foremost. He belonged to many associations, some Jewish, some not. Of course he was aware of being a Jew, but I'm quite sure it's fair to say he was neither proud nor ashamed of it. It was just one of the facts of his life, but there's no doubt that he always, all his life, felt more Czech than Jewish.

I remember him saying more than once to my mother: 'So many things make up who you are. The way you look, whether you're a man or a woman, tall or short, whether your eyes are blue or brown. The place you grow up in. It's all part of you. What makes you what you are. Being Jewish, well yes, that's on the list. But why should it be something special? To me it seems no more important than all the rest.'

He had not one ounce of sympathy for Zionists. He detested their self-obsession, always putting themselves first. Their fanatical pursuit of a homeland in Palestine – that was something he couldn't share. Anti-Semitism well, that was different of course. That you would have to fight if it actually reared its head. As a matter of fact, he never encountered it personally all the time he was growing up, or later during his student years at the University in Berlin. It was only in the nineteen thirties that he was, like all the rest of us of course, forced to confront it.

In the late thirties, many Jewish families had started moving out of Germany and Austria into Czechoslovakia, to escape Hitler's increasingly draconian measures. Then, after the Munich Agreement in 1938, more of them started streaming north into Bohemia out of the Sudetenland. Naturally it was impossible not to recognise the iniquity of anti-Semitism and the way it was poisoning society. But even then, he insisted on seeing it as just one species of intolerance and injustice among all the many others.

He didn't think of it as something that had any special reference to him personally. Nor did he share my mother's view of it as the supreme injustice, pre-eminently appalling, the most heinous of all crimes against humanity. He believed in the possibility – the necessity, even, of co-existence. He never lost his faith in human nature as fundamentally good, compassionate and tolerant. He said it was wrong to cut yourself off from the rest of humanity. People *should* be able to live together in peace. He said why not? Why make a problem of something so obvious, so simple? Surely it's easier to love – or at least to look for the best in people – than to hate, isn't it? My mother would shake her head as if to say: 'you poor deluded man!' and make that peculiar sucking-in noise of hers and say: 'well, it's a pity we don't all think that way isn't it?'

And my father would go on, with increasing irritation in his voice: 'What's the point of dreaming of some kind of utopia planted in the middle of a barren desert? Impossible! Crazy! The whole idea is ridiculous!'

He said as far as he was concerned it was Bohemia he loved. That was his country. That was where he wanted to be, now and for ever. Generations of his family had lived and died in this place.

'Just think of this,' he pointed out emphatically, 'we've been here since the tenth century! Why should I want to move my family thousands of miles away to some Middle-

Eastern desert, some god-forsaken back of beyond dried-up piece of the earth, Jew or no Jew? Give me one good reason!'

I remember huge, bitter arguments between my father and mother. They didn't argue about many things. But these were stupendous fights. Shrieking and roaring like a pair of hyenas, for what seemed like hours on end. She would repeat over and over, tirelessly and passionately, about her dearest wish that was to see *her people* finally settled and at peace in their own country.

'To come home to their rightful land at last!'

And my father would shout back furiously:

'*Your* people! *Our* people! What do you mean? What do we have in common with all those *other* people? Be sensible! They live all over the world, in virtually every country you can name: France, Britain, Spain, Morocco, Russia, Australia, the United States, and the rest? People who just happen to call themselves *Jewish*. They don't look the same, they don't speak the same language, they have different ways of life, they don't dress the same, or even eat the same... How can you possibly think of them all as one people, one nation? And don't tell me they have the same history. They don't! They are neither a nation, nor – and even less so, a *race* – no matter what that bunch of misguided Nazi lunatics are preaching to the world over there across the border. How on earth can you talk about one people – 'our' people – when we have far more in common with the Hajdikovs down the road than with some faraway family in Vladivostok or Paris or London or Marrakesh? There is no common link, whatever you say. I don't accept it. It's a myth! They're no more *our people* than Catholics in Spain, or Moslems in Arabia, or Methodists or Presbyterians in... wherever. We all belong to the human family. That's the only link worth talking about. And *that's* all I'm going to say on the subject!' he uttered with finality, banging his fist down on the table. But it wasn't, of course. He generally just carried on, always finding more things to add.

'The way each of us chooses to express his religious faith – or the lack of it – as the case may be, well, that's up to him or her. Maybe faith creates a kind of bond – yes I suppose you could say that. But it doesn't make nations. All this rubbish those Nazi thugs are ranting on about – all this, believe me, it will soon pass. It's nothing but a flash in the pan. It won't last. It can't because it's all based on obviously false science and myths and ideology.'

Then he looked straight at my mother and wagged his finger accusingly at her: 'And you – you with your *one people* and *my people*, you're simply playing right into Hitler's hands. It is people like you who make the situation a hundred times worse for yourself. You'd do better to hold your peace!'

My mother for once was reduced to silence, but she was no more convinced by what she'd heard than she had been to start with. That was obvious from her pursed lips and her frown and the angry way she glowered at him from beneath her thick black brows. But he was undeterred.

'*Here! Here* is your home!' he insisted. ' *Here*! Is it so bad here?'

And truly, at that time, it was not so bad. Not bad at all. On the contrary. My father taught English and Philology at the German University in Prague. I honestly don't remember any prejudice at all in my early childhood. Believe it or not, I didn't know what the word 'anti-Semitism' meant, even. It didn't come into my life. Not until I was about eight, in the months leading up to *Anschluss*, when Hitler had taken charge first of Germany, then Austria, and soon after that, the southern part of our own country. Then obviously everything changed.

My father had a wide circle of friends, most of them academics, journalists and colleagues from his student activist days. What drew them together in the early days was the nationalist ideal. Independence for the Czechs. They wanted to make a separate nation, and to make it one of the great nations of Europe. They were enraged by the crushing, suffocating burden of Austrian rule. And I can tell you this for sure: he was more roused by this than any real or imaginary persecution of the Jews.

Your grandmother, naturally, was forever accusing him of betraying *his people*.

She would say over and over again: 'You devoted yourself to a cause for which people will never thank you. And think about this! You have no interest in a Jewish homeland, yet you were willing to lay down your life to achieve independence for the Czechs! Pah!'

He was not phased by this oft-repeated argument, but back he would go again to his favourite subject:

'What is nationhood?' he would ask rhetorically. Then straight away give the answer: 'A nation is defined by language, history, geography. There are Jews in almost every country you can name. What do they speak? Yiddish? Maybe some, but not all. But how do they communicate with everyone in these different countries? They speak the language of the country they were born in of course! French in France, German in Germany, Polish in Poland. Should all Catholics be given a country of their own? All Lutherans? All Baptists? Or all atheists, for God's sake? The idea is ridiculous!'

The creation of Czechoslovakia had been an ideal worth fighting for, he said. Throwing off centuries of political oppression: a noble cause. Creating a Jewish state had no meaning for my father. 'There is no such thing as a *Jewish nation*,' he would declare, to my mother's fury. 'And there never will be!'

His apparent indifference to anti-Semitism only because he had never experienced it personally both astonished and grieved her.

'You think you're free from this?' she would challenge him. 'You think it won't touch you? Well, I'll tell you this: it's all around us. No Jew is immune. No Jew is safe. It's our fate and our burden to be hounded wherever we go. You may not see it now, but it's there beneath the surface, festering, just waiting to erupt.'

'Nonsense!' he retorted, unmoved. 'Don't give me this melodrama. Anti-Semitism is a product of ignorance. It's a minority thing. A fringe group of bullies and thugs, the kind that finds pleasure in torturing animals. Such people will always exist. They will always find some group or other to victimise. This is of no importance.'

My father used to love recounting to me every detail of the fateful day: 28th October 1918, a date engraved in his memory, when the Ferdinand Boulevard in Prague was filled with crowds of demonstrators, running and shouting 'Down with Austria!' And from early morning the sounds of brass bands could be heard all over the city. Everyone knew it was only a matter of hours before the Czechs would finally be liberated after three hundred years of oppression. When evening came, the Prague National Committee declared Czechoslovak independence. It was a time of tremendous euphoria. A new beginning! A new democracy in the making!

My father told it with so much passion, I felt as if I'd been there at his side, sharing the experience with him. I felt the people's exultation, the sense of history being made. And I was so proud of him: my father, the history maker.

He didn't even know my mother then. That meeting came almost ten years later. And then, soon after that, I was born: into a brand new republic that had existed for barely more than a decade.

In the beginning my parents' arguments went over my head. But as I grew older, it gradually started to make sense. I saw what was happening. The Nazis were on the rise. Everything was changing.

I started to lean more towards my mother's standpoint than I ever had before. The growing victimisation of the Jews in Germany, the way it was gradually spreading beyond the borders of the Reich – though I was only a child, even I could see this and the senseless discrimination that was beginning to creep into our own country too. And this led inevitably to a feeling of solidarity. I was able for the first time to gain an understanding of what my mother meant when she spoke of 'our people'. I understood the love and passionate commitment she felt. Something that would never be extinguished, no matter how powerful my father's attacks on it were, no matter how often he attempted to demolish it or ridicule it.

And I must confess that the indefinable feeling of 'Jewishness', which I fully accept cannot be explained either historically, or biologically, or even rationally, has always been something strong and deep-seated inside me. A sense of kinship, of belonging to a wider family – made up of people I will probably never meet, but nevertheless people with whom I know somehow I share common traits, all kinds of similarities, a common understanding. And this indefinable feeling has stayed with me all my life, ever since those horrible events long ago (though not *that* long ago, I have to say) that made it impossible to stay any longer in our beloved homeland.

CHAPTER FIVE

She stands in her studio at the top of the house. She stares at the painting in progress. Contemplates it for a while. She sees forms, juxtapositions of colour, whole passages she didn't realize were there until that moment. Twenty-four hours' absence makes everything look new and surprising. She starts to make decisions as she looks. Selecting areas to develop, others to lose or change. She picks up the palette knife and scrapes out a small section on the left which doesn't fit with the rest. Then takes the brush and spreads thick wedges of burnt umber and sienna in loosely parallel curves round the base of the canvas.

She paints the music that fills the room: Miles Davis playing *Blue in Green*. Enthralled by sound, she voyages on an ocean of light. The music embraces her and she melds with it. She has become the instrument of its longing to be seen. Standing at the intersection of two worlds. A link between one universe and another.

She uses brushes and knives to build up layers of colour. Rich, delicate harmonies, subtly and intricately constructed. This is not just a paraphrase of the sounds. The musical inventions give rise to the painting, but after a while the painting starts to take on its own identity. Sudden and unpredictable, a moment comes when it begins to exist independently. A watershed. Then the stage of floundering and uncertainty comes to an end. The final stage begins; the resolution moves closer. Not long now…

Michael's voice, jarring, edgy, like a blade slicing through the underbelly of a fawn:

'Do you know what time it is?'

She jumps. Looks at her watch. Half-past one.

'Sorry. Had no idea…'

'Aren't you coming to bed?'

He peers myopically at the painting. Moves closer and frowns. Without his glasses, his eyes resemble a child's, soft and blue, guileless. She watches him as he bends over the canvas, his fine broad brow, his hair thick and still pale blonde, hardly grey at all, except at the temples a little. He still has the capacity to touch her, even now. An overgrown child, his thin ankles and long narrow feet poke out from beneath the ridiculous Disney pyjamas. A jokey gift from the girls one Christmas.

She busies about, cleaning brushes, replacing lids on tins of paint, pretending not to notice him. Finally he turns to her to offer his verdict:

'I don't really get the point of this. I mean, there's nothing solid about it...'

He stops. A brief silence hangs between them.

'It's not finished…' she begins defensively. Tailing off. He waves his hand dismissively.

'Yes obviously. I know that.'

A pause, then he goes on:

'But there's something that happens with your paintings. I try to... understand them, but somehow I always end up feeling lost somehow. They do have a pleasant look about them, I mean they're certainly nice to look at... Yes, very nice...Decorative, I suppose, you might say. But...'

He pauses again, then stares straight into her eyes. He grimaces, making a show. She can see that.

' But what do they *mean?*'

There. He's said it. Naturally. She was hoping he wouldn't, yet knowing he would. Effectively saying to her:

'What is this shit?'

She pinches the brush-head with the rag, over and over, as if she wanted to squeeze the life out of it. She utters in hardly more than a whisper:

'Perhaps they don't mean anything.'

He won't be satisfied with that.

'But paintings have to *mean* something, don't they?'

Just needling her. She knows, yet she cannot resist rising to it. He continues to provoke her:

'Paintings *have* to have a meaning. You said yourself art is a language. If it says nothing, it's just decoration. Isn't it?'

Verbal dexterity is Michael's forte, but not hers. She finds it hard to counter it, particularly at almost two o'clock in the morning.

'Yes. That's right. Art isn't decoration. There's always something more…' she tails off.

Silence again. He saves her.

'Well, anyway. Let's go to bed now. It's late. We're both worn out.'

Lying beside him. His slow breathing. She can't sleep. Her brain is going round in circles. Art isn't art if it has no meaning. Art without meaning. Mere decoration. Wallpaper. Furniture. Prettification. So what does it mean? How to put it into words? If you can't put it into words… This painting is about… What?

Alice sits in the small back room that overlooks the garden. She calls it her office. Stares at the computer screen. Pages down a list of names. She comes to a stop and turns to the man facing her. He is leaning back in his chair, slim legs outstretched, faded jeans, his head at an angle resting lightly on his curled fingers, his elbow on the chair arm. His pose is easy, elegant, confident. His look is Mediterranean – dark hair almost black, his skin brown and warm against the plain grey T-shirt – but this is belied by his speech. English public school trying to apologise for itself by blunting the edges.

Aspiring to ordinariness because ordinary is cool. It's exactly the way her children speak. He smiles at her across the desk.

Glancing back at the screen she tells him she's sorry. Nothing much to offer him at the moment.

'About three. Or perhaps four. You said you do piano, didn't you, as well? And theory?'

He nods.

'Saxophone... it's not something we have much call for, really. Unfortunately. Well, you know. It's mainly schoolkids I deal with. Extra coaching for exams. That kind of thing...'

He totally understands, he says.

'If you can just keep me on file. If anything comes up, you know.'

'Of course.'

He makes as if to get up. She says hurriedly:

'Your CV – it says your main instrument was piano? So...'

'Yes. That's right. At college. The sax came later. Still play piano sometimes. When I'm working things out. You know, chords... arrangements...'

She listens intently while, with sudden and unexpected candour, he launches into the story of how he got into jazz in the first place, started up his band about ten years ago. His voice is quiet and intense. Each word is measured, his sentences unhurried, his words carefully chosen, entirely free from flippancy or cheap attempts to impress.

'We get to travel. That's the good part. Playing what we want. Wherever people want to hear it. The downside of course: not much cash. Not enough to pay the bills, usually. Still, what the hell… There's more to life than paying bills…'

When he's gone she reads again through the life he has offered her, compressed into a page and a half of double-spaced type. Born where and when. Single. Her mind drifts beyond the dry record of numbers and facts. She sees his face, the boyish grin, slightly askew. Without wanting to, she finds herself comparing ages. The difference is less than ten years. Just about. Place of birth: Wimbledon. So, only a few miles apart too. Hardly any distance. Then off to some boarding school…

The colour of his eyes is hard to define. A kind of earthy greenish-brown. Trees, hedgerows. The woodland floor in autumn after rain. A blend of fallen leaves, oak, ash and beech mixed with ivy and brushwood. All crushed together into a wet mass of colour. Warm, subdued, imponderable.

Bertie's sharp insistent bark echoes through the house. Alice hears his paws sliding and skidding over the parquet as he careers through the length of the hall towards the front door. It bangs shut and the barking stops. The sound of Chloe greeting him, in the tender voice she reserves exclusively for Bertie.

'How was your day?' Alice calls through the open door, but Chloe is already ensconced in the kitchen, nosing through the fridge, opening and slamming cupboard doors, the TV turned up to full volume. Some inane soap with people screaming at each other, a paean to hatred.

She waits for the first howl of complaint.

'Mum! MUM! Where's the normal baked beans?' insistent, impatient, demanding.

Alice walks into the kitchen and switches the TV off.

'Mum. For Christ's sake...'

'These are better for you,' Alice bangs the tin onto the table.

'I hate these crappy healthy ones.'

Alice shrugs. 'Take them or leave them.'

Chloe opens the freezer, rifling through it. 'What's happened to that pizza? I bet Florence ate it. Damn her!'

Half an hour later Florence phones to say she's gone to MacDonald's with some friends. Will be back 'some time'. Alice puts the phone down and wonders what these two beings actually have to do with her. The connection is gone. When or how, she cannot say.

I am nothing but a multi-functional servicing centre. Everyone's needs fully catered for. Cleaning, clothing, feeding, mucking-out, transport. And most important of all: limitless finance, no questions asked.

Added to which, they think she's weird. Why isn't she like their friends' mums? Why doesn't she do normal things like shopping in London, having coffee with normal people, going out to lunch, reading *Homes and Gardens*, spending time in the gym or the tennis club, watching daytime TV even? What's with our mum? Why does she spend hours in that room at the top of the house she calls her 'studio' painting peculiar pictures that don't look like anything?

Michael thinks she's weird too. She knows that, though he's never said it. But she knows what he's thinking. In fact, he thinks she's going through a phase of oddness that sooner or later will pass. Probably her age. Mid-life crisis …

It started about four years ago. Seemed insignificant at the time. She woke up one cold and bright January morning and somehow, out of nowhere, the decision was there. Without preamble or obvious reason, she knew she was going to start painting again. By evening she had already been out and purchased paints and brushes, boards and canvas. She hauled her old easel out of the attic where it had lain forgotten for fifteen years. Made a start straight away on a painting. She was on a high. She had no studio but there was a room at the top of the house, not used for anything but storing junk. It was L-shaped and had windows at either end. It was light for most of the day. Perfect.

At first Michael was full of enthusiasm. Even helped her clear the room. He offered to get the builders in and improve it, but she said no, it would do as it was. What she needed most of all was peace and quiet. Michael was an enthusiastic believer in people making use of their qualifications. What's the point in having a degree in fine art if you don't use it? 'Great!' he said. 'It's about time you started thinking about yourself for a change. A new chapter in your life. Go for it!' So she went.

But as the months passed, his enthusiasm waned. At first he thought: a pleasant pastime for Alice. Something to distract her from the mundanities. Might even use it to raise his own standing. *'My talented wife!'* He could boast about her to acquaintances. But it got to be more than just a pastime. It got to be serious.

At first he looked forward to a succession of pretty flower pictures or romantic landscapes he could hang up round the house. He would point them out to people when they came round for drinks or dinner. *'My talented wife!'* But Alice started to spend more and more time closeted in her studio, rushing up to get on with what she called 'her work' at every possible opportunity.

He would spend evening after evening sitting in an armchair beside a glass of whisky or brandy, listening to the faint tones and rhythms of jazz as they wafted down the stairs. He sat alone and felt abandoned.

And at the end of all these hours of dedication, there would emerge strange contortions of coloured shapes spread thickly over boards or canvases, that he found totally mystifying. If they had been out-and-out abstracts he could have assimilated them. Equally so if they had been recognisably figurative. But they were neither. He remained in the dark and Alice did nothing to enlighten him.

Alice knew she could have made more strenuous efforts to guide Michael, at least towards an understanding of her way of working. It might have helped him to read her paintings. Not to feel completely at sea. She could have, but she did nothing.

She could have invited him into her world. Her other world. She found peace there. Even a taste of something you might call eternity. She could have, but to tell the truth and she was nothing if not honest, she didn't want him there. She thought in any case he would not be capable of reinventing himself, reshaping himself to fit through the doorway which gave access to that world. It was hers. Her domain.

They are eating dinner, just the two of them. The girls are out with friends. As always, Radio Three helps to relieve the leaden weight of silence that permeates the house in the children's absence. Tonight it's a Brahms concert performed by the LSO. They have almost finished eating when Michael suddenly proposes: 'Let's go away for a few days. Would you like that? A break. You're looking tired...'

Alice puts her knife and fork together and shakes her head. 'How can I do that? It's the middle of term.'

'They could board. No problem.'

'No, really. I can't. I've got to get my work finished. You know. The exhibition?'

He sighs. 'Exhibition... Why are you doing this? You don't need the money.'

She sighs. Strives to keep her voice quiet: 'You know it's not that.'

'But they'll be up for sale, won't they?'
She says nothing.

'That's what galleries are for, isn't it?' he persists, 'to sell things...'

She looks him straight in the eye. 'Yes, but that's not the point – for me.'

'So what is? Why do you feel compelled to hold your *works of art* up to public scrutiny?' The familiar raised eyebrows, the twisted smile.

Pausing for a moment, she replies: 'I don't know exactly... It's to do with communication, I suppose. When you've done – created – something you think has merit, well... you want other people to ... I mean...' she falters can't find the words. He waits, without speaking or changing his expression, enjoying her discomfiture.

'Why?' he asks finally. 'Is it fame you're after?'
She waves her hand impatiently. 'No. No. It's not that. Not at all… It's … a kind of… reaching out…some way of touching someone. You know?'

Basically, she doesn't know why she bothers. With Michael, it's a case of 'silly bitch! Get real!' And anyway, neither of them actually wants him there, in the alternative world. For him it doesn't even exist. For her it's a place she has no real desire to share with him.

They start to clear the table, working together in silence. Then he starts up again, from the kitchen, raising his voice so she can hear from where she's piling up plates on the dining-room table. 'So if someone happened to take a liking to one of your paintings, would you sell it?'

She shrugs indifferently. 'I suppose so.'

'You wouldn't mind then, about it disappearing from public view? Being shut away in someone's house, never to be seen again?'

She thinks about this for a moment. 'Well, of course, I *would* mind, in a way… But I've got no option…'

'Yes, exactly! There you are! It's just a business, isn't it, like any other, this gallery thing. And you've opted right into it. This mystical *reaching out and touching people* stuff. It's all crap really, isn't it Alice?'

CHAPTER SIX

Winter hangs over the fields and woods in an endless pall of tenebrous days and freezing nights. Life is nothing but a succession of days, each indistinguishable from the next. The tired rituals of Christmas trundle along their deep-worn tracks. The annual charade with its weary exchange of cards and gifts masquerading as cheer, leaves Alice too dispirited to paint. She longs for the resumption of the school term so she can recover solitude and the control of her life. A new year dawns. New only in the change of a single digit. Everything else is the same.

The man with eyes the colour of crushed leaves returns. Still looking for work. This time she finds something for him. Extra coaching in music theory – a fifteen-year-old boy. His broad grin delights her. When can he begin?

When he comes to collect books and sign forms she offers him coffee. He stays for an hour. They talk continuously about themselves. Why, she wonders, has he done so many different jobs, most of them unconnected with music? She breaks off. Sorry, none of her business.

'No, don't worry. I think...' he pauses, gazing out of the window at the branches of a willow tree as it bends and stretches in the wind. 'I guess music is so important to me... I couldn't just do it, anything or anyhow. Just for the money.' He turns back to look at her. 'I mean. I'd rather do something completely different. I didn't put everything down on that CV you've got there. I've done some pretty weird things. Once packed food for airlines. That was a breeze.' He laughed. 'Then I was a gardener – well, gardener's assistant. Wasn't much good, I'm afraid.' Another laugh. 'Teaching. Yes, that was OK. Two or three years. You saw that. Peripatetic. Pathetic more like. When they make cuts, the pathetic ones are the first to go…' He stops and turns to the window again. Says nothing for a moment. The wind howls round the house.

Alice begins to speak, but he's already turned towards her. He lowers his voice, speaking with intensity:

'See, what I really want to do is just play jazz. Make the sounds.' He opens out his hands, palms upturned, fingers outspread, as if setting a butterfly free. 'Anything else. No good. Couldn't do it. These three guys I play with sometimes. They're not like that. They're OK with – well – anything really. Birthday parties, weddings – whatever. Me? Sorry, no. Can't do it.' He shakes his head. 'No. Not on. I'd rather dig holes in the road.' He looks up. Maybe that's hard for her to understand?

No, no. She demurs. Absolutely not. She hears words spilling out of her out of her control. Words till then reserved for the second self that lives secretly inside her. Thoughts and feelings never shared before with a single person. How she might have become a concert pianist, was on the brink of it, but turned away, changed direction. How it wounded her parents who never understood why. How she herself couldn't put it into words until much later. The absence of freedom it would have meant. But at the same time the terrible wrenching, tearing herself in two because of her passion for music. When she heard Charlie Parker play for the first time, it was *'Out of Nowhere'* – that was the one. How she knew from that exact moment what freedom meant and how she would never be able to get hold of that freedom herself. Not that way. The straitjacket she was in. The freedom she craved. And yes, that was why she chose art and not music.

Voiced for the first time, the words stream forth incoherently yet he looks as if he understands completely. Not taking his eyes off her. Resting his chin on his hand. At the end he says:

'It's seeing the world in colour after a lifetime of black and white. For me, music is the drug of choice. Better than the rest. Doesn't harm your health anyway!'

And a little later:

'And so, did art give you freedom?'

She can only say 'yes, but…'

'But what?'

Not enough, she tells him ruefully. Not enough. Not the ultimate experience. Not yet.

When he's gone, Alice remains in her seat by the window, watching the violence of the wind as it bends trees and bushes to the ground, mercilessly, almost to breaking point. Rain begins to fall, at first just a mist, then more and more heavily, flinging itself in waves across the garden towards her, clattering like handfuls of grit being hurled against the panes.

Michael is highly suspicious of phrases like *the ultimate experience*. He enjoys deconstructing them to demonstrate their emptiness. Alice takes care to keep her poetic inclinations to herself. Sometimes, inadvertently, her guard falls, letting him glimpse her uncharted inner world, but always, straight away, she kicks herself for it. Because he will instantly seize on the situation as a chance for sport. His favourite sport, which is, of course, verbal combat. Mercilessly he pokes and goads with the steel of his logic till there is nothing left of an idea but a few scraps of flesh left bleeding and squirming on the ground.

Once years ago, the girls were still small, she and Michael sat in deckchairs in the garden, drinking wine. It was late summer. The sun was setting, but there was no chill in the air. Just the faint hint of a breeze fragrant with honeysuckle from the hedgerow along the lane. No sound apart from occasional trills of blackbirds and thrushes at the day's end.

The pleasure of the moment lulled Alice into an urge to share intimate thoughts. As the light slowly faded and the birds fell silent, she said quietly: 'Have you ever felt that there's another kind of existence going on around us? Something we can't access with our senses, but something real. A kind of other dimensional life?'

Michael responded with amusement. 'Sounds a bit sci-fi to me. A bit *new-agey*...What do you mean?'

Alice struggled to make it clearer but all she could come up with was 'It's just a feeling I have. I've always had it...'

He was just a shadow now. Through the gloom she heard the creak of his chair and then his voice: 'Don't put your trust in feelings, Alice. Hard facts, that's what you need in life.'

'It's more than a feeling though...' She felt that was wrong, but she couldn't just leave it like that. 'I mean, I know. I just know it. Not life after death. I'm not talking about that. But some kind of parallel life. Going on now, right this minute. Outside our senses...' She felt frustrated and impotent. She waited for the demolition job.

He prefaced it with a dry laugh. 'But how do you *know*? What kind of knowledge are you talking about? This so-called parallel universe or dimension is, by definition, not accessible to the senses, so there's absolutely nothing you can say about it. Least of all that it exists.' He stretched his arm towards her and patted her knee. 'You're such a dreamer,

Alice. But maybe that's why I fell in love with you.' Yet still she persisted. 'But I have glimpses of it sometimes,' she whispered. He withdrew his hand. 'Glimpses?'

'Well, there has to be a catalyst. It's often music... Or being in the middle of a huge landscape... Or maybe walking by the sea... Or...'

'With nobody there but you...' he laughed. 'Come on, Alice. I don't buy this. Airy-fairy stuff. Romantic rubbish!'

'But there are ways of experiencing things. Not through the senses, but...'

'Yes. Dreaming. That's one way. You might as well face facts. This is the only world we can know. The boring old everyday world. There ain't nothin' else. The sooner you accept that, the better off you'll be. Come on. Let's go in.'

She didn't move. 'No,' she insisted. 'There must be something else. There is, I know it. There has to be. Why do we sometimes get the feeling we've moved into a kind of different mode of being?'

'I never feel that!' he interrupted sardonically.

Ignoring his derision, she continued: 'But you do. You must do. When you listen to music that moves you. The way it makes you feel... Why should this happen? There must be something more than just – surviving. Keeping yourself alive, till something happens to make you die. Or your body just gives up... There is something else. I know it. These feelings of somehow transcending everything... Moving into a higher sphere. I don't know…' She ended lamely, not finding the words. There seemed no way of saying it without sounding either trite or absurdly seraphic.

His response was predictable. 'Why do you feel euphoric after a couple of stiff gins? It's the brain. No mystery about it. Exactly the same with music. There's always a scientific explanation. Trust me.'

She wanted to pull away from his touch as he patted her shoulder but she made herself stay put, her body as tense as stone.

'There's nothing else, you know. This world – it's all there is. Like it or not. Everything else is fiction.' He patted her again.

She could see nothing but trillions of white lights in an ocean of black.

But perhaps, on the contrary, her world was the true reality. The times when she let the music of being flow into her with its colours and forms and sounds were the times when she felt most complete, most in touch with truth. They flooded into her when she let go. Did absolutely nothing. She felt she was truly real only when she ceased to be Alice, wife of Michael, mother of Florence and Chloe.

She must shed every mark of identity and become as nothing. Then enter somewhere rich, textured and joyous. It is different in nature from anything experienced in that other life: the named, finite existence, circumscribed by time and space. The world that people call *real* is synthetic and opaque in comparison.

Not that it's a place, of course. More a mode. In truth she is living two lives. Two lives in one. She thinks of each as belonging to its own spiritual universe. She thought of names for them some years ago: the *Chronic World* and the *Halcyon World*. *Chronic* because everything in it is dominated by the clock and the calendar. Whatever happens, enjoyed or endured, is dragged through the sludge of time. The Halcyon World is weightless and untrammelled. Unencumbered by identity in a sea of others, you can fly.

Once Alice did a small painting which she finished in one day. It was sharp and bright, a round bubble of light floating in a blue desert. Inside the bubble were two figures like insects or leaves caught in amber. They were tiny but you could see that they faced in opposite directions.

When Michael saw it, he looked puzzled. He commented 'It's odd. Not like your usual style. What's it meant to be? Looks a bit like a glass. Or a paper-weight. Is it a still-life then?'

Alice said 'Yes. It's a sort of still life.'

CHAPTER SEVEN

A cold morning in early February. Watercolour sky. Pale lilac wash streaked with random pink, melting rose into orange. Colours leach into one another, floating and dissolving. Alice walks along the high-banked lane that runs between Stokers Wood and the flat wide fields of Tringley Farm that stretch from over the hedge right up to the line of purple-grey trees on the horizon. From time to time she closes her eyes, to intensify her other senses, focusing on the feel of different textures beneath her feet, listening to the various bird calls and barely perceptible rustles emerging from the movements of small creatures in the wood. She opens her eyes now and then to survey any holes or other obstacles ahead into which she might fall or over which she might trip, then shuts them again. Bertie has disappeared. Alice can hear him rustling and scuffling through leaves and undergrowth, following the scent-trail of some rabbit or pheasant. The sky is cloudless and there is no wind. Despite the cold, the bright sunshine reminds her of spring. One or two clumps of primroses are already emerging along the banks.

Opening her eyes, she comes to the end of the wood and turns into a field where the ground is completely covered with thick layers of oak and beech leaves, still lying where they fell months before. Some of the brown leaves are sugared with frost. Traces of ice crunch beneath her boots.

She calls Bertie, then whistles twice and he scampers up, darting out between the trees. There is still hardly any green, just the dark, shiny, lush ivy climbing up the trunks and, here and there, a holly tree, and at the foot of the trees, along the edges of the wood and the headland, the healthy tender green of young nettles.

A glimpse of pale yellow catches her eye. She stoops to take a closer look. A lesser celandine, with its star-shaped petals. As she moves on, she notices others dotted about the headland, and a single dandelion.

She hears the sound of running water and stops to investigate. There is no sign of a stream, but she notices a dip in the ground, a shallow crater, like a dried-up pond. The sound seems to be coming from beneath there. She pictures the water flowing underground. Bertie sits beside her, panting.

They both look up at the sound of a vehicle approaching rapidly behind them along the edge of the field. She turns and recognises Ralph's black Range-Rover. The car stops beside her. Bertie starts barking defensively. Ralph winds down the window.

'Good boy! Good boy!'

Recognising Ralph, the dog falls silent and wags his tail enthusiastically.

'How're you doing?' he gives Alice a half-wink.

With a sharp sense of mortification, she recalls the recent bathroom incident. Thankfully, he makes no move to get out of the car. She flashes him a quick, neutral grin. Then looks down, bending to pat Bertie.

'Enjoying this beautiful weather!' she says, smiling up at the sky. 'What a change to see the sun!'

'Absolutely!'

He's in a hurry.

'Well, must go. See you later. Enjoy your walk.'

She nods, relieved at his departure.

'Oh, by the way,' he adds, as he starts the engine, 'do thank Mike for me, will you. He's been a great help with the Potts woman. It's all sorted now. Well, so long!'

Then he's off, leaving an oily smoky trail hanging over the lane.

That evening Alice quizzes Michael.

'Who's the Potts woman?'

He looks at her swiftly, the carving knife and fork held motionless above the roast leg of beef.

'Where did you get that from?'

'Ralph. I saw him today when I was walking with Bertie. He said to tell you thank you for your help with her – the Potts woman.'

Michael shakes his head, looks back at the joint and carries on carving.

'It's nothing,' he says. 'One of the houses on the estate. Nothing important…'

'But this Potts woman,' Alice persists. 'Who is she?'
He shrugs impatiently. 'She's one of his tenants, that's all. He's had a bit of a problem with her. Nothing important. Is that enough meat for you?'

'What problem?'

'A legal thing. Trivial. Let's drop the subject, shall we?' Then suddenly she remembers. Something clicks. The Potts woman. She's the girl who lives on her own in the cottage at the end of Green Lane. The one with the 'Local Honey' sign hanging over the gate.

Later in the week, on her way home from Jennifer, Alice, on a whim, takes a right-hand turn into Green Lane. She brings the car to a halt in the driveway that lies just beyond the 'Local Honey' sign.

Sarah Potts has indigo blue eyes, unexpectedly, compellingly blue against the dark curls that play around her pale, oval face. Her mouth is firm and grave. It seems to underline a wilful spirit. To Alice she has the look of a stubborn elf. Curious to know more about her, Alice engages her in conversation as they stand inside what was once a garage, by a trestle table laden with honey jars of various sizes and colours, ranging from pale narcissus to deep amber.

When Alice tells her she lives just down the road, Sarah says:

'Would you like some tea?'

They sit facing one another across a pinewood table that bears the scratches and stains of generations of mealtimes. A small black terrier sits protectively at Sarah's feet. She pours tea from a dark brown pot with a cracked spout. A ginger cat sprawls out full-length, fast asleep, on the arm of Alice's chair, its paws sticking up at odd angles to reveal the white fur on its underside.

She tells Alice she has lived here all her life. Alone for the last two years, since the accident that killed her parents. She was in her last year at school, she says, about to take her A Levels, but they had to go by the board, of course. No time for all that any more. It was a question of survival.

'I couldn't imagine leaving here. This is home...' She breaks off abruptly. She points to the plate of biscuits.

'Help yourself!'

Alice takes a tea biscuit and asks her about the honey business.

'How long have you been doing this?'

Sarah smiles.

'Oh, years and years. Dad started it. It was just a hobby for him. He taught me everything. Then, when he – died – I carried on. Developed it.' She pauses. Looks out at the garden through the window to her left. The branches of a weeping willow bend and sway in the strengthening wind. Then turning back to Alice, she begins to speak, the words tumbling forth:

'They're trying to get me out. You know that, don't you? I've got letters. They've been ringing me. Over and over. The lawyers. Badgering me. They tell me they're giving me notice. *Notice to quit*, it's called. Can you believe it? You're one of his friends, aren't you? In his circle. That's true, isn't it? That awful woman. Emily, his wife. Oh God, I'm sorry if she's a friend of yours… Sorry. Don't mean to be rude, but – for God's sake. She's the one, I'm sure. She wants me out so she can have it – the house – for her precious son. They don't need it…' She stops. Stares at Alice, her blue eyes pleading *help me*.

Alice is about to speak when Sarah begins again. Her composure regained, the corners of her small straight mouth lift into a conspiratorial smile. Her face reddens.

'They can't do it, though, you know. Get me out, I mean.'

'No?'

She shakes her head. A black curl falls over her left eye. She brushes it back with an impatient flick of the hand.

'I've got this document, you see.' She nods defiantly. 'Ralph Stigwood's granddad – he signed it. He made a promise to my dad. Written down and signed. All those years ago. I've got it. They'll not get me out. Just let them try!'

'So what's the deal with this Potts woman?' Alice asks Michael casually that evening, as if to say *'well I'm not really interested. Just making conversation'*.
They are watching the seven o'clock News. Michael looks at her suspiciously.
'Why do you ask?'
'You remember. I mentioned it the other day. Just wondering. What's happening about her?'
He looks back at the TV. His attention caught by a Middle East story.
'Sschh...' he tells her. 'Hang on a minute...'
When the report ends, he returns to her question, dismissing it with a curt:
'Don't know. Rob's been dealing with it.'
'So she's staying then?' Alice goes on, refusing to be brushed off.
He turns to face her.
'What do you know about this?' he asks her.
She smiles knowingly.
'Well?' he looks irritated.

She shrugs and gets up, gathering up their two glasses to take to the kitchen. As she leaves, she remarks over her shoulder, throwaway fashion:

'Sarah's a friend of mine,' adding 'she's not so stupid, you know.'

Michael follows her to the kitchen. With a frown, he tells her:

'Don't get involved with this. It'll make it immeasurably more difficult for me if you do.'

'Don't know what you mean,' she replies innocently. She washes up the glasses and places them carefully face down on the draining-board.

'It's nothing to do with you.'

'Isn't it?'

'It's just work, that's all,' he says dismissively.

She wheels round, fulminating with a sudden surge of anger.

'Work! Yes, of course!' Her voice has risen a pitch. 'Ralph's work. Your work. What kind of people are you?' She feels hot.

He stares at her in astonishment.

'What the hell's brought this on?'

'It's just not right. That's all,' she replies. Her voice returns to normal. She's regained control. 'What you're doing. It's just – immoral. There's no other word to describe it.'

'Huh!' He laughs drily. 'It's law. What's morality got to do with it?' A second laugh. 'Surely you've cottoned onto that by now, after twenty-odd years?'

Finally, in a tone that is new to Alice, quiet and dark, he warns her:

'Don't meddle with this, Alice, I'm warning you.'

Then he turns tail and goes back to the News.

She wastes no time. Next day, as soon as Michael's out of the house, she sets to. Tense and determined she scrolls down his emails. It doesn't take long. Ah! There it is! Triumphantly she reads: *'Mike to Rob: Re S Potts: She's prob got 60/40 chance, so v.i.p tell her it's not worth the paper it's written on. She'll believe you, no worries'*.

'But I can't afford solicitors...' Sarah laments as Alice gives her the name of a local firm.

'Trust me. Give them a ring. Listen: I've checked the document...'

'But what about this?' Sarah waves a letter she's just received that morning. It's from Rob.

Alice takes it and gives it a cursory read-through. She shrugs.

'Ignore it!'

Sarah stares at her in disbelief. 'But how do you know?'

'I just do,' Alice says. For added reassurance, she mumbles something about knowing a bit about the law. 'Had thoughts of becoming a solicitor once years ago. Soon changed my mind. Not for me!'

'You married one instead!' Sarah retorts ironically. (*Touché*)

Alice briefly wonders how long before she'll have to come clean with Sarah. But not yet.

'Let me know what they say'.

Looking back at a faintly bewildered Sarah, she closes the gate behind her, gets into the car and waves encouragingly before driving off.

A smile of quiet triumph spreads over her face, a smile that recurs irresistibly many times during the short drive home. She hasn't felt this buoyant in years.

Jack lives alone with his dogs in a ramshackle house surrounded by a hundred acres of grassland. Fifty years ago it belonged to a landowner, whose cattle grazed the land. Now the land is rented out to local sheep-farmers and the house is owned by a property company in London.

'I feel like a pioneer in the mid-West living here,' he told Alice. 'When the wind blows up over the marshes, it howls like a hurricane. Sometimes it's so fierce you can imagine it tearing the house from its roots and whirling it away. Like in *The Wizard of Oz*.

Alice stops the car at a lay-by to consult the crumpled paper on the passenger seat. It was hanging around in her bag for weeks, squashed into her wallet among supermarket receipts and old shopping lists.

'You won't find it on a map,' he said. 'It's just a dot. I'll draw it for you.'

She remembers his hands. His fingers long and narrow. His hand trembled a little as he held the pencil above the paper. He raised his eyes to meet hers. 'It's here, see.' He ran his finger along the wavy line he'd drawn, that snaked up to a box shape in the middle of a circle. 'You come off the road here.' He pointed to an arrow next to another box. His smile was slow, slightly lop-sided. 'You'll know when you come to a white building with a big sign on the wall that says *Builders' Merchants*. Follow the lane up for about half a mile. There's a gate halfway along. I've drawn it here, see.' He looked at her again. 'It's never locked. You can't miss my house. It's the only one there.'

She didn't want him to draw a map. It made it more difficult for her. It started with a flippant remark. Something about genuine rural living and if she wanted to know what it was really like…

She never gave it a thought. Only when she came to clear her bag of its detritus. Then there it was. Popping up again. She screwed it up once, threw it into the wastepaper basket, then took it out once more, stuffing it back into her bag.

She hadn't planned to come today. After leaving Jennifer with a pile of exercises to work through till next week, she drove away from the Morgans' house towards the supermarket. Then abruptly turned round and drove in the opposite direction.

From the lay-by, she can see no sign of a builder's merchants. She starts up again and drives a bit further. There it is. She turns off the road onto a rutted, pot-holed track. To the left is a tangle of mixed woodland; to the right, flat, empty fields stretch for miles to the horizon. No sign of habitation. The light's already beginning to fade. Rounding a bend, she comes to an ancient five-bar gate on which is nailed a wooden notice. Paint that was once white has peeled away, most of the letters gone. It reads 'D-A---NS -ARM'. She gets out of the car to open the gate. She struggles with its weight, dragging it over the humps in the track, then finally heaves it onto the grassy verge, wondering why she is there. A moment's hesitation, but it's too late to turn back. She's come too far.

His ancient blue Land Rover is parked in the muddy yard. Growling and barking start up from behind the house as she drives up. She turns off the engine and two enormous Alsatians come bounding up to the car, their barks almost deafening her. She doesn't move.

He emerges after a minute from the house, waving and smiling, calling the dogs back. When she steps out, they rush up to her, friendly now, sniffing round her legs. They follow her into the house and park themselves at her feet as she takes a seat.

'They like you,' he says. 'That's good. They can always tell.' He nods and smiles.

He kneels at the fireplace, piling pieces of kindling wood into a pyramid. His boots discarded by the door, he pads around in thick grey socks.

'I'd have had the fire going,' he says, 'if I'd known you were coming.'

She watches him as he bends forward and back, forward and back again onto his heels, building up the fire, with screwed-up newspaper, then logs. His feet encased in their schoolboy socks. He brings her hot green tea, which they drink from mugs as they squat on leather-covered stools close to the fire. Then salty biscuits on a blue plate covered in orange stars.

'Have you heard this?' he asks, leaping to his feet. He presses a switch releasing glorious torrents of music, shapes of shimmering colour. Like meeting a friend after a lifetime of absence: John Coltrane: *'Body and Soul'*.

Listening carries her to a place she once knew and loved, a place where she was happy. Walking along familiar roads, exactly remembered. Every tree and shrub, every garden, house, every view of park or street glimpsed between twisting passages, shifting patterns of light and shade, morning sliding into evening. Nothing changed. And the same entrancement. Waiting for every familiar note, every phrase, every twist and turn of sound. Sounds eliciting love, immutable and unconditional.

It was late.

'I must go.'

Next day she is sitting on the tall bar-stool in her studio. Not painting. Not physically. Focusing intently on the large canvas which stands against the opposite wall. She has reached an impasse. Nothing's working. She has scraped the paint off different areas in turn, then laid on more paint, then furiously scraped it all off once again. This process so many times repeated, now she can do nothing but look.

Lost in contemplation – it must have been several hours by now. When she started it was light, now it's dusk and she can scarcely distinguish tones or colours. Not even music can help this time.

Thoughts drift in and out, flashes from yesterday and the day before. Michael left for Berlin yesterday. Before he went, they talked in a way that was rare between them. She was intent on driving him into a corner. She wanted to bite into the cosy complacency that clung to him like a second skin.

'Always so damned – *satisfied* with everything!' she snapped. Battle-lines drawn.

He raised his eyebrows in the familiar pose, affecting surprise. They'd watched a television film about a politician in the government of a fictitious country, an idealist aiming to bring freedom and democracy to the country. He witnesses the gradual chipping away of his ideals by people intent on lining their own pockets. People who were once like him. He finds himself isolated and abandoned. Thrown out of office, all he can do is stand by while his country becomes riddled with corruption and descends into anarchy and despair. In the end he commits suicide.

Alice was moved to tears, but Michael's verdict was: ' Totally implausible! Nobody would kill themselves for that'.

'Why not?' she challenged.

'He'd have found some way of coming to terms with it.' He shrugged. 'People always do.'

Then she accused him of complacency. 'Never anguishing over anything. Why is everything so simple with you?'

He shook his head. 'No. You're quite wrong, Alice.' He was pouring himself a second whisky. 'What I am saying, though, I suppose… there's always a compromise to be found. If you try hard enough.' He placed two cubes of ice into his glass, gently, so as not to splash a drop.

Alice wriggled impatiently in her chair. 'You're just – infuriating! I mean, can't you accept that sometimes people just don't have a choice? Despair. Utter despair... So death is the only option.'

'Speaking generally, of course, there are circumstances...But we're talking about the film, aren't we? I was merely saying that in real life, I don't think it likely he'd have killed himself. He'd have carried on somehow. People do. Probably he would've got out of politics altogether. Maybe gone into social work, or something.' He grinned. 'People who want to change the world. They can't do too much harm there.' He glanced at his watch. 'Better be making a move...'

But Alice wasn't finished.

'The trouble with you is,' she said, with increasing agitation, 'is that you divide everything up into either work or non-work. Work means whatever you do to earn money. Non-work is everything else. And that doesn't count. It's just unimportant, apparently.'

He put his hand up, as if to say: 'Whoah! Calm down!'

'Sorry? I can't see what this has got to do with...'

'It's got everything to do with it!' she interposed fiercely. 'You just can't conceive of anyone doing something out of sheer love. Or because of an ideal. Something good in itself. Not for money. That's just playing, for you. It doesn't count. How can it? It's just a diversion. Art, music, playing golf, having a few drinks… It's all the same for you, isn't it? Just add-on value.'

He sighed. 'So we're back to this again, are we?' he said quietly. He got to his feet. 'I really must go now. I've a plane to catch first thing tomorrow.'

'You don't have to,' she retorted. 'Doesn't matter what time you get to the hotel, does it?'

'I *would* like to get *some* sleep tonight.' He spoke calmly, humouring her, refusing to be roused.

Which only made her doubly furious. 'Always taking the moral high ground…'

He was on his feet, about to pick up his bags and go out to the car. When she spoke, he sat down again, impatience oozing through the cracks. He was tired. He didn't need this.

'What do you mean, Alice?' he asked wearily.

She glared at him belligerently. 'I mean this… I mean… you always act as if you know everything. As if you're always right. But the truth is, there's something really important that's lacking in you. You know that?'

He sighed again. Half-closed his eyes. 'And what's that?'

She felt like hitting him. 'It's like a whole sense that's missing. It's the same with all your bloody family. *And* all your so-called friends, too. You're all the damned same!'

He said: 'So we're all in the line of fire, are we?' Smiling, he got to his feet again, brushed her cheek with his lips. 'Look. I'm off now. I'll call you later.'

She didn't get up. She heard the front door slam shut, then the car door. The engine starting, the car pulling out of the drive. Then the sound faded away. She continued to sit where she was, motionless. Later she moved to the kitchen. She made herself some coffee and sat staring at Fingal curled up asleep beside the Aga. After a while, the cat woke up, stretched, stood up and walked away. Alice continued to stare at the spot where the cat had been.

Michael called her, not from the airport on his way out, as he usually did, but two days later from Berlin. By then her outburst had lost its edge. The intervening days and the sound of his voice restored the status quo. It was hard to remain for long at war with Michael. Too good-natured. Too caring. He had a way of disarming the opposition with his charm. He generally ended up on the winning side without a shot being fired.

So what's actually wrong with Michael?
Well, nothing, really.

Another time. Further back. Months before. Michael by the kitchen window fiddling with something electrical. She was doing pencil sketches of him. His head bent over his work, outlined against the light, the exquisite delicacy of his hands as they manipulated small pieces of metal, wire and plastic. She wanted to capture his intentness, the beauty of his absorption.

'Does it look like me?'

'I want it to be a picture of what you are. At this exact moment. It's not about how you look.'

He was having trouble trying to fit a screw into an awkward place. It kept dropping out of his fingers onto the table. Eventually he got it in place. Then raised his eyes and said: 'So it's not appearances then. What things actually look like. That's not what you're after, is it?'

She replied, without taking her eyes off her work, 'Well, you know that already. You should by now.'

'Yes I know. But why?'

'Why what?'

'Why are you sitting there studying me so intently when how I look doesn't matter?'

She thought for a moment. 'Mmm... Fair question. But I already told you. Your physical reality isn't what I'm after. It might not end up like a human being at all. It might just be a series of abstract marks. I don't know.'

'My *inner being* then, is it?' he mocked.

She was silent.

He fiddled some more with his screwdriver and then: 'But how will anyone know it's a person doing a repair job if it's just a series of abstract marks?'

'They won't. But that's not the point.'

He moved his hand impatiently. 'But surely there has to be some resemblance. Something you can recognise?'

She tore out the sketch, placed it on the table beside her and started another on a new page. She could see through his *faux* innocence – he must know that, and it was beginning to be irksome to her.

'There is,' she said shortly. 'In some art it's less obvious, that's all.'

He returned to his work and she to hers. Communication at an end.

As she worked, Alice reflected on what she was doing. She acknowledged that she was not able to explain even to herself what happened when she made art. It always ended up a muddle in her head. A corner of her was even attracted to Michael's scepticism as commonsensically valid. A scepticism with which, perversely and against her better judgment, part of her was drawn to concur.

Yet at the same time there was the overriding sense that art had a nobler purpose. She started to speak again, trying to overcome his resistance.

'Art is communication…

'Yes, I've heard that enough times,' he interrupted peevishly. 'But what a poor way to communicate! Figuring out puzzles? People don't have the time. Art should be clear, direct, obvious. If it's so obscure only the artist knows what it's about – it's not communication, it's solipsism. What's the good of a picture that looks like nothing on earth?'

Nothing on earth. *Nothing on earth.*

But exactly! That was precisely what Alice wanted. To make art that left the commonplace behind, miles behind. Art that invited others to follow.

She was nothing if not tenacious.

'No,' she said. 'My art is … it's about suggestion. It's a kind of … offering. I reach out. You take it, absorb it. Turn it round in your mind. It's a dynamic. It's actually *more* than communicating. What it is… is…' she was struggling, 'is … it's only the diving-off point. You see… it's a fluid thing. There's no limit to it. It's like a pebble thrown into a lake. The ripples are what you're after. That's really the point.'

She broke off. Michael had stopped listening. He held the electrical object up to her with a triumphant 'Done it!'

I can't speak to you if you block your ears. I can give you nothing if you turn away. I can't lead you to heaven if you refuse to leave the earth.

'Will you walk a little faster?' said the whiting to the snail,
'There's a porpoise close behind us, and he's treading on my tail…'
'Will you, won't you, will you, won't you, won't you join the dance?'
But the snail replied 'Too far, too far!' and gave a look askance –
Said he thanked the whiting kindly, but he would not join the dance.
Would not, could not, would not, could not, could not join the dance.

CHAPTER EIGHT

For Alice and David: a little memoir
A New Life

My father had some good friends in Berlin. Once or twice a year he would travel there to visit them. Jan Heinzl was Jewish; Eva not. My mother generally stayed at home with me. She used to go with him to Berlin at first, but when I was born she stayed home. I think now, looking back, she used me as an excuse. She felt uncomfortable there. Jan was an artist, Eva a journalist and poet. They lived together but without being married. So many unorthodox features about that couple. It was all too much for your grandmother to cope with.

My father met them first when he was studying at the University of Berlin and all three had stayed friends for fifteen years, all through the twenties and early thirties. His regular visits to Berlin gave him an insight into what was happening in Germany. He observed, first with mild interest, then puzzled amusement, then finally, with deepening incredulity and alarm, the curious phenomenon of Adolf Hitler as he gained prominence on the political stage. He found it difficult to understand how the German nation, which had always in his mind stood for the highest degree of culture, wisdom and refinement of spirit, could now, apparently of its own volition, be hurtling headlong into a ravine from which there could be no escape. The Nazi machine had geared itself up and was rolling relentlessly onward, crushing everything in its path.

He came home from Berlin recounting talks he had had with his friends and others. He was increasingly perplexed and sought answers which might make some sense of it all.

'What are the German people doing? Have they gone mad?' he exclaimed, but Jan was more sanguine.

'Mad perhaps… but maybe not so mad. Forget the Jews, forget the communists, forget the capitalists. Think about the masses. Think about the young. Those are the ones he wants. It's them he needs. He wants to be adored, unconditionally. That blind "we'll follow you to the ends of the earth" thing. Total control. And he'll do it of course. Elementary. Appeal to the darkest, the most destructive elements of the soul. Stir up the embers. They're never far from the surface. It all seems so innocuous doesn't it? This instinct we all have to categorise, make divisions, order things into groups, particularly ourselves. Like seeks out like. Clubs for everything. Them and us. My tribe and yours. Nothing wrong with that, you might say. But the potential for evil is there. That's where it starts. The tipping point being when difference becomes a reason to condemn. Hitler's no genius, but he's damned cunning. He's stirring up the shit that lies inside each one of us. Poking, prodding, digging till it rises to the top. Then glorifying it. This is the making of the New Great Noble German Reich! And all the better of course if you can shift the blame away from *us* onto *them*. *They* were the cause of the war. *They* were the reason we lost it. Nothing wrong with us. Nothing at all. It's all *their* fault. So get rid of them!'

I saw how my father's faith in human nature was eroding bit by bit. He still wanted to believe that good sense and reason ultimately prevail, but his optimism about the fate of Europe was fading with every passing day. His arguments with my mother didn't have the ring of conviction any more. More hesitant. Even I could see that. And she took full advantage of that. You know what she's like!

She'd seen all this coming long before Josef was forced to accept it. Before there was even a hint of the *Anschluss* to come, she knew Hitler's greed for land made the nazification of Europe inevitable. And that could only mean one thing for us. She knew we had to escape before it was too late.

We had relatives living in England, distant cousins who had settled there in the early twenties. She started to urge your grandfather to up sticks and get out. He would have none of it. He dismissed what he called her 'ravings'.

'You're just dramatizing everything as usual!'

But she kept on and on. Day after day after day.

'Have you taken leave of your senses, Edda?' he would ask. 'You're talking about pulling up our roots. Leaving everything we know – our friends, family, our home. My job, for God's sake! Julius's school. Emigrate? Never!'

He responded with shock and amazement. You'd think she were suggesting flying to the moon. But she would shake her head vigorously, saying: 'No, no, no. Not *emigrating*!' She was emphatic about that.

'Not for good. Only for a while – maybe a year. Who knows? Just till the danger has passed.'

And then my father would look at her with exasperation. A look that meant: 'Why must you be so tiresome?' And he would speak to her in a quiet, patient way, as if explaining something to a child:

'Danger? What danger? At the moment there is no danger to the Czech people. If it comes, we will face it then.' And that was an end to it. For a while.

But not for long. Because she was convinced, beyond a shadow of a doubt, that her decision was right. She was the one who usually gave way to Josef, but this time she wasn't budging.

My father said whatever was going on in Germany was a matter for Germany alone. She would have none of it. She simply retorted each time: 'Josef, your head is in the sand!' and stormed out.

I got sick and tired of hearing the same old arguments. I used to make my escape from the house whenever they started up. I ran and ran, as far away as I could. Finding friends to play football or have races with in the public gardens. I wanted to close my ears, not have to think about the words or what they meant. I sensed that my world was coming to an end. The happy life I'd known till then, I had the feeling it was about to be destroyed forever. A premonition. I just knew in my heart my mother was right. I couldn't bear to hear her ranting on about it. By closing my ears I thought I could somehow pretend it was not happening or at least stall it for a bit longer.

One day I was sitting at breakfast with my father. The usual argument had run its course, my mother having disappeared into the kitchen. He turned to me and was silent for a few moments. Both of us were acutely aware of my mother's distress, which seemed somehow aggravated by her absence. The silence was broken by a baby's distant cry from somewhere in the house. It was my sister, Irma, about eight months old at the time.

Then my father spoke at last, looking not at me but down at his hands. He spoke more to himself than to me. 'Well,' he said quietly, 'I suppose I might as well write to London. It can't do any harm.'

I didn't know what to reply, so I said nothing. My mind was racing. I tried to imagine what London could be like.

But no pictures came. I was about ten or eleven. I'd never been outside of my own country. I just felt numb. I sensed by the change in my father that a bridge had been crossed and there would be no turning back.

Looking back now I don't think he would ever have gone if it hadn't been for us. There were powerful instincts inside him urging him to stay and fight. The idea of running away was abhorrent to him. But now he had three other lives to think of. But still even so and despite that, I think he would have stayed if it hadn't been for your grandmother incessantly getting onto him. So Alice and David: you have her to thank, really, for your lives.

When it grew impossible to go on believing that what was happening was confined to Germany, it became obvious that if Hitler stayed in power and also managed to escape getting assassinated, war was inevitable. My country was under threat. Not least because of the huge German population living along its southern and western borders. The Sudetenland, it was called. Those people – the ethnic Germans – would like nothing better than to sever their attachment to Czechoslovakia and be taken back into the fold of the Fatherland. It was only a matter of time now. Two thirds of them were already members of Henlein's Sudeten German Party, not a million miles away from the German NSDAP.

And of course, for us, in our situation, being Jews, we were the most endangered people in Europe now. My father finally had to face up to the truth. There was no way he could argue away the fact that the anti-semitic hysteria being whipped up in Germany would inevitably have repercussions far beyond the borders of the Reich.

It seemed we had been living in a fool's paradise. As I told you before, I never even knew what the word 'anti-Semitism' meant for the first ten years of my life. None of my family or friends ever experienced discrimination of any kind. I went to the local school. There were both Jews and non-Jews there. My father was highly respected in academic circles; never held back in his career on account of being Jewish.

But anti-Semitism is like a spore. It never dies. It lies dormant till the conditions are right. Then it bursts into life once again. My mother was right.

The turning-point came in 1936, when Jan and Eva wrote with news that Jan's commissions had all but dried up. The Nuremberg laws which had the absurd object of 'protecting German blood and honour', whatever that could possibly mean, were hitting one profession after another. Artists couldn't work unless they belonged to the League, but Jews, as you might expect, were forbidden to belong. So Jan and

Eva were making plans to emigrate to the United States. Jan's brother had been living there for a number of years.

I still have Jan's letter. I want you to read these extracts from it. I think you will find them enlightening. My translation, with apologies to Jan. As accurate as I can make it, anyway:

We are being systematically reduced to a people without legal or civic, even basic human rights. Forget the isolated, but increasingly frequent, cases of intimidation, humiliation and violence. Forget the smashing of windows, the burning of synagogues, the boycotting of Jewish shops, authorised bullying by men dressed up in handsome brown or black uniforms, intoxicated by power. All that is relatively insignificant. We could live with that. We've lived with it before. It passes. You just sweep up the mess and start again.

What's different here is something more sinister, something of an altogether different nature. This is the beginning of a systematic programme of disenfranchisement of a whole community. The highest authorities in the land have actually designed and sanctioned this. It is a programme which cuts across every facet of our existence. Though it seems inconceivable, it is clear to me that what they're planning is to actually eliminate us completely – to wipe us out. So we no longer exist as a people. In fact to them we are not a people at all. We have been reduced to a "question" requiring resolution, a "problem" to be solved. Nothing more.

They are spinning a web around us, growing stronger and tighter by the day. Soon we will all be trapped in the centre, unable to move.

Every day you hear of a new regulation, a new decree intended to alienate us ever further from German society.

And how do they justify this? Quite simply by blood. The "right" blood, the "wrong" blood. Aryan blood. Non-Aryan blood. What the hell does this mean? For generations we've been German citizens. Now suddenly we're not. It's crazy, isn't it? How can this be happening?

They're now trying to destroy friendships between Jews and Germans by making it illegal to even socialize together. Can you believe this?

The other day I telephoned a colleague I've known for nearly ten years. When he knew it was me, he just slammed the phone down.

You know of course that Eva and I are committing a grave offence against the Reich simply by living together. By loving her I am committing Rassenschande – Defilement of the German Race! Can you actually believe this? I am daily risking imprisonment or maybe even worse (who knows?) just by living with her. Eva, too, is running a big risk of course, despite Hitler's assurance that no German woman will suffer from the fault of a Jew. But that's no guarantee. It's common knowledge that Heydrich has other ideas... These cronies of Hitler's, they're loose cannons most of them. They're all capable of absolutely anything...

...One day all this will belong to the past. This insanity will have run its course. People will read about it in books. I can see them now, shaking their heads. I can hear them: "How could this be possible?" Hitler and the Nazis will be dead, but right now it's only just beginning. It's bad now, but I'm sure it's going to get far worse. There

are terrible things in store. I don't know what, but I'm sure as hell not waiting round here to find out!'

That was the last we heard from Jan and Eva till the end of the war. They wrote to the only address they had: our old home in Prague. Their letter travelled halfway across the world, circling Europe and finally arriving at our London address, by some miracle! Its journey started in Columbus, Ohio, the postmark on the letter. For me, as a teenage boy, these names, like most American names, held magical resonances. They conjured up thrilling pictures of Indians in headdresses made of multicoloured feathers, horses galloping across vast plains, cowboys in Stetsons with holstered guns: Hollywood-fed images, which could not be further from the truth.

Eva and Jan wrote us that they were now married. That was the good news. Also they had a son. They called him Samuel, after Jan's father. The bad news was that Samuel, the elder, had perished in Auschwitz, together with Jan's mother, Esther.

They could so easily have been saved. Like Jan and his brother, the could-have-been victims. Like their sons, they too could have soared like songbirds across the ocean to the land of the free, hanging onto the good bits of their past and leaving behind the bad ones, the daily humiliation, the fear. They had the chance, if only they had followed Jan to Ohio.

It was quite possible. It would have been easy. In the beginning Jews could leave Germany, were even encouraged to go. The Nazis were happy to get rid of them. When the war started, it got more difficult. But still it wasn't impossible. It was largely a question of money. If you had enough to pay the emigration tax. They did. And the limit on money you could transfer out of Germany would have made no difference to them – they didn't have enough to worry about anyway. And also if you had people who could vouch for you in the States. They did, of course. They could so easily have gone. Jan and his brother, Otto, were continually exhorting them to leave. But pig-headedly they stayed.

And there's the rub. They could have lived if it hadn't been for their accursed Jewish stubbornness. Dogged, idiot, everything-will-come-right-in-the-end, crazy, impossible optimism. Believing against patently overwhelming odds that somehow, some time, things must – will – get better. The big problem was they loved Germany. It was home, their fatherland. For generations it had been home and they decided they were staying, through thick and thin.

Even right up to the end they thought that somehow as long as they carried on minding their own business, being law-abiding, doing whatever the state required of them, they would be safe: sanity and balance would surely return.

Something would turn up. It had to. It was just around the corner.

'Don't worry, boys,' they wrote, 'it'll all be over soon and we'll be together again, just like it used to be.' A few weeks later they were rounded up and loaded onto the trains.

Jan described to us how he'd trudged the streets from one end of the city to another for almost a year looking for jobs. Advertising agencies, publishers of every kind, big and small, translating firms, newspapers, magazines, even theatre companies. In the end he found work as an illustrator and layout artist with a small magazine.

It was a huge relief to all concerned when he and Eva at last moved into an apartment of their own. By then the forbearance of his brother and sister-in-law had been stretched as thin as it was possible to go without splitting apart. Eva too – even gentle, angelic Eva, for whom it was difficult, almost impossible to speak harshly about any creature, who almost always managed to find some excuse or another for even the most abject behaviour – even she found herself more and more frequently on the point of erupting into a major row with Ilse, her sister in law, over just about anything. Silly minor details of daily existence: had the bread been cut straight or at an angle? Should an egg be boiled for two minutes or three? Surely it was two, not three? Had she forgotten to buy flour for the bread when she knew they needed it, or was it Ilse's fault, because wasn't it she who was the last to go shopping?

Even the most generous, tolerant and forgiving natures can become warped by breathing other people's air for too long. Absence of space enlarges the most insignificant facts of our lives to grotesque proportions, blanking out everything else. It wasn't that they weren't grateful to Otto and Ilse for taking them in. How could they be otherwise? But when they escaped at last from that claustrophobic second-floor apartment in downtown Columbus, they felt like a couple of bears, stretching and blinking in the sunlight after an endless winter sleep. They felt like plants that had lain motionless in the dark silence of the soil and could now erupt into bloom and vibrant colour.

By the time we received their letter it had been almost seven years since we'd left Czechoslovakia. By an odd quirk of fate, the timing of our departure had coincided with *Anschluss*, when Hitler absorbed Austria into the Reich. We left Prague in the early hours of March 11th 1938, and travelled west through Austria towards the Swiss border. Just as we were leaving Austria that night, Hitler's troops were marching in from the opposite direction.

The next day, as we were getting close to France, the troops entered Vienna and Hitler was shouting to the world how he had rescued Austria from chaos. The Austrians waved their little German flags and laughed and cheered in gratitude at the honour of becoming incorporated into the noble Reich. There were some Austrians born and bred who didn't share the communal euphoria, however, for reasons I don't need to go into.

My parents' decision to leave, urged relentlessly by my mother for months and only agreed to with huge reluctance by my father, undoubtedly saved our lives. Just think what that means or might have meant: no Alice and no David in the world!

Barely six months later, our own nation was simply abandoned, left alone in the wilderness by all those she believed were her friends. Left at the mercy of an ogre, a demon, possessed by greed and delusions of world domination.

At Munich, the French and British caved in before the rants of Hitler and Mussolini, hardly raising a whimper. Like weaklings on the beach, they simply stood there inert while the bullies flung sand in their faces. They carved up our country between them like a cake. You have this bit. I'll have that. Poland and Hungary got in on the act and grabbed their chunks too. The little that remained was gobbled up a few months later. A year after we arrived in England, Czechoslovakia ceased to exist. And after only a mere twenty years of life!

In 1945, my little sister – your auntie Irma – was in the first stages of her English education at a local school in Bayswater, near to where we lived. She was the only one of the four of us, of course, who had absolutely no recollection of living anywhere except England. She was about eight. I was nearly eighteen. As her schooling began, mine was ending. A very chequered affair, I have to say! My schooling I mean.

By the time war broke out, I was about eleven or thereabouts. My command of English was not brilliant, but just about adequate for me to follow what was going on in lessons. But then, unfortunately, the school was shut down. All over London children were being shipped out into the countryside to carry on their schooling somehow or other. My school relocated to somewhere in Oxfordshire. All its staff, except for those who joined up, went with it, together with all the pupils who wanted to go. I didn't want to go. And neither did my mother. She didn't want to break up the family. So I stayed. We all stayed on in London.

My father still felt desperately guilty. He saw himself as having abandoned our country in its hour of need. A big part of him yearned to be back in Prague fighting alongside the Czech Resistance. There was something called the Czechoslovak National Committee in London at the time. Benes, our former president, had founded it when he resigned in disgust and left the country after Munich. Your grandfather offered his services to the Resistance but they told him what he already knew really – he was too old. They told him he would be more useful to the cause by staying put and working for the Committee in London. So that's what he did. And so began a political career of sorts, which carried on for some years even after the war ended.

In the beginning, the Committee just organised emigration but after a short while it turned into a political thing. Benes was the head of it all. In less than a year the Committee turned into the Provisional Government in Exile with Benes as its president.

So my father was from then on committed to remaining in London for the foreseeable future. And we, of course, stayed with him.

There followed what was, for me, quite an enjoyable year. My mother was searching around to find a suitable school for me. While she searched, I spent most of my time wandering round London, exploring this new city and generally doing whatever I felt like. I read some books, German and English. I played my violin. As you know, I started violin lessons in Prague when I was six. Both my parents loved music. My mother very soon found me a teacher in London. She was desperate that I wouldn't fall behind.

Dr Redei was an aged Hungarian gentleman of extremely short stature. Though still only eleven I was already taller than him. He was a brilliant musician and an inspiring teacher. Since the end of the First World War he had lived in England. He was actually a naturalised British citizen, but you would never know it. He still spoke a central European variety of English in a thick, barely intelligible Budapest accent. Somehow we managed to communicate, hobbling along on a mixture of German, Pidgin English and a lot of sign language and singing.

Practising was never a bind for me. I don't know at all how many hours I practised in a day. It varied. I picked up my violin whenever I felt like it and just played. My mother had always a special smile on her face then. She never once asked me to stop. All that changed when I switched to the saxophone. But that was much later.

As to my general education, it staggered along in fits and starts. My mother got in touch with the Jewish Council which recommended some ladies, who came to the house two or three times a week to give me school instruction. I suppose it was better than nothing. But I was not a responsive pupil. It must have been hell for those well-meaning Jewish ladies. A succession of them came and went. All terribly sincere, wanting to help. But I resented them. My opinion was that my English didn't need perfecting. It was fine already. I didn't need lessons. I found out how wrong I was when I eventually found myself in a school classroom surrounded by English children. But in the meantime, there I was, all alone with only my inflated ego for company. The ladies set me homework, reams of exercises which I scribbled out answers to in the most perfunctory fashion. I just scrawled something down on paper, anything, in the least possible time so I could get out again into the fascinating London streets and pursue my explorations.

When the Blitz started over London and other British cities in 1940, a house just three doors away from ours received a direct hit one night. I ran to look at the rubble which was all that remained. That was the day my father put his foot down. My mother begged and entreated. He ignored her tears.

'You can cry as much as you like,' he told her. 'I'm sending you away where it's safe. I'm sorry. It won't be forever. Only till the bombing stops.'

We ended up in a village in Gloucestershire. My father stayed in London because of his work for the Committee. He got us installed in a small cottage – a holiday place belonging to someone he knew. Then he returned to London and the bombs. My mother was left with the task of once again searching round for a school for me. Not easy. Many schools had closed down for the war. And not all the functioning ones were prepared to take refugees. Anyway, we finally found somewhere – a small private school quite near to where we lived, which agreed to take me in as a day boy.

I remember my mother being miserable for weeks. But gradually she adapted to life without my father. He wrote to us often and visited whenever he could. That was about every two or three months. Not more. We thought at first we would be going back to London in a short time – certainly no longer than a year at the most. In fact, it was another five years before we were able to resume life together as a family again.

We always planned to return to Prague when the war ended. But it didn't work out that way. We never regarded London as a permanent arrangement. We were so naïve. When Benes got friendly with Stalin at the end of '43, we stupidly thought this would be a good thing for us. We actually believed Czechoslovakia would go back to what it had been before Munich. Wishful thinking! How could we be so blind? Benes was our president in name, but in reality he ended up as nothing but a puppet of the Soviets.

When the war ended we were euphoric. We saw the Russians as benefactors, liberators. We were like children, totally trusting. Then when Benes went back in the spring of '45 the first thing he did was to kick all the Germans out of the country. Stalin had no problem with this. My father was appalled. He saw it as an act of blind revenge.

'Look what he's doing!' he said in disgust. 'Exactly the same as before. Only now it's us doing it to them. What is the point of all this? It's not right. And we've been through all this ourselves. Uprooting people from their homes. I despair! I despair! Will we never learn?'

My father was a genuine idealist. As pure as they come. Justice was his guiding light in everything. I never once saw him choose personal advantage over principle. He lived his life that way and expected everyone else to do the same. He wasn't meant for politics. Which is probably why he never got anywhere in public life. He expected too much from people and people constantly disappointed him. When they fell below his standards, he was unforgiving.

But on the other hand, as a father, he was wonderfully understanding. If my sister or I broke something or spilt something on the floor, or did badly at school or spoke out of turn – things that would rouse my mother to paroxyms of fury, he would calmly shrug and say: 'Don't worry. It's a mistake. It's not important. It can be rectified.'

For him there was a radical, absolutely uncrossable, line between things you could put right and things that were so irredeemably wrong they could never be eradicated or forgotten. He said those kinds of things were like a stain on the human fabric, there forever.

'Our actions leave a trail behind us,' he used to say. 'Nothing is lost. You may think you can just turn your back and move on, but you can't. Collective memory won't let you off the hook.'

When Benes began to curry favour with the Soviets, my father branded him without hesitation a traitor. Not just to the Czechs, but also to him personally. Benes was someone he had worked with and believed in for a long time. He never forgave him.

There was no question now of returning to Prague. Not that we gave up hope of things getting better. Against all the odds, we still hoped against hope for a while. We gave up hoping in '46, when Gottwald became leader and turned our country into a communist satellite of the Soviets. From then on, the situation went from bad to worse. From friends still living in Prague we heard that they were grabbing people's land, nationalising factories and forcing huge tax increases onto intellectuals and writers. Even conducting a vicious witch-hunt against anyone suspected of being anti-communist, in every kind of organisation – big or small, public or private.

Everything my father and his friends had struggled so hard to achieve for their country thirty years before – all destroyed. One kind of oppression simply substituted by another. His detestation of Soviet Russia was boundless.

I remember him railing against the tragic fate of the Czech nation to my mother, but she usually just listened in silence, her head bent over a book or something she was writing in one of her ubiquitous notebooks.

'Why do you just sit there saying nothing, Edda?' he would demand angrily. She would look up and tell him he had already said everything that could be said about the situation. There was nothing she could add.

In truth she was little affected by politics. She had no sense of nationhood or patriotism. The only solidarity she felt was with the Jewish community and that transcended national boundaries. For several years after we came to England she wrote letters to Hanna, her sister. She continued to hope that eventually some reply would come, some news of her. Maybe she had moved out of Prague and someone would forward her letters. But all through the war we never heard anything.

When the war ended, my father made some enquiries. There was no trace of her, or Jacob, her husband, or their little boy, Stefan. My mother still continued to write, never giving up hope. Till one day, in '46, we received a letter from some people who were living a few doors away from where Hanna and her family used to live, the only address we had. A letter from my mother had been delivered to them in error.

'*I am returning your letter,*' the man wrote, '*because the Bergman family left Number thirty-three some years ago. We were told they were taken to Thereisenstadt some time in 1942. I believe they were later sent from there to Auschwitz'.* And as an afterthought, he adds: *'Very sorry'.*

Just that: *'Very sorry.'* I'm sure he was sincere. But those two little words. To end a letter like that… But then I suppose there are no words that could ever do justice to such a tragedy as that.

We never spoke about Hanna again. I learned to keep my mouth firmly shut about any part of our former existence in Prague. The one time I made a mistake – it was winter and a few light snowflakes had started to float past the window of my bedroom – without thinking I blurted out: 'Look Mama! But it's not *real* snow, is it? Not like we used to get at home!' I saw her back and her shoulders tense up and that stopped me in my tracks, but it was too late. She whipped round from the pile of clothes she was folding and turned to face me with a look I'd never seen before. Her eyes were as cold and hard as two pistols pointing straight at me. I thought she was going to hit me. But she just said to me in a quiet, intense voice: 'Never speak of that again. All that is over.'

I have to confess that I was less bothered by these unhappy events than my parents. To tell the truth, I was blissfully happy. I had no desire to leave England. In '46 I was eighteen. I'd lived here for eight years and I felt I belonged. The country I was born in had the feeling of an alien place.

So when it became more and more unlikely that we would return, I felt secretly relieved.

Added to which, I had recently been propelled into two new and utterly mesmerising worlds: American popular music and GIRLS! Either of these on its own, let alone both together, had the power to overshadow everything else that was going on around me.

As far as the music was concerned, it was a permanent backdrop to everybody's lives in those days. It drifted into homes over the airways, into movie-houses, theatres, hotels. As I grew from childhood into adolescence it was a familiar, reassuring sound. It made me feel good, but in a distant, half-conscious way. Like coming into a warm house on a winter's night. My head was filled with melody. Cascades of instantly hummable tunes, with witty lyrics and infectious rhythms that lightened up the post-war years.

But it was only when I left school that I started thinking about it seriously. It was quite a sudden thing. I can remember the exact moment when the course of my life changed. A dreary afternoon. Rain beating against the windows of the basement which Irma and I had always used as a playroom. She was there with me, playing with her dolls. She was lining them up in a succession of different arrangements, speaking to them in a stern voice like a teacher. My mother was on the floor above, ironing in the kitchen.

The radio was on – *wireless* as we used to call it. Me sitting in an old easy-chair next to it, half-reading, half-dreaming. Suddenly these wonderful sounds came flooding into the room. It was Artie Shaw playing *Begin the Beguine*. I was transfixed. I'm not kidding: it was like falling in love for the first time. Sorry, but this is no exaggeration. The melody came through with this jaunty lilting quality, as clear as a mountain stream, the exultant rhythm section pounding along all the way insistently, a perfect foil for the solo.

Those three minutes were an epiphany. I fell irredeemably in love with that music. A love affair that's gone on ever since. And I knew from that moment that the inevitability of my future as a concert violinist was drifting off rapidly into space. My parents for most of my life up till then had taken that future for granted. I was the should-have-been maestro performer, destined for greatness, all set to captivate concert audiences throughout the Western world. They were convinced of that. It was one of their deepest satisfactions, listening to me play and dreaming their dreams. But me: I didn't give a second thought to them or their disappointment. I was just overwhelmed, taken over, hooked.

The love affair that started was as much with the songs as with the bands. All those sublime melodies. *'Body and Soul'*, *'Honeysuckle Rose'*, *'In a Sentimental Mood'*, *'Sophisticated Lady'*, *'Deep Purple'* to name just a few... The profusion of them: incredible. Tumbling forth, one after another. A cornucopia that never seemed to run dry. Why I hadn't seen it before I don't know. I guess I just wasn't ready till that moment. You live with someone for years hardly noticing them and then out of the blue one day you see how stunningly beautiful they are. Why? I really have no idea.

I couldn't call it a choice. I had no alternative. In my euphoric state I felt I had to tell somebody. Straight away. I seized my sister's hands and she stared at me, as if I'd gone mad. My heart was bumping so hard I could hardly breathe.

'Irma,' I gasped, 'I'm going to play the most beautiful music in the world!'

'What – now?'

A little deflated, I replied: 'No, of course not. I'll do it as soon as I've learnt to play the clarinet.'

'The what?'

She was only about eight at the time.

I retained enough respect for my parents' feelings, particularly my mother's, not to ditch the violin. As a matter of fact, it turned out to be not a bad decision. It was a valuable source of finance in the early years. I went on having lessons and practising. But I was like a man caught in a loveless marriage continually lusting after his mistress.

At first I thought it prudent to keep my plans to myself. I found a job as a shop assistant in a place near Tottenham

Court Road, which sold musical instruments and sheet music. I earned extra money three nights a week playing second violin in a string quartet entertaining guests in a hotel near Hyde Park. I saved enough money in the end to purchase a second-hand clarinet from the shop where I worked.

What a day! Without doubt the most memorable day of my life till then, excepting only the day Artie Shaw had unwittingly pointed me towards my true destiny.

I shall never forget my parents' stunned expressions when, with some trepidation, I opened the battered black case and reverently lifted out the precious instrument to show them. Naturally they hadn't failed to notice my growing obsession with American band music, but I'm sure they saw it as just a hobby, no more significant than other phases I had gone through, interests come and gone: stamp collecting, model building and the like. Even after I showed them the clarinet they weren't too worried. They correctly assumed my career would be in music, but for them that meant two things: classical music and the violin. Despite my mother's initial horrified shriek I don't think they seriously imagined I was about to veer so radically from the expected path.

Knowing them as I did, I accurately predicted their reactions when I opened the case. My father took one look and said flatly: 'So who do you think you are? Benny Goodman?'

As always with Josef: right on the button. Whether by accident or intuition or maybe it was just self-evident, but at that time I identified one hundred per cent with Goodman. East European Jewish émigré: that was me, absolutely. Him and me: two of a kind. Except that he was a star and I was a nobody.

Edda managed to combine in a single utterance the hysterical prophesying of doom with the matter of fact worldliness which, together, typified her approach to everything. A high-pitched: 'What a tragedy, Julius! To be throwing away your life and your talent!' was followed by accusatory finger-jabbing targeted at the clarinet, accompanied by a contemptuous: 'And you'll never make a living out of *that*!'

Those were her last words on the subject. Neither she nor Josef tried to dissuade me. I guess they knew it would be pointless.

I then fell abruptly off the mountain-top to find myself face to face with reality: how to learn the technique of playing a wind instrument from scratch. I bought myself a book. '*How to play the clarinet in I don't remember how many easy lessons...*' Not so easy actually. So I found myself a teacher. Joe Silberman, he was called. One-time leader of a six or seven-piece band that toured the country playing in small venues in the thirties. He was the father of a friend of a colleague of mine – also working in the shop. Joe had given up playing at the time I met him. He ran a tobacconist's and newsagent's shop now, somewhere off the Portobello Road. His jazz past reduced to supplementing his income from teaching wannabes like me.

Joe taught me all the rudiments. I managed to pay for six months' of lessons, an hour a week. But then I ran out of money. So it was back to the book. And the records. I practised day in day out, for hours at a time. I started directly I got home from work. Kept on sometimes into the early hours. Luckily the house was built on four floors and solid enough for my horrible squeaks in the basement not to wound anyone's ears but mine.

I learnt the meaning of terms like *the bridge, riff, vamp,* that I'd never heard of before. I played the small collection of seventy-eights I'd managed to acquire over and over again, till the grooves were almost worn through. Recordings of Artie Shaw, Benny Goodman, the Dorseys, the Duke Ellington band, Count Basie: I learnt them note for note so I could exactly reproduce the solos and improvisations. Then I started making up improvisations of my own.

At the same time I pressed on with my violin. As my mother predicted, it provided me with a useful source of income. Thank goodness I had the sense to realise I might as well make use of the ten years I'd already spent sweating over one instrument. I had no idea how long it would take before

I got good enough to earn anything from the other one. A long, long time: that was all I knew.

As you know, this wasn't the end of the rainbow for me, despite my love affair with Swing. After a couple of years I was looking for something new. Jazz was changing. Goodman and Shaw were, I had to admit, beginning to sound dated. With the fickleness of youth I dumped them, without a backward glance, in preference to a new idol: Lester Young, and a new instrument. If you ask me what happened to my old friend, my faithful companion whose keys had nurtured my first stumbling attempts at making jazz, well, I'm sorry to say I handed it over in part exchange for the tenor sax – second-hand again, but a precious thing which turned out to be my pride and joy for many, many years.

In the meantime, before I graduated to the sax, between serving in the music shop, playing palm court violin in hotels, and working up my jazz clarinet technique, I was developing a taste for a new kind of pleasure. I had had very little contact with girls till then. I'd spent most of my life at a boys' only school, so there was little chance of ever seeing a girl, except from afar, let alone talking to one.

Over the years, since we'd lived in London, my mother had accumulated a fair clutch of lady acquaintances – not friends exactly... No, I wouldn't go so far as to describe them as *friends*. Anyhow, she socialised with them quite a bit. Meeting up now and again for lunch in town, or tea. They were all nice Jewish ladies just like her, some from émigré families, some English-born, and some of them had daughters round about my age.

When I left school she started to invite some of these ladies round to the house more frequently, particularly the ones with daughters. She made a point of including the daughters in her invitations. These occasions invariably followed the same format and were, on the whole, a pretty excruciating experience both for myself and the girls involved.

Thanks to some mysterious atavistic influence at work in her psyche, Edda clung to the notion that now I'd reached my seventeenth year I was ready for the initiation rites which would result in the grand and glorious rainbow's end for every decent Jewish household: the discovery of the perfect match. I believe there lurked somewhere deep within her a lingering nostalgia for the warm, close-knit world of the *shtetl* of her ancestors. It wouldn't surprise me if somewhere amongst that crowd was one who had actually exercised the revered profession of Official Matchmaker.

These occasions usually took the form of tea-parties. I would be forced to put on my one and only suit and a tie chosen by Edda. I had to smarm my hair down flat with water, a pointless exercise, since as soon as it dried, the curls would bounce up again and return me to my normal dishevelled appearance. At precisely half-past four, the doorbell would ring, causing my heart to lurch with apprehension.

We would sit, rigid with embarrassment, in the third-floor sitting-room, the lady and her daughter on one side, my mother and I on the other. As the afternoon wore on, increasingly desperate attempts were made to ward off the ever-threatening silences. Anything that could conceivably be used as a subject of conversation – the weather, the state of the economy, Mr Attlee and the excellent things he was doing for Britain, my career plans, the daughter's career plans, the latest Rita Hayworth film – was dredged up till the bottom of the barrel had been reached. At that point, usually after about forty-five minutes, Edda would rise to fetch tea and cakes.

The other mother would invariably leap up as well, offering to help with a big smile on her face and a meaningful nod towards the daughter and me. She would never have sunk so low as to actually wink. But the nod was as good as.

This left the hapless daughter and me alone together, forced into casting thin smiles at one another across acres of faded blue and beige carpeting. I remember this as a particularly painful moment. The supply of serviceable talking points having been used up, there was often nothing left but to drag them out all over again, albeit with a new slant.

One of this long succession of girls was called Sophie.

'So you're planning to go into the retail business then?' I began brightly, praying she would come up with some details I didn't already know. Her mother had proudly announced earlier that *'my Sophie'* was about to start a course as a trainee buyer with a well-known West End store. 'Always such an excellent eye for fashion!' she told my mother, and both turned admiringly to Sophie, who seemed unusually intent on examining the design of the carpet, and did not look up, as if they were talking about someone else.

Sophie replied to my question in choked bursts, her eyes fixed on a point on the wall, somewhere to the right of my head. Her discomfiture magnified my own and also aroused in me an agony of sympathy for her. I struggled to help her along by finishing her truncated sentences for her, as you do out of sympathy for a stammerer.

'Yes… Going to learn…' she stopped, looking for the word.

'About fashion?' I prompted. Her head gave a series of nods, that reminded me of the clown-toys which carry on nod-nod-nodding once you've set them off.

'When will you start?' I continued, trying to sound relaxed.

'In… after…end of…'

'The summer?'

'No! No!' Nods gave way to shakes.

'September?' I hazarded.

More shakes.

'October, then?' I tried, feeling increasingly desperate.

Nods once again.

'Yes... Middle of...'

'The middle of October! Ah yes!' I was beginning to feel like a primary school teacher coaxing a child through the first stages of literacy.

Then all of a sudden she began to produce torrents of words that tumbled out of her mouth in a seemingly unstoppable flow of information and opinion. It was as if an ignition switch had finally made contact after dozens of false starts.

Once the spark was lit, it was impossible to halt the forward motion. In the space of a few minutes, her entire life history was reeled out, all her immediate family members named and classified – age, social status, level of intelligence, marital situation, and so on. Her academic record was detailed (impressive) as well as her reasons for pursuing a career in retail clothing (the most important being that her father owned a women's clothing business).

When she finally stopped, it was for want of breath rather than things to say. By the time the tea and cakes arrived with the mothers, her breath was back and she started up all over again. I was halfway through my tea and onto my second cake by the time she ran out of steam.

Of all the unfortunate girls forced by their mothers and mine to endure the pain of the tea-party experience – and there were a great many – Sophie is the only one that remained in my memory. Not only did she have a sharp intelligence and wit, she was also extraordinarily pretty. Her hair was a mass of bubbly black curls, her eyes an unusual shade of deep violet, her skin smooth and pale, like the inside of a lily.

We saw one another intermittently for about six months. I remember sitting tensely beside her in the dark of cinemas. Every time her arm or her knee brushed accidentally against mine, rivers of fire gushed through me. As for her, she maintained a consistently passionless exterior. I was never able to detect whether anything was going on inside her. She never gave me even a hint that things might go further between us, given time. And I lacked the courage to take any kind of initiative.

She was a well brought up Jewish girl after all. I was terrified that any advance from me would be angrily thrown back in my face and whatever was developing between us would be brought to an abrupt end. So we carried on that way, me burning up with secret desire, her quiet and icy-prim.

When we were apart, in my turbulent imagination we journeyed together through gardens of orgiastic delights. We thrashed about in every conceivable mode of carnal congress. But in the few months we spent together, the closest I got to quenching my desire was a swift kiss planted in febrile guilt one evening onto her cool, closed lips. She reacted to this with as much passion as a white orchid encased in glass.

I can't recall now when we stopped seeing each other, or why. I think it was something that faded away naturally, like a song that has nowhere else to go. I don't remember any specific breaking apart event or moment. No particular pain. There were just the two of us. And then there weren't any more. Maybe something happened. Memory fails me.

I can only surmise. The months we spent together before the start of her new career were perhaps a void she was willing to fill with whatever came along. I, with my puppy-like devotion, was as good as anything else I suppose. As for me, the temptation of Sophie's beauty and my state of permanent frustration probably led me to a sense of relief when finally the demands of the clothing industry took precedence over me.

I bumped into Sophie again years later. We were both in our forties. I walked into a ladies' dress shop and there she was. She had put on a bit of weight, but I recognised her at once. The same dark curls, the same lilywhite skin. My heart lurched at the sight of her. I'd leapt back thirty years. She didn't see me at first. I watched her in profile, while she spoke to another, younger, woman beside a rack of evening dresses. She appeared to be giving instructions to the woman.

I wondered 'shall I speak?' Your mother was with me. She was over at the other end of the shop, looking at suits. But while I was debating with myself, Sophie caught sight of me. She walked over to me, frowning, trying to place me.

'I know you,' she said. 'My God! Julius? Is it you?'
The shop belonged to her. So did a whole chain of others. She reeled off the details of her life, all in the space of about five minutes, just as she had before at the tea-party a lifetime ago. It was difficult to take it all in. Twice divorced, two children – a son and daughter both in their twenties.

'And you, Julius?'
But I had no chance to tell her because by then Estelle had seen us and was approaching with intense curiosity.

'My wife,' I said. 'Sophie, this is Estelle.'

So it goes. Life is strange, isn't it? Meetings and partings. I even found myself wondering some years after that, when your mother and I were no longer together, would anything happen between Sophie and me should our paths cross once again? I found myself in the same street again once. I had to deliver some arrangements I'd done for a recording. The address was just a few doors away from the shop where I'd seen Sophie that time. When I'd dropped the music off, I thought, 'well I'll just have a look. You never know…'

She wasn't there of course. I made no enquiries. It wasn't meant to be. Not yet anyway. The wrong time.

So, anyway, going back to the early years, when Sophie and I went our separate ways, my mother resumed her matchmaking forays. By then I was increasingly bored with the whole exercise. I was even starting to vent my impatience on the wretched girls and their mothers. Very unfair of me. I became surly and truculent. A poor match for any girl. It infuriated my mother, needless to say.

At one disastrous encounter I reduced a plumpish girl to tears by suggesting, in an innocent voice, that she might improve her chances of marriage if she cut down her intake of cream cakes. She was just reaching for the third time to grab a cake from the piled-up plate.

Her mother at this flew into a rage and stood up, pulling her daughter onto her feet in the same action. In a shaky, high-pitched voice she accused me of such rudeness as she had never before heard in all her life. She then turned on my mother and shouted: 'And you, Mrs Levy, what kind of an upbringing did you give to such a boy? He brings shame on your family!' Whereupon the two of them stormed out of the house, pursued by my mother's wails of contrition.

I can still feel the sting of my mother's hand on my cheek. I was faking defiance, but inwardly quaking. She spent the next hour reviling me and fulminating against me, fuelled by all the pain of a woman dishonoured in the presence of her peers.

'I can't understand what's happened to you, Julius,' she ended sadly, once the rage had subsided. 'Where is the nice, pleasant, happy boy we used to know?' She shook her head. Then suddenly, as if a penny had dropped, she leapt into a venomous attack. 'It's that – that *jazz music!*' She spat out the words with the disgust reserved for a turd deposited on the pavement by some inconsiderate dog.

'That's what it is! Of course! It's turned you into a stranger. I don't recognise you any more. And that's a fact!' And that was the last of the tea-parties.

It was then I started to go on hunting expeditions of my own. Even in those times, there were girls to be found. You didn't have to look too hard. Girls who were not too worried about the *proper way to behave*. Ironically enough, Edda's assumption that jazz had made me into a different person contained a grain of truth, though not in the way she meant it. As I relentlessly searched around for free-spirited girls to share good times with, I soon realised that being a bandsman – even an embryo one – conferred an aura of glamour. It gave me a definite edge over other guys.

Though my standard of playing was still pretty mediocre, the mere fact of describing myself as a *jazz musician* had a magical effect on females. Never mind that in reality at the time I was still standing on the sidelines. My connection with the world of American popular music was tenuous. I'd had one or two gigs playing saxophone with some friends at parties, but that was it. Still, it made me more interesting than if I'd been just a bank clerk or a librarian.

It was about three years after I started playing professionally in bands that I first set eyes on Estelle. I was about twenty-five, still just an average sax player, but managing to scrape a living, the bulk of it still coming from the violin. I didn't need the music shop job any more. I was also still living at home, which helped the finances.

The chamber group I'd played with from time to time in the hotels took me on as a permanent member. I was the youngest: all the others were in their late thirties and forties. We played a wide repertoire. Anything from Mozart to genteel renditions of hit tunes from musicals of the day: *'Oklahoma'*, *'Annie Get Your Gun'*, *'Lady Be Good'* and the like. The cello player was also our agent and business manager. He was smart enough to realise that the wider our range, the more work we'd get.

The music we supplied was of the wallpaper variety. Agreeable, non-intrusive background noise: I suppose people would call it 'lift music' these days. Not the kind that makes you want to dance or fall into raptures over. It was *music-to-go-with-something-else* music: music to talk to, music to eat to, music to do anything in the world to, apart from actually listening and experiencing it for itself.

What did I care? I was OK. I was leading a double life. One: controlled, civilized, soporific; the other: inspirational, unpredictable, passionate. It really hit home those times when a number I was playing with the strings in the afternoon reappeared in the band's programme at night. That happened quite a lot. One example that springs to mind was '*Summertime*'. The chamber group was hired to play for a group of ladies down from Yorkshire on a day trip to London.

The string ensemble was enlarged that time to include a flautist and a harpist. Thanks to an incredible feat of arranging, this quintessential jazz classic came out like a totally unswinging, yet at the same time rollicking cross between '*The Sailor's Hornpipe*' and '*It's a Long Way to Tipperary*' or even '*My Old Dutch*'. I could hardly keep a straight face. I nearly dropped my fiddle at one stage when I caught the eye of the other violin-player in the group – the only one of the lot who shared my sense of humour. It was just farcical, but the ladies seemed to love our rendition. They gave us a great hand at the end. I wonder whether they had any idea what tune they were actually listening to, or what it should have sounded like.

That same evening I found myself on a makeshift stage in the works canteen of a factory that made machine parts for something – I forget now what. It was their annual staff party. I was playing tenor sax as one of the Billy Rowson sextet. *'Summertime'* was once again on the programme. Comparing the two versions I played that day, apart from the title and the basic chord sequences, there was not a thing they had in common. If the Yorkshire ladies had been sitting in the audience with the workers, they wouldn't have recognised it as the same tune.

They probably wouldn't have recognised me either. This time I played from the heart. I was flying. Everything came together at last. I reached a new level that night. It was a watershed: everything up to then had been a big effort, trial and error – with plenty of errors. But that night all those hours of practising in the basement finally paid off. It felt great. Incomparable. In hindsight, it probably wasn't, but it certainly felt like it.

The other guys looked at me differently from that day forward. I'd shifted up several rungs in their estimation. I felt like a professional for the first time. The kind I longed to be, not the pallid, tired, play-by-rote, going-through-the-motions-to-earn-a-few-pennies fiddle player I was in my other incarnation.

The opportunities for band-playing were erratic and none too frequent. We might get two gigs a week, then go for five or six weeks with nothing. The six of us practised mostly at my house, because of the famous near-enough-sound-proof basement. Billy was our trumpet-player. He was the named leader because he was more experienced than the rest of us and he'd put the band together in the beginning. But it was a loose kind of arrangement. We each of us searched around for work all the time as individuals too. We might hear on the grapevine that a bandleader was looking for a sax player or trombonist or whatever, then we'd rush off to get in first. There were literally hundreds of bands around in those days. Or we'd go down to Archer Street and tout for business, together with other out-of-work musicians, hoping for a break. Sometimes we got lucky, mostly we went away empty-handed.

I found a job one time with an orchestra that was booked to play for a short run of a musical review at the Apollo Theatre. I was looking for work on clarinet or sax, but as it happened, they needed fiddle players, so I got the job. It was a pretty nondescript review: forgettable tunes and mediocre arrangements. I don't know how it made it to the West End. It closed after six weeks. The cast consisted of half a dozen men and about ten girls, all singers and dancers. It was called some ridiculous name, like '*Young, Carefree and Gay*' – I don't remember exactly. But it was profoundly significant for me because one of the cast was a lovely blonde actress by the name of Estelle Bouret.

You've seen many pictures of your mother at the time. You know how stunning she was. No surprise, then, that I was smitten with her as soon as I saw her. I didn't think I stood much of a chance, but for some reason she responded favourably to me. God knows what she saw in me.

Estelle craved fame. I thought she had a beautiful singing voice – I told her so over and over. She accepted the compliments I showered on her rather condescendingly, I remember. One thing she never lacked and that was confidence. An essential element of a stage career. I also thought she danced divinely. Perfection, in my book. Yet somehow fame continued to elude her. She never rose much above the chorus line or bit parts. Maybe her acting wasn't quite up to scratch. I don't know. Given the enormity of my infatuation, I was not the best person to judge.

By the time I met Estelle, she'd been treading the boards for seven or eight years. As soon as she could, she left school and rushed straight into the business. After all those years of never getting anywhere, she was starting to get tired of the struggle. She told me she could have slept her way to success, like some others she knew, but that wasn't her bag. So she told me, anyway. And I believed her...

So when she met me, she was close to being ready to settle down. I was lucky. A year or two earlier, and my life might have turned out altogether differently. You wouldn't be in the world, for one thing...

I was only twenty-seven myself, though, and I reckoned I was entitled to a few more years of freedom. I really could not see myself in the role of a married man. But unfortunately, I was besotted. I tried to force the issue by walking away. I stopped seeing her. Took out a succession of other women. I tried to extricate myself from the web by gobbling up every new delicacy that came my way.

But it was a pointless exercise. I was like a condemned man frantically trying to squeeze a lifetime of freedom into the few weeks he has left. I couldn't get Estelle out of my mind. She was the only one I wanted and the only way I could get her was to marry her.

My decision to marry Estelle was my final and definitive fall from grace as far as my mother was concerned. It was bad enough when I turned my back on the glittering concert career she'd been planning for me almost since the day I was born. But this beat everything. To marry outside the faith! This was something she could never have predicted or imagined, even in her worst nightmare.

She spent weeks in a state of suppressed panic. Walking from room to room, perpetually tidying up, re-arranging the furniture, constantly on the move. It was painful to witness. And all this was set against the *basso continuo* of her incessant, sinister mumbling to herself as she worked.

This stage was superseded by outbursts of rage, that erupted without warning. At these times I was afraid to go near her in case she picked up the nearest blunt instrument and hurled it at me. Other times, she would affect a mysterious, coldly logical approach and would, with unnatural calm, discuss with me ways in which the disaster of what I was proposing might be mitigated.

'Why don't you spend some time apart? Six months, perhaps, a year...?'

'A year?'

'Yes. To test yourselves.'

I looked at her nervously. 'I already tried this, Mama. It didn't work.'

She shrugged. 'So try it again.'

I shook my head and moved a little distance away from her. She thought for a moment, pursing her lips and frowning deeply.

'Then go away! Do some travelling. See the world! A young man like you...'

I shook my head again, edging further away. 'It wouldn't be any good. I'd just want to take her with me.'

She clucked her tongue with impatience. Silence again. Then she looked up, her face suddenly illuminated with a broad smile. 'There is only one way, then!' she concluded triumphantly. 'Estelle must convert to Judaism. Then at least your children will be Jewish!'

An expression of satisfaction passed across her face. It passed away again rapidly the moment she heard the explosions of mirth I could no longer contain.

In the end, she had to bow to the inevitable. Our wedding was so quiet it was almost invisible. We were married at the local registry office. Nobody came except for my father, Billy from our band and Julia, a friend of Estelle's. Afterwards the five of us went out for a meal at a restaurant nearby. My father paid. He took to Estelle right away. He couldn't have cared less about her not being Jewish. Her parents were Catholic but religion was of no more importance to her than to him in any case.

Your grandmother, on the other hand… Well, you remember what she was like. At first she said we should move out of the house. At least then she would not be forced to have her shame paraded before her eyes day in day out. We stayed because we couldn't afford to go. To tell the truth, the house was big enough to take at least three other couples and not even my mother could bring herself to evict us. My father would have put his foot down anyway.

Your mother found the whole thing very difficult for the first year. She and your grandmother took strenuous care to avoid encounters in or out of the house. We lived in the basement, which we used as a self-contained flat. We had a small kitchen put in and there was already a bathroom downstairs. We were like two separate families. Whenever their paths crossed, as they had to sometimes, they treated one another with a kind of stiff courtesy, like an impeccably-mannered dowager and a distinguished house-guest. They only just stopped short of bowing to one another. It was too ridiculous to contemplate without wanting to laugh out loud. But neither of them saw the joke.

Of course this couldn't go on. Something had to give. But the almighty row everyone thought would erupt at any moment never happened. The event that wrought the most miraculous transformation in my mother, turning grim antipathy to rapturous affection, was your birth, Alice. From the moment she held you in her arms when she came to visit you and your mother in the hospital, you – just a few hours' old, the redoubtable battle-axe vanished forever, never to return.

CHAPTER NINE

As far back as she could remember Alice had lived with the alchemist's dream. She encountered it at different times and in different guises. Music was the first and remained the most enduring key to the transfigured world. A world that hovered on the edge of reality, a promise of sublimity. Sometimes it was only glimpsed for a moment; sometimes experienced for longer and more profoundly. She gravitated towards it like a plant to the sun.

Music and dance permeated her very earliest memories. Her mother and father seated either side of a window through which sunlight streamed; so blindingly bright she could barely see them; she dancing ecstatically to the sounds that flowed from a gramophone in the corner; pirouetting, leaping and bending, flinging her arms into the air, stretching her legs, pointing her toes. She was no more than three or four. She heard her parents' delighted applause, but the energy and passion of her dance was for the music, not for them.

And later, she must have been about seven or eight, she sat on the floor of the living-room, hugging her knees. The circular rug was the colour of her mother's bath soap and edged with two interlinking rows of small pink roses. Her father was playing the Adagio from the Max Bruch Concerto. It was the first time she had heard it. She rested her head on her knees. The sounds infused every inch of her body with a joy that made her eyes fill with tears.

Some music affected her so profoundly that listening alone failed to do it justice. It moved her physically as well as emotionally. It filled her with an intense desire to mirror the sequence of sounds and rhythms with the movements of her body. The melodies and harmonies took form as shape, colour and motion. The music was re-creating itself through her physical being.

When she was little, her parents and grandparents frequently took her along to concerts and ballets. She could not explain to them how agonising it was for her to be trapped in her seat in the darkness when every muscle and nerve pleaded to fly free.

Estelle, eager to nurture what she perceived as the dance gene which her daughter appeared to have inherited from her, enrolled five-year-old Alice in a ballet school in Ladbroke Grove. Here, every Saturday morning from ten to twelve, Alice was schooled in the techniques and disciplines of Russian ballet by one Natalya Morozova, a gnarled and fearsome lady, always clad from head to toe in black, whom one was expected to address at all times as 'Madame'.

To Alice, Madame appeared incommensurably old. She had been one of the stars of a ballet company from Kiev which toured Europe in the twenties wowing audiences with the spectacular skill and showmanship of its dancers. During the company's visit to London, Madame, then just twenty-two, fell passionately in love with an English actor and subsequently contrived not to accompany the group when it returned to Russia.

Though the love affair did not last, Madame remained in London. She never returned to Kiev. After some years she became a British citizen, but her speech never lost the characteristic inflections and complete absence of the definite and indefinite articles that revealed her Russian-Ukrainian origins. 'Point toe, not foot! What happened to knee? Arm is like stick! Soften! Soften! Make it like stem of flower bending in wind!'

When her career as a prima ballerina ended after the war, she opened her school in a derelict church hall in Ladbroke Grove, a couple of streets from the flat where she lived.

Her reputation preceded her, ensuring that she never needed to advertise for pupils. Her parsimony disinclined her to make any structural alterations to the premises other than the bare essentials: wall-size mirrors at either end of the hall and wooden practice barres that extended along the two long facing walls. She also purchased a second-hand upright piano. By the time Alice joined the school, only the loud pedal worked and the hammers were so worn that several keys refused to emit a sound, no matter how hard they were thumped. This resulted in a series of resonant twangs interspersed with thuds as substitutes for missing notes, which made everything sound vaguely African, a combination of voice and rhythmic drumming. This presented an unusual species of piano accompaniment for ballet classes and probably accounted for the high turnover of Madame's pianists.

Alice was a pupil at the school for twelve years and during the whole of that time no attempt was made to remedy the growing dilapidation of the premises, apart from the replacement of one broken window through which a football had been propelled by some boys in the adjoining playground. Thus Madame was provided with a comfortable income for the rest of her days.

Despite her advancing age, Madame insisted on conducting every class herself. Alice later came to the conclusion that this was not so much a consequence of her distrust of anyone else's ability to do the job as her reluctance to divert even a small fraction of her income to someone else's advantage. The small fee she was forced to pay over to the pianist was painful enough as it was.

She directed the class with the help of two aids. One was a stout walking-stick which thumped onto the floor, regulating the rhythm of the dancers' feet, and accompanied her commands: *'pli-e!' 'en-dedans!' 'haut de bras!' 'je-te!' 'entre-chat!'* screamed at high volume so as not to be drowned by the discordant clangs of the piano.

The stick served a dual purpose. By means of an occasional adroitly placed rap on calves or back, she made sure that there was no drift away from the perfect positioning she insisted upon. Intense parental ambition meant that no murmur was ever raised in objection to Madame's teaching methods.

The second of her aids took the form of an older pupil, selected by Madame to demonstrate the more energetic steps she could no longer manage herself. To be chosen by Madame was an honour comparable to being plucked out of the *corps de ballet* to dance the role of the Princess in 'Sleeping Beauty' or the White Swan in 'Swan Lake'.

The position was, self-evidently, unpaid and lasted for one term only – during which the chosen one was expected to make herself available for every class taught to school-age pupils, at every level, from infants to the most advanced. This entailed working three evenings a week and all day Saturday. All this time and unpaid labour was a small price to pay for the supreme honour of being chosen as star of the school for a term. It would have been unthinkable to refuse.

In the final term of her last year at the school, Alice was informed by Madame that the prestigious position was to be hers. Her delight was as nothing compared to the ecstatic response of Estelle.

'My God, darling! This is unbelievable!' She wrapped Alice in a perfumed embrace that left her gasping for air.

'Such wonderful news!' And the day after the announcement was made, she hauled Alice off to an exclusive establishment in Bond Street, where she bought her the most expensive ballet shoes in the shop.

Alice's memories of her mother were clouded with an overarching sense of blighted hope. Estelle seemed to have spent her life attached to a roller-coaster that carried her incessantly from aspiration to disappointment. It was hard to understand how someone blessed by fortune in so many ways could have missed out so consistently. She combined beauty, grace and intelligence with larger than average measures of stage talent. But for some reason, she never gained entry to the world of the universally envied and nothing else could have brought her true fulfilment.

For years she fiddled about with minor roles in small productions, dancing and singing in nameless chorus lines from end to end of the country, always hoping for the elusive Big Break that never came. As she approached thirty, she reluctantly recognised that she'd reached the end of the line. The success she craved was not to be hers. But Estelle was never one to mope. She re-invented herself, transferring the burden of unrequited stardom onto the shoulders of her family. That way she thought she might at least get to touch the golden laurels, if not actually to wear them. A kind of consolation prize.

Julius had settled for the life of a jobbing musician. Unlike Estelle, his moments of beatitude were not contingent on applause. Those moments lived in the minds and memories of musicians and those that listened. They arose spontaneously, without warning. It might be a group of instrumentalists that sheer chance cleft together, a union carved out of time, its elements a symbiosis generating a unique experience of emotion, triggered by the sounds. It might be listening to other players, or working something out by himself, struggling to make it fit, then suddenly hearing it all come together, like the point at which the multi-coloured strands of a tapestry cohere and suddenly a picture appears.

Every time he set out for a gig, he expected nothing in particular, at least no more than the satisfaction of a job well done. On the whole that was the limit of his return. On rare occasions, a musical encounter produced an experience that carried him way beyond the flawed here and now. At those times he felt privileged. Not knowing why or how it happened, just grateful. He didn't know to whom or what.

In between these rare visits he was content to meander along the trail of music as a business, which after all was not such a bad life.

'I'm a service provider,' he used to say, without a trace of bitterness. 'Have instruments. Will travel. Our aim is to please: no request too extreme! Gypsy violin? Done! I'll even put on my gypsy costume and walk round the tables serenading you. You want dancing for your son's bar mitzvah? No problem. Something sad to mourn your grandfather? Fine. Music to cry to, music to laugh to, music for babies, music for lovers… I can do it all. I can provide the sounds for every occasion!'

His lack of ambition infuriated Estelle. She was so hungry for acclaim, she couldn't understand how Julius, who clearly possessed the raw material of fame, could be so indifferent to it. Alice felt her mother actually resented her father's contentment. How dare he be happy? She blamed him bitterly for being happy. He had no right. He owed it to himself and everybody else, his family, his public-in-waiting, to propel himself out of the slough of anonymity into the Elysium of fame.

'Why do you waste your talent on people who don't appreciate it? You're wasting your life.' But Julius said nothing. The idea of celebrity left him cold. Estelle would never understand that. So he let it be.

Estelle had met Julius at a time when the vital energies that fed her stage career were ebbing away, yet his had barely been tapped. His brilliance astounded her. Her objective was to drag him up to where he deserved to be, whether he wanted it or not. Soon after they married, she decided to nominate herself his 'agent-manager'. Despite pregnancy, she worked tirelessly to promote him, pursuing every conceivable avenue that might lead him into the limelight. When Alice was born, she simply carried on, hardly stopping for breath. A year later, she found herself pregnant again with David, but not even two babies under two could phase her.

She had a hard task. She had to fight not only Julius's indifference, but also the changing face of popular music. The advent of Rock and Roll rapidly making musicians like Julius surplus to requirements. Few options were left to them. It was no good sniffily turning their backs on the new style. If they did, they'd be out of a job.

An alternative was to go classical. But the market was already full to bursting. You mostly had no choice but to join the backing-music band-wagon, everybody competing with everybody else for places in bands cobbled together for live shows in theatres, radio or TV, for film tracks or studio recordings. As a last resort there was always the party and wedding circuit.

Estelle tried everything, repeatedly and tenaciously. The relentless pursuit of fame was eventually reduced to the more banal quest of simply finding him work. Whatever brought the highest returns. He wasn't choosy. If it made her happy… Thanks to her, he was never without paid work; playing music of one kind or another.

Soon after Alice was born, he put together his own small band. They played from time to time in clubs and bars. They were paid, but it wasn't for the money. Estelle had no patience with it. He gave up trying to describe to her the rapture that infused every cell of his body as the fragments of sound coalesced into a perfect whole.

Arguments that erupted between them were rooted in her inability to comprehend the intensity of his need.

'I've already booked you for next week, for God's sake! How can you do this to me?' she wailed when he said no, he couldn't, and that was that.

'Some God-forsaken dive. For peanuts! Are you mad?'

'For you it's madness,' he said. 'For me it's what keeps me alive.'

When Alice was five and David four, Estelle branched out. She took on other artistes. She discovered she had a flair for sniffing out success. She'd finally found her vocation. By the time Alice was ten, Estelle was running one of the biggest theatrical agencies in London.

Yet beneath the success, she remained in thrall to the stage. A corner of her still harboured the old hankerings.

David, her only son, early on demonstrated an unexpected obsession with science and mechanics. 'Where on earth does he get it from?' she would wail, to which Julius would shrug and reply 'Search me! Nothing like that in our family background, as far as I know! But why worry? You have a regular genius in the making here. Is that a bad thing?'

But it was a source of huge regret to Estelle that David showed not the slightest interest in the performing arts. As far as she was concerned, David was a failure. She rarely missed an opportunity to tell him so.

'It's unbelievable! How can it be? You can't even sing "Happy Birthday To You" in tune! I give up.' And she did, eventually, one attempt after another to get him to play an instrument having ended in dismal failure: the piano, the trumpet, the violin – even the drums... A final forlorn hope. Nothing worked. If David had been a more sensitive child, he might well have suffered indelible hang-ups and a blighted life ahead of him, but the stubbornness of his nature was in every way a match for his mother's mockery, and nothing she could throw at him, however cruel, could deflect him from his passion. In any case, Estelle's was a lone voice. Everybody else in the family was filled with rapture at the prospect of a world-renowned scientist – nuclear physicist or the like, destined to bring glory upon a family who had always and without exception, trodden the humanities route – music or letters or law *'not without success, by the way!'*, but never, as far back as anyone could remember, the hallowed pathways of science. So David, for most of his family, was a hero. It was of no matter to him that in his mother's eyes he was an abject failure. That was her problem.

'What happened? A whizz at mathematics! Brilliant at science! But no sense of rhythm! Tone deaf! Are you sure he's mine?' Julius used to needle Estelle, his intention being to infuriate her, which never failed. But what really got to her was his exaggeratedly effusive expressions of wonder at David's natural aptitudes and achievements, coupled with a correspondingly disparaging comparison with music, art, dance and theatre – in other words, all those things which to Estelle were sacred.

Alice was well aware, even at the time, that these were not intended for David's benefit or reassurance, since the approval of others mattered little to him. No – the point of it all was simply to cause mischief: typical of Julius. His take on life was to look for the funny side of everything. His jokes and quips were a source of endless hilarity to the rest of the family. And yet, Alice got to thinking years later, perhaps there was something deeper to his teasing of Estelle. Something that maybe he was not even aware of himself. Many times she tried to figure out why it was that the stout cloth her parents had woven together with so much love and care, thread by twisted thread, over the years, the cloth that had seemed to bind them inextricably together for all time, could have frayed, thread by twisted thread, grown thinner and weaker, in the end disintegrating into rags, like a sail on a boat that has made too many voyages.

As for David, despite his early promise, he never turned into the world-renowned nuclear physicist, neuroscientist, brain surgeon or microbiologist he had been so confidently expected to become by all the family. Having gained a First in computer science and technology at Cambridge, he went on to pursue a career in I.T., eventually setting up a small business specialising in creating websites for companies and individuals. Profitable? Yes – no-one could deny that. A good living that provided David and his rapidly growing family (one wife and four children, at the last count) with security and a comfortable life-style, that was for sure. But a far cry (it had to be said) from the exalted future that they had all been predicting for him ever since the day when, at barely five years old, he succeeded in figuring out the solution to a puzzle, originally found inside a Christmas cracker, and which had been perplexing everyone in the family, young and old, for days. 'A regular genius!' they cried, over and over again, as, with a few deft twists and turns of his still baby fingers, he transformed a tangle of metal and plastic into a fully functioning miniature motor-car, which he placed carefully onto the table in front of his awe-struck grandmother, before running off to some other, more pressing preoccupation, neither waiting for, nor expecting praise, in which he had no interest. Practical problem-solving was his abiding passion, the finding of the solution being all the reward he needed. Public recognition was as unimportant to David as it was to Julius.

'So what if people don't know about you?' Julius would retort whenever Estelle reeled out her customary string of laments at both his and David's indifference to glory and renown. 'What does it matter whether what you do is known about by five people only, or five hundred, or five thousand, or five million? If you love what you do, you'll go on doing it in any case. Being famous: that's not the reason you do it. OK – maybe you make a bit more money, but that's not the point of life, is it?'

Try as she might to remain dispassionate, to look at both sides of the argument equally, with every ounce of objectivity she could muster, Estelle was simply not made of the same basic stuff as Julius, and, however many years they should be destined to live side by side, neither would be able even to comprehend the other's position on this point, let alone find any common ground to share.

In David's case, what made things even worse for Estelle was the fact that her only son, having inherited her fine blonde hair and grey-blue eyes, did not, sadly, take after her in any other way. The delicate, sensitive eyes had been marred by a congenital squint requiring several years of correction, leaving him with a permanent reliance on thick, ugly spectacles. As for his stocky build and comparatively short stature: in those respects he could not have looked less like his tall, elegant mother.

Mostly she kept to herself her profound sense of disappointment in her son. She did her best to suppress it because of loyalty and compassion, but occasionally, when driven by some circumstance or other, prompted by David, into states of frustration or anger, her true feelings would erupt uncontrollably into streams of cruel words, along the lines of: 'Why did I have to be landed with a son like you? Everything I didn't want! Why should I have to be ashamed of my own son? What did I do to deserve this?'

The terrible flood of invective would then instantly be succeeded by remorse, her attempts to assuage her guilt taking the form of excessive demonstrations of generosity – sweets, treats of all kinds, and hugs lavished onto the poor child. But David, as Julius often remarked, had a skin as thick as a rhino's hide, and always on the look-out for the main chance, was not put out in the slightest by his mother's diatribes. On the contrary, since he knew they were invariably a prelude to a bonanza for him. At Christmas and birthdays, for the same reason, he was always particularly well-served: Estelle showered him with gifts – far more expensive than any she gave Alice.

Alice herself had inherited her colouring from Julius, being as dark as David was fair. She had also been blessed with her mother's slim build and grace of movement. So Alice became the focus of Estelle's ambition. Alice was her last hope.

So it was that when, following her selection as star of the ballet school, Alice was chosen to dance the title role in the school's summer production of 'Petrushka', Estelle thought the Fates had finally chosen that moment to intercede.

The Morozova school at Ladbroke Grove had a longstanding reputation for excellence. Its annual performances were so popular they were staged on three successive evenings at a local theatre. They were open to the public and all seats were paid for. Madame allowed no exceptions. Absolutely no free seats, even for the loyal band of volunteers who every year dedicated weeks of their lives to sewing costumes, building sets and painting scenery.

The performances were publicly promoted as charitable, all proceeds dedicated to an organisation that went by the name of *'The West London Russian Ballet and Ukrainian Folk Dancing Trust'*. The programmes always printed this information in bold lettering on the front. Underneath, in much smaller letters, were the words: 'founded and administered by N. Morozova and D.Vassiliev'. The identity of D.Vassiliev remained a mystery. Nobody had ever seen him, nor did Madame give any clue as to who he was or might have been. The suspicion was that there was no such individual and never had been, but no-one would have dared to put Madame on the spot.

The days leading up to the performances, Alice found it difficult to sleep and could barely eat. Rehearsals occupied most of her waking hours. Madame was without mercy. Her insistence that the dancers' every step and movement should be flawless made no allowance for frailty or fatigue. The individual was unimportant: everything must be sacrificed to the performance.

When the big day arrived, Alice danced every step precisely as instructed. Her nervousness melted away when her feet touched the stage. A protective haze surrounded her. She danced effortlessly, without thought, her body seeming to float. At the end of the show, the riotous applause returned her to earth with a jolt. People were clapping and cheering. Madame, beaming, gazed across at the audience from the wings, luminous, transfigured.

For a few weeks Estelle was exultant. A succession of delightful images jostled for attention in her mind. She could see the wasted, fraying strands of her life, after years of ineffectual flapping about, weaving themselves into a tight, golden coil. She felt that long dormant seeds were about to germinate and burst into flower. Seeds that time and destiny had fostered: now the time had come for her to pass the precious gift on to her daughter.

But the anticipated flowering never happened. Alice rejected the gift. When the elation of the show subsided, she found herself re-living the purgatory of muscles and limbs excruciatingly contorted. For Estelle and Madame, all this was justified in the name of The Spectacle. But Alice got to questioning its rationale. She came to the conclusion that others might willingly sacrifice themselves on the altar of Terpsichore, but she would not.

She saw the stage as the scene of an elaborate lie. The ballet a ritualised sequence of motions and postures, without freedom or creativity. She baulked at her mother's incessant pestering and eventually let rip.

'No! It's a stupid charade! I won't do it! Just because *you* failed...'

Words uttered and almost simultaneously regretted. Words that left a jagged tear in the seam that held them together.

CHAPTER TEN

Eight months have passed since the launch of William's gallery. Alice is invited to lunch at Gitte Blomberg's country house. It lies on the border between Surrey and Sussex. Gitte's invitation to Alice is handwritten, against a background of pale lilac. At the bottom she adds a note: 'So looking forward to meeting you again. DO COME!'

William urges her to go: 'you absolutely *must*!' he repeats, as if the success of the gallery depended on it. But Alice has already decided to go, curious to see where Gitte lives.

She turns off the dual carriageway and drives along a narrow, tortuous road which runs along the ridge of a deep valley. Wide swathes of land covered with dense pine woods alternate with ploughed fields. The land slopes abruptly down along the side of the valley into an undulating landscape of small fields, orchards and sporadic farmhouses, cottages and barns. On the horizon she glimpses the tower and spire of a church, with rural dwellings clustering around it – a community not yet touched by urban sprawl.

The road twists and turns, first climbing steeply then plunging again. It passes beneath an iron bridge, then veers sharply to the right, past a single cottage perched on the brow of the hill, then down a gentle incline for about a mile until a pair of tall iron gates come into view on the left. They are almost concealed by a dense coppice of trees bordering the road for over a mile.

Alice brakes sharply and turns in through the open gates. At first no house is visible. The drive extends for about half a mile. Every few metres there are steep humps and signs which exhort visitors to *PLEASE DRIVE SLOWLY*. The drive is flanked on one side by banks of trees and shrubs of many different varieties. On the left, a breathtaking vista of parkland dotted with trees, over which groups of deer browse, the land falling gradually away towards a distant lake.

The road twists finally round to the right, leading into a crescent-shaped courtyard, entirely paved with rose-coloured stone. Rising from the centre of the pink floor is a steel sculpture, about two metres high. Its interplay of positive and negative space suggests a running female figure with flowing hair. Set a short distance back from the paved crescent stands the Blombergs' residence.

For a few moments, Alice contemplates the building from the car. It resembles nothing she has ever seen. A bewildering hotchpotch of styles and influences, incoherent and puzzling.

She's arrived much too early. No-one else is about. She gets out of the car, still mesmerised by the house. Built entirely on one level, the front elevation is made up of a central section, flanked by two wings, which extend forward round the edge of the pink crescent. At first sight the design looks minimal to the point of dullness. It is constructed almost entirely of massive concrete blocks, painted white, with a curved green copper roof. Squat black and white chimneys look like boxes someone dumped on top. The blocks are laid out in an angular U shape. The front door, black and forbidding stands at the centre of the U. Then she catches sight of a narrow strip of glass, lurking apologetically near the door. The house gives off a sense of blind hostility. It barks at you: 'Be off! You're not welcome here.'

It would be indistinguishable from any modern, out-of-town industrial unit, were it not for the decorative details at each corner of the three sections. These are heavy, rectilinear columns built into the walls, extending from ground to roof. They look like a cross between flattened-out factory chimneys and Renaissance pilasters.

In startling contrast to the plainness of the rest, they are painted in a variety of gaudy colours: orange, purple, green, yellow, red and pink, all arranged in parallel, horizontal bands which cover each column from top to bottom. Psychedelic sticks of rock.

She walks round the house to the back. Here there's a different look entirely. It is almost entirely glass. The three wings have been brought together onto the same plane. If anything, structurally, it is even plainer than the front. The whole is a series of box-like units, unrelievedly rectilinear, like a giant display cabinet. Once again, false columns painted in riotous colours intersect the floor to roof panes, but here they look more like a row of pantomime soldiers, each one standing to attention beside eight huge, wall-sized windows.

Viewed from this angle, the house with its glass walls reminds Alice of a municipal swimming-pool or leisure centre. She turns round to face an impressive panorama. The house stands at the top of a terraced slope of marble steps and lawns, which fall away into shrubberies and woodland walks, leading down to a magnificent deer park and the glinting waters of a lake. All this accounts for the giant windows.

Walking back round to the front, she looks once more at the windowless walls and massive concrete blocks. Now she can see echoes of ancient Egyptian temples. Their stillness and sombre power.

Several cars have arrived. More driving up, gradually filling the paved crescent. The door is open. Alice walks through, closely followed by Ben Grantley. He's dressed all in black, as usual. Silk polo-neck sweater and tight jeans. She looks round. 'Hi!' she says cheerfully. He nods, smiling thinly.

Gitte waddles towards them. 'My *dears!*' Her plump arms are outstretched, her squat body swathed in a cotton dress seemingly fashioned from bathroom curtain material: blue and yellow roses proliferating. Gitte grasps one each of Ben's and Alice's hands in her own. Gives them a firm squeeze. Ben bends low to receive her double kiss. Alice also has to bend towards her. Air kisses done, they move on. Gitte looking beyond them to greet new arrivals.

The spacious entrance hall is octagonal, its wood-panelled walls are light-coloured pine contrasting with dark mahogany and beechwood strips inlaid in a trellis design at the centre of each wall. The floor is of white marble, displaying, over most of its surface, a circular Roman-style mosaic laid out in a formal pattern, which suggests the sun and its rays. The colours are mute greys, pale yellows and almond green.

Alice walks through the wide double doors leading from the hall into a wide reception room, where guests stand talking in groups and sipping drinks. Facing the door is a huge patio window. The view thus framed appears more spectacular even than when seen from outside.

Someone taps her on the shoulder. It's Josie Wishart.

'How ya doin? Wanna drink? 'Ang about… I'll get ya one.'

She bounds off, returning a moment later clutching two glasses of white wine. Her hair is still cropped short, but not multi-coloured any more. It stands out from her head in spiky orange tufts.

'Hey! This is some kinda fuckin place, innit?'

Alice notices her teeth are chipped at the front and stained with nicotine. Josie takes a gulp of wine, then catches sight of Ben. Though he stands quite close, she screeches out his name, making heads turn.

'Hey, Ben! How ya doin? Saw you on the box last night!' She laughs as he approaches. Then, more quietly: 'What the fuck was you on about?'

She lights a cigarette and takes a deep drag. Grantley views her with distaste.

'What do you mean?' he asks.

'You know. All that stuff you was talkin' about. Insides and outsides…'

He turns away from her, gazing into the middle distance.

'Yes, well. I think most people who know my work understand the major themes …'

Josie grins. 'Yeah… themes…'

Ben turns to her. 'Why so combative, Josie?' then adds, looking meaningfully at Alice, 'Perhaps you're wishing it was you on the box?'

Josie blows out smoke in a contemptuous cloud.

Alice says nothing. She finds Ben's remark odd, since Josie, as the current *enfant terrible* of the art scene, is constantly in the public eye, unlike him. Last night's Channel Four interview was screened to plug the opening of a retrospective of his work at the Whitechapel. The reporter was polite, but viewers were left in no doubt about the general consensus: Ben was basically a has-been, his work no longer relevant.

Alice remembers an article she read about him recently in some review. She read it several times because she was fascinated by the pretentious pyrotechnics. The words so absurdly generalised they could apply to just about anyone. Ben Grantley was just a pretext for the author's attempt to display his mastery of erudite art-speak. She recorded some choice extracts in the notebook she keeps by her bedside under the heading: *'Cobblers et al'*.

'The perpetually repeated interaction between the physical and the spiritual...the erosion of sculpture's traditional totemic significance... the image of the body as a site of tension between inner and outer experience...'

The work itself has disappeared completely. The work itself is six feet under, suffocated and interred beneath the rubble of meaningless verbiage.

Grantley's off again. Banging on about the interview. It's starting to get serious.

'You see, Josie, this is what you've got to remember...' his tone is didactic, a muscle twitches beneath his left eye, 'There are still a few of us left who believe art should be about things that go beyond culture. Things that belong in the realm of Man as Man...'

'And Woman as Woman...' Josie interposes. He ignores her, continuing:

'Humanity. The human collective. That's what art's all about. Or should be. Man face to face with the Unknown! Both inside and out...'

'Yes! I knew it!' Josie yelps gleefully. 'We're back to insides and outsides again! Can't resist it, can you, Ben?'

Without responding, he continues, his voice descending almost to a whisper. 'Let me ask you something,' he says. 'Have you ever thought about Infinity?' There is a faraway look in his eyes. He might be gazing at the lake, serene and sparkling island in a sea of green. 'I mean *really* thought about it? No beginning, no end. The zillions of people that have lived and died. People living now, people yet to be born. And each one – each one of *us* – we fight all our lives to find ways of making our random existences *un-random*. It's a game no-one can win. But we can't stop playing it...'

'Not necessarily,' Alice observes in a matter-of-fact voice.

He twists his head down towards her, frowning impatiently.

'Pardon?' he snaps.

'Well, not everyone believes that. I mean, for some people, it's the opposite. Some people have a really strong feeling that things are meant to happen. Including their own existence. Why should they be wrong? Why should you be right? And anyway, why waste time asking questions that can't be answered?'

Before he can speak, Josie intervenes. 'Thought we was talkin' about art,' she grumbles. 'Not this philosophy stuff…' Triumphantly, he pounces. Seizing the moment.

'Yes! Exactly! That's just my point, Josie. That's just what art *is*. It's philosophy without words. A way of telling people things. Ideas. Making them think…'

Alice again: 'How can you be sure?'

'Sure of what?'

'Sure you're making people think what you think – if that's what you mean.'

'Well,' he replies irritably, 'I can only try. That's all any artist can do of course. Try and hope.'

Alice wants to ask him why he believes his featureless iron figures are a good way of making people think about infinity and randomness. She also wants to know why he chose art rather than writing. But Josie gets in first. Dragging on her cigarette, she remarks: 'Yeah… *I* wanna make people think too. React, anyway. Art's no use if it's just *oh-isn't-that-nice-and-what's-next?* kinda thing. Art that's *nice* ain't fuckin' *art*!'

As drinking and chatting move imperceptibly into thoughts of lunch, Gitte's guests start to melt away. A succession of goodbyes and sounds of departing cars float through the house to the room where those remaining wait for a sign as to what's next.

It comes in the shape of Laszlo, the butler. Suddenly he is in their midst, his arrival unnoticed, a tail-coated ectoplasmic apparition. With soft-toned authority he announces that lunch is served and would everyone follow him please.

There are eight of them, including Gitte, who sits with her back to the window. It's a modestly-sized room with walls the colour of cinnamon. Through the great window, the same view of park and lake, an irresistible draw to the eye. They sit round a circular mahogany table, waited on by Laszlo, who glides silently between kitchen, sideboard and table, impeccable in his grace and timing. His pale grey eyes behind the small, rimless frames dart everywhere. No detail escapes him. His lips are permanently fixed in the half-smile of deference born of a lifetime of service.

William, who engineered the lunch, sits at Gitte's right. At her left is an American, Bill Vant, a video artist. Alice knows his work but has never met him till now. She sits next to Tom Gerhardt, who appears to be absorbed in examining the food on his plate, every morsel having to pass scrutiny before it is placed gingerly between his lips. The process occupies his attention to the exclusion of conversation. After several attempts to engage him in talk, resulting only in monosyllabic replies, Alice gives up. Josie, witnessing the scene, giggles.

'Lost in his own little world!' she whispers to Alice.

Lunch proceeds, exquisite flavours delicate and light as gossamer, impeccably served, overseen by Laszlo, doyen of butlers. A sense of quiet opulence permeates the scene. Original signed Picasso prints adorn the walls, polished surfaces abound with carvings from the South Seas and elegant pieces of Swedish glass. All conspires to mesmerize. Controlled euphoria infuses the company and as lunch proceeds, discourse floats from awkwardly stilted to warmly expansive, almost approaching love.

Gitte Blomberg casts a motherly eye over the gathering and smiles contentedly: each guest is her protégé, both past and present. All, in varying degrees, still in hock to her munificence. Even those who have now reached prominence were desperate once for her patronage in the days when the struggle for recognition seemed hopeless. For Gitte still continues to support them. Like a mother who clings to her adult brood, she is incapable of letting go.

She sponsors in part or in full shows of their work. She regularly purchases pieces by Grantley and Gerhardt. Several of Grantley's iron figures are encountered in odd places in the gardens or even the park. They startle unsuspecting ramblers, looming incongruously from out of some shrub or atop a wall – mummified trolls in a nightmarish fantasy.

The Dupre Gallery was largely financed by Gitte, though it bears William's name. It gives her the opportunity to indulge one of her fondest ambitions: the accumulation and display of contemporary art personally selected by her. Monetary value is of no significance. Properties and investments she leaves to Lennart, her husband. Money matters are unremittingly tedious to Gitte. The gallery showcases her enthusiasms, her individuality, it represents her personal mark on the world.

When questioned by others, William replies that her tastes are best described as 'eclectic, one might even say whimsical'. No guiding rationale underlies her choices, other than gut feeling and passion. And these could be aroused by just about anything – an abstract piece, a symbolic pile of stones, a multi-media installation, or anything else. And in equal measure. She is driven by a rare purity of motive, unfortunately for William, bound as he is by a different set of priorities.

When the Du Pre's launch show ended, Gitte insisted that the next should be a display of, as she put it, 'everything worth seeing in British contemporary art'. 'Everything' for Gitte means whatever excites or has meaning for *her*. She presented William with a vast list including three times as many artists as are now seated around her table.

It took William weeks of reasoning and cajoling to get her to accept the simple notion that there had to be some measure of cohesion, otherwise it would be impossible to curate such a show. His threat to wash his hands of the whole thing had no effect on her.

'So what?' she said. 'If you go, I'll get someone else to do it instead.'

In the end, she agreed to reduce the list only when he promised to hold a second show at a later date featuring all the artists excluded from the first.

'Absolutely! Diversity is the thing, is it not?' she directs the question at Bill as she dabs the corners of her mouth with a scarlet napkin, of the same shade as her lipstick.

Bill, taken by surprise, was about to wipe his beard clean after consuming the last remnants of the *Tarte Aux Pommes*. He nods emphatically. He clears his throat. A few buttery crumbs cling to the coarse grey tangle that infests the lower half of his face. 'Yes, absolutely,' he agrees. 'I do think the diversity of today is remarkable. An exhibition like this would certainly be an eye-opener. I mean, the public – they – they on the whole, don't they, they have this kinda cynical view of art.'

Grantley, deciding to intervene, observes 'What might be a problem though, is, you know, actually finding a common thread. You know, pulling the thing together?'

He stops, looking at William for support, but the latter simply gives a non-committal 'Hmmm'.

'So it seems to me,' he continues, 'we've got to find a common denominator in all this. Otherwise... well... there won't be much sense to it. A bit of a mess, even...'

Gitte is staring hard at the crumpled napkin in her lap.

The silence is broken by Josie, who inquires: 'What're we gonna call it?' The question finally inducing William to speak.

'Yes, well that's the crucial thing, isn't it?'

'Art in Britain today?' volunteers Tom Gerhardt. This gives rise to a communal groan. *Too lame too lame. No spark. Boring.*

'How about " British Art: the Full Picture" ?' proposes Bill. Another groan.

'And anyway,' Josie remarks, 'you can't call it that. You're American, ain't yer? Don't matter 'ow long you've been 'ere.'

Bill, whose beard has yet to rid itself of the tenacious crumbs, retorts that by 'British' he obviously means 'produced in Britain', 'that goes without saying, doesn't it?' But Josie is adamant that people won't see it that way.

Gitte is looking increasingly annoyed. This is a far cry from her exalted plans. Suddenly, she claps her hands sharply together twice, like a head teacher restoring order. Instantly the bickering stops. For a few moments nothing happens. Everyone sits motionless watching Gitte, who stares back at them, her eyes like sapphire pinheads in a lump of freshly-kneaded dough. At last, as if after long reflexion, she speaks. Her voice makes Alice jump.

'My dear friends,' she begins, 'of course you are all *absolutely right*! *Absolutely!* We have to find unity in all this diversity. Some order in all this wonderful *dis*-order. No question. Yes. But where?' She moves her eyes around the table, fixing them onto each of the group in turn.

Not a word is spoken. Pausing a moment, she resumes: 'I really am beginning to think there is *no* common thread at all. I mean, what can there *possibly* be in common between – say, one of Josie's dolls, a video piece by Bill, or one of Alice's paintings?' Once again she looks around, studying each of them in turn. 'What are all of us actually doing here? I give it to you, my friends! The ball is in your court.' At that she hands over the problem, stretching her arms out towards them, in a symbolic gesture of offering.

What is Gitte playing at? Is she about to call the whole thing off? What answers does she want? Is this an elaborate charade? Some kind of test?

Without forethought, nor the least sense of what she's about to say, Alice finds herself breaking the silence. She begins to speak hesitantly, conscious that everyone's eyes are upon her, William tense and apprehensive, like a cornered rabbit.

'But surely it's you, isn't it, Gitte?' she blurts. 'You're the link between us. Your belief in us. Yes, it's true. We're all so different. But each of us – we all really believe in what we're doing, don't we? It mean, it's totally *honest*. Nothing fake. And you – you can see that, Gitte. That's what this show's all about, really, isn't it?'

She breaks off. Her face feels hot. Wishing she'd kept quiet. *Clumsy, over-emotional. Overdone it as usual. And how true is it anyway? How can she know? Sham? Honest? She can only speak for herself. And even then...*

She looks up. Gitte is smiling broadly. Any question in her mind that her judgement might have been flawed now dispelled.

'Yes, my friends: I think we have our title now. Yes indeed! We will call our show: *Inspiration and Belief: the Refusal to Pretend*. Wonderful! You: the inspiration. I: the belief. And all of us: the refusal to pretend. Perfect!'

Soon after lunch ends the party breaks up. Grantley is the first to leave, saying he has a plane to catch to Milan that evening. Embracing Gitte, he whispers in her ear, then is gone. In the hall as Alice prepares to leave, Josie sidles up to her and nudges her.

'Buncha dick'eads really,' she comments in a loud whisper, jerking her head in the direction of those still making their farewells to Gitte. Alice says nothing.

'Speakin' honestly,' she goes on, 'I don't reckon much on your stuff... But you're all right. Yeah. Not like them.' She turns away. 'Hey, Bill! You off? Speak soon!' Then she too drifts away.

By the door, Alice shakes Gitte's hand. Holding onto Alice's in a tight grip, Gitte says: 'My dear! Lovely to see you. Goodbye now. We meet again soon, yes? Next month. Let me see more of your paintings. Goodbye, my dear. *A la prochaine!*

CHAPTER ELEVEN

Weeks have passed since Alice visited Jack. The memory of their meeting is blurred, infused with a dream-like quality, its initial intensity buried beneath layer upon layer of day-to-day minutiae. It has the feeling of something she might have read or heard about, something that happened to someone else. Yet tonight without warning it surges back, vision after vision, as she lies on the brink of sleep.

Random images and sensations materialize, then fade, to be replaced by others, outside logic and in no particular order: the musky fragrance of apple-wood smoke, her gaze held captive by dancing flames, red, gold and white, the explosive crackling when he throws more logs and twigs onto the pile, the fire an insatiable beast, devouring, devouring. The heat so fierce at one point she sees herself retreating into the room, whilst the dogs seemingly impervious, remain sprawled across the hearth, within singeing distance. The socks he is wearing, thick and grey, with blue stripes encircling the tops, like a schoolboy's. The soles of his feet, beguilingly soft and woolly. She hears the song, played over and over, Billie Holiday in 1940, enticing you into her grief, the lament of loss, her voice the quintessence of female martyrdom, woman as willing victim. '*My days have grown so lonely... I spend my days in longing...My life's a hell you're making...I tell you I mean it, I'm all for you body and soul...*' Then the same melody, wordless, played by a young Freddie Hubbard.

'An idol of mine,' Jack tells her, of the trumpeter. 'One of the few real giants in our business...' which were just exactly the words her father had used, she remembers it clearly, long ago, when she was about ten or eleven. He was talking about someone else, though: a saxophone player, 'Lester Young, I think'.

She and Jack listening as one, neither moving nor talking, enraptured by the painful beauty of Hubbard's invention, melodic and rhythmic structure flowing with its own energy, a creature perfect in every way, yet never losing touch with the fountainhead, the song that gave it life.

Alice knows the recording as well as the sound of her own breathing. Listened to countless times, long before she met Jack, its melodic phrases and harmonic twists and turns produce their own unique essence. She can hum them with perfect accuracy from beginning to end. Sometimes she sings the founding melody itself whilst following the improvisation by ear. Other times, she does the reverse, singing the invented phrases and thinking the basic song simultaneously. Whichever way it goes, her enjoyment is the same. So to find someone else who thinks and feels the same is pretty exceptional. Not something she ever expected to happen. No way.

She is hearing it right now in the silence of her mind's ear as she stares into the darkness, every phrase, every melodic turn. She is wide-awake now. No chance of sleep. Outside, in the other prosaic world, there is Michael's breathing, slow, regular and increasing in volume. It gets so loud it starts to impinge on the music, on her pleasure. He irritates her by the sheer insistence of his presence. *Listen to me! I'm here! Don't forget me!* he seems to cry silently even while lost in the depths of sleep. Guilt seeps into her, confounding all her attempts to shift it.

Michael is a heavy sleeper, not easily roused, mainly because of the pills he takes to dampen down his permanently active brain. Even so, she is careful to remain as still as she can. Any disturbance might lift him onto a level of consciousness which will inevitably lead to his reaching out to touch her. Touching, handling... *How does the song go?*

'I love you Porgy, don't let him handle me, don't let him handle me with his hot hands...'

So when did *that* turn into *this*? Impossible to put a time on it, or a place. Where was the bed? Here? Provence? Greece? Italy? New York? London? There have been so many beds, so many places, so many times. When did need, yearning, hunger, the hunger to *cleave* ... (interesting biblical word *'cleave'*; of similar ilk is *carnal*. 'Oh, I only know him casually.' 'Really? I know him *carnally*'. And quite odd that *cleave* can also mean its exact opposite. Split. Separate. *Cleft*.

Or *cloven*. And how her father used to reduce them all to fits of helpless laughter with his talk of the Jewish eating laws, the *cloven-hoofed animals*. 'You have to eat only the animals with the *cloven hoof!*' he used to yell in the exaggeratedly Eastern European accent he liked to affect, underlining *cloven hoof* with a delighted yell accompanied by a joyful banging of the nearest flat surface, as if it were the most ridiculous, the most laughable absurdity that had ever been invented and trust the Jews to invent it!)

So when did that urgent, overwhelming desire to *cleave one to the other* transmute into this pathetic fear – dread, even, of waking him in case, God forbid, his hands should intrude into the private space of your body? When did *cleave*, sense one, u-turn into *cleave,* sense two? Why does a touch once loved and desired turn into one which leaves you totally cold? It must be something to do with her. Mustn't it? At least, that's what he thinks. And here comes the avalanche of guilt hurtling down once again. But why? She has *nothing* to feel guilty about. She is furious at the very suggestion. She is not responsible for this.

He tries to make it seem so, of course. In his ever-so-carefully-polite way, yet there is no doubt about his meaning.

Nothing to do with me. You're not trying hard enough. You must be some kind of freak, either that, or just plain selfish. Don't forget me! I'm here! You owe me, anyway...

Not that he actually uses those words. He is far too delicate for that.

But the trainload of guilt refuses to dislodge itself. But when? When and why? The pull in the loins... '*Loins*' another of those biblical-type words. *Now it only conjures up visions of meat, chunks of pork, pinky white, hairless and ever so slightly slimy.* So how did all that loin-pulling turn into this pitiful indifference?

When did she become a *thing* to be handled? An instrument of another's few paltry seconds of derisory and ultimately pointless pleasure? A means to an end which is not hers, from which she stands utterly alienated. And that someone else, a person she *owes*?

When did coaxing fingers that peeled her slowly open, layer by layer, like the heart of a rose being sweetly bared, petal by petal, anticipation of pleasure deepening and excitement quickening with every breath she took, till she could scarcely breathe at all, when did those instruments of silken sorcery become transmogrified into tools of molestation? Why did something that once was experienced as rare and fine come crashing down to earth in a form so shabby, so base, so commonplace?

Which bed? Which place?

There was a summer. She recalled it vividly. It glowed like a lotus-flower painted in primary colours. They rented a villa in Provence. A small village outside Arles. The children, nine or ten, perhaps, no more: in and out of the little pool all day. Alice beneath a canary-yellow parasol watching as they leapt into the water, clowning around, shrieking with laughter. Chloe: half her face hidden behind outsize red goggles – a diminutive visitor from an alien planet, pink-suited and brown-limbed, in perpetual motion. Florence was just a year older, but quite different, reflective and circumspect. Her appearance was always of tremendous import to her. Every morning she deliberated at length over which tee-shirt to put on, which shorts, which jeans, which swimming costume. Everything, from pony-tail ring or hair-slide down to socks and trainers, or sandals, had to be perfectly attuned. Chloe had no patience with this. Throwing on whatever was at hand, often clothes still strewn over the floor from the previous day, then dashing out to the swing that hung from a tree at the back of the house. Her blonde curls permanently matted except for the times when Alice managed to sit her down and force the brush through, impervious to her howls of indignation.

While the children played, Alice would draw or paint watercolour sketches and Michael would read, stretched out on the grass in the sun. An oil portrait of her daughters created from sketches made during that blissful time still hangs in her bedroom. It is the first thing she sees when she wakes and the last when she turns off the light to sleep. Florence is pictured with her face half-turned to look at a golden oriole perched on the overhanging branch of an olive tree. Her right hand is raised with her index finger pointing to the bird. Chloe stares straight ahead, challenging the viewer, her wide green eyes proclaiming her fiercely independent nature. The double portrait had been long and hard in the making – many months. Alice had wanted it to stand as the definitive expression of love – her own personal experience of love without limits, which is not something you can say in a few, loosely applied brush-strokes.

The villa was surrounded by pine trees, olive trees and oleander bushes, dark-leaved against scarlet, rose-pink and white blooms. Purple bougainvillea invaded every whitewashed wall. Many varieties of wild flowers had been allowed freedom to grow wherever they pleased, decorating the tough scrub-like grass helter-skelter with patches of bright pinks, blues and orangey-yellows, dotted here and there with points of white, like scattered stars.

Beyond the hedge that bordered the garden to the south, vast flat fields stretched to the horizon. Much of this low-lying land was devoted to rice-growing. When the rice was harvested, it was processed in a small factory, a stone's throw from the house. You could see the end product displayed in brightly-coloured boxes, labelled '*Riz du Camargue*', in shops all over Arles and its surrounding villages.

Alice was not keen on its stodgy, sticky texture. But she bought several boxes anyway, out of loyalty and gratitude. She took some back to England when they left Provence, as if the memory would somehow be preserved inside the crimson and indigo boxes. She never opened them. Years later they still stood, dusty and forgotten, on the top shelf of a cupboard dedicated to things too precious to be used.

Because of their proximity to the rice fields, the villa and its pool were plagued with large and aggressive mosquitoes as soon as the sun began to set. Dusk was the signal for Michael to start rushing about, feverishly slamming doors, windows and shutters, spraying insecticide as he moved from room to room.

It was Alice's job to set up the electric mosquito killers in the bedrooms and each day he would repeat to her word for word exactly the same instructions on how this was to be done. She never bothered to tell him she had no need of his instructions. She knew perfectly well how the devices were activated and operated. She chose to leave unchallenged his assumptions of her ineptitude in the *man-things*: electrical repairs, car maintenance, plumbing. She played obediently along with the charade of female helplessness, because this was what he wanted. After all, it was of no importance to her, one way or the other.

Miriam would have screamed and screamed in protest at this. She would have pinned Alice mercilessly to her guilt like a butterfly to a tray, fixed by her fierce black stare. Miriam never compromised. They had met as students and soon became friends. Miriam was pure and transparent, and tough as a block of crystal. Several years older than Alice, and as canny as Alice was naïve, they made an unlikely pair.

Miriam had had several false starts before alighting on art as the path best-suited to her objectives. She was a committed crusader for left-wing causes, the more radical the better. Passionate in her quest for social justice and fiercely inimical to the rich and privileged. From her early teens she had embarked on her quest to rid the world of capitalism. She began training as a social worker, but quickly gave it up in disgust and exasperation at the system's ineffectiveness, its resistance to change, ultimately its impotence to help the poor and vulnerable.

She then tried the academic route, launched into a law degree, which she very nearly completed, but that too ended up by the wayside. Halfway through her final year, she concluded that once again she'd taken the wrong path. She would never change the world by joining that particular club. Joining the legal establishment would mean selling out to everything she most despised.

'Direct action, that's the *only* way,' she declared to Alice soon after they met, her eyes like blobs of molasses, glowing and intense. They stood at easels in the stifling heat of the life class. They worked side by side in contrasting ways. Miriam produced a succession of bold, rapidly executed sketches in charcoal. Alice laboured stolidly over two or three carefully detailed, fine pencil drawings, with lines many times erased and corrected. She envied Miriam's panache and confidence. She was impressed by her sure touch and the brilliance of her draughtsmanship. Beside her, Alice felt timid and inadequate.

At seventeen, Alice was largely unconcerned with the world that existed outside the warm bubble that had held her safe all her life till then. She was vaguely aware of a war going on thousands of miles away in Vietnam, but was indifferent to why it was being fought and had no interest in why it should excite such violent reactions amongst her peers.

Thanks to Miriam, her initiation into political consciousness was brutal and swift. In a matter of weeks she was spending sleepless nights helping Miriam and others create posters and flyers denouncing the war and the vile USA. She marched through London with the rest, brandishing banners and shouting slogans. She trailed behind Miriam like a grateful puppy.

Miriam lived alone in a bedsit in Hackney. One afternoon, after a shouting match between Miriam and Oswald, her tutor, Alice eventually managed to calm her down and they returned to Hackney together. They ended up spending the evening there, imbibing cheap Beaujolais. Bitter words had been exchanged. Oswald told Miriam to stop wasting her and the college's time with her political activities; she threatened to walk off the course. It ended with his yelling: 'Well, you'll never get anywhere in the art world anyway!' before storming out of the studio. The scene was witnessed by a group of horrified first years, too stunned to speak.

They sat on cushions on the floor as the light faded, their backs propped up against a divan pushed into a corner of the tiny room. Miriam lit up a Gauloise. The treacly smoke settled into an appetising fog above the table-lamp. They finished excoriating Oswald and, having run out of expletives, fell silent.

'I've been thinking,' Miriam began, staring into the gloom. 'It's more than just politics.' She refilled her glass and offered the bottle to Alice, who declined. 'I mean, it's people, really, isn't it? States of mind...'

Alice said: 'You mean – getting rid of capitalism isn't...'

'Not the solution.' She swallowed some wine. 'No. Not the answer. It's people. They're the problem. Greed. Stupidity. Pride. Even if you did – get rid of it. Change society... Wouldn't make any difference. I mean, it'd just happen all over again. For sure.' She stopped.

Alice racked her brains to find something wise to say, something reassuring.

Miriam went on, miserably: 'Sometimes I think: what's the point?'

Yet despite the hopelessness which periodically overwhelmed her, she continued to pursue her mission with obstinacy and dedication. Alice went along with it all, blissfully and unquestioningly, swept away by the nobility of the cause.

For a time, her view of art itself became re-shaped by Miriam's Marxist theories. The economics of power, Miriam declared, generates, at worst, art that endorses it, or, at best, the art that's required to change it. Art was a waste of time and space unless it served a revolutionary, or at the very least, a critical purpose.

'Art is nothing but a reflection of its time,' Alice intoned time and again to anybody who happened to be listening. 'It's power politics. The controllers versus the controlled.' She recited this mantra to Estelle, who listened politely but distractedly. She did the same for Julius, who smiled in a manner Alice regarded as despicably patronising.

She grew to despise her parents as typical examples of the bourgeois mentality soon to be swept away by The Revolution. Her behaviour towards them became studiedly insolent. The ruder her behaviour, the more satisfaction she experienced. Her life seemed suddenly infused with meaning. The tiger of rebellion had seized her in its jaws.

Julius and Estelle, by now living apart, were both equally baffled by the change in her personality.

'What's happened to you?' her mother fretted one afternoon, shouting after her as Alice threw her bag onto the floor and raced upstairs without a word.

'I don't recognise you any more.'

Alice slammed the door.

A few days later she walked into the kitchen where Estelle was preparing dinner and announced bluntly: 'I'm leaving. I can't live here any more.'

She was eighteen. She could do what she liked.

Entreaties, tears and threats were to no avail. She had money. The money Grandma left her. She'd be fine. 'Don't worry.'

When Julius heard, he was philosophical.

'Let her go,' he said. 'She's not yours any more. Not ours.'

It wasn't only Alice who fell prey to Miriam's fervour. Most of the other students were eager to follow her lead, Marxism being the prevailing fashion. Even those like Alice, middle class and fresh from school, whose political consciousness was virtually non-existent, spurred on by Miriam's infectious ardour, were rapidly gathered up into the fold. It bore all the marks of a religious conversion.

Ordinarily college administrators would have paid little attention to it. Just a phase. But the ethos of St Anthony's being what it was, the simmering radicalism spreading through the student corpus threatened to undermine the founding principles on which its whole approach to art education was based.

St Anthony's was an old-established place that favoured traditional methods based on very narrowly-defined views of what Art was and ought to be. These did not include the use of Art as a socio-political instrument. In the eyes of the academic board, Art belonged in a stratosphere akin to religion. It spoke to and about the higher reaches of the human spirit. The dissension being fomented by Miriam among the rank and file was seen to jeopardise the entire reputation of the school as a respected guardian of traditional values in a fracturing world.

At meetings of the board, the issue of *what to do about Miriam* was frequently debated. It was resolved that she be given a series of formal warnings. Essentially: bring yourself into line and curb your activism – otherwise, you're out.

Needless to say, the warnings had no effect. She simply carried on exactly as before. The board could have expelled her, but it had to do a balancing act. Miriam, despite her unorthodoxy, was too good to lose.

CHAPTER TWELVE

It was not long after Alice left home that she first met Michael. She was at a party at the house of a friend, Georgie, in Notting Hill Gate. Michael, a friend of Georgie's brother, was a trainee solicitor in a City firm. Alice was in two minds whether to go. Almost didn't, but then changed her mind at the last minute. She arrived late, around ten. Michael was standing quite close to the door, the tallest in a group of men and girls exchanging jokes. Raucous laughter rising periodically above the background of chatter and music by the Beatles and the Rolling Stones. People were dancing, some alone, some in couples.

They caught one another's eye at the same instant. He was like a silver birch, straight and elegant, his blonde hair, pale as honey, fell across his broad brow in silky touchable strands. He exuded stillness and calm, like a Nordic fjord.
He detached himself from the group to approach her and within minutes she found herself relating the story of her recent trip to the Greek Islands, as if she'd known him for years. His eyes were cobalt blue spattered with gold specks. They looked straight into hers, his attention focused intently upon her and her tales. He made her feel she was the most exciting person in the room.

'So what happened then?' he asked, with bated breath, seemingly hanging on her every word. 'And where did you go next?'

It was no mere show, she could tell. He possessed a genuine curiosity about others, and his honesty shone through, softening the aloof set of his mouth – a half-smile beneath permanently raised eyebrows: the unconscious legacy of generations of privilege.

She told him how she'd been roped into going, initially without enthusiasm. Dragged along to make up numbers with a bunch of people she had little in common with, how she'd parted company with them early on in the trip to head off on her own. She told him Greece had been a revelation. Six weeks in the Cyclades, but wishing she could stay forever. She told him of the dozens of sketches and paintings she'd made, the breathtaking beauty of the Greek coastline with its rocky coves and inlets, whitewashed villages with their flat-roofed houses clambering up hillsides, the fragrance of oregano and thyme growing wild in the mountains, the aroma of freshly-caught mullet and lemon-scented *souvlakia* being grilled over charcoal in beach-side *tavernas*, the exuberant bouzouki music which burst into life at dusk, the sight of the sun sinking blood-red into a purple sea.

He listened. He seemed enraptured. As she talked, Alice was intensely conscious of the impression she was making. She saw herself through his eyes: dark hair falling loose about her bare, tanned shoulders, the primrose-yellow dress that hugged her body, her long, slim legs, delicate feet strapped into black sandals.

They continued to meet now and then. He took her to concerts, ballets, the theatre, the cinema. He had a flat overlooking the Thames. It belonged to his parents, who, he told her, lived most of the year in their country house in Hertfordshire. She went back to his flat sometimes at the end of an evening together, but never stayed the night.

With infinite delicacy Michael waited. She wanted to please him. She was enamoured of his tenderness, his generosity, his charm. But...

'I don't feel ready. Not yet,' she would tell him.

He never imposed. He would wait, he said.

But it didn't happen. Alice waited and waited for something to happen to her. A tidal wave. An avalanche. Something powerful and irresistible. *What's the point*, she thought, *without that?* But nothing did.

In the end Michael's patience ran out. He got tired of waiting for Alice to feel ready. He began seeing someone else. A girl he'd taken out a couple of times before. Jenny was a cool blonde with an unpleasantly shrill laugh and a good body, a secretary at the firm where he worked. Jenny was out for a good time, unattached and besotted with Michael.

From then on, everything changed. He continued seeing Alice, but he became irritable, even irascible towards her. He blamed her for forcing him into a situation he didn't want to be in. He felt it was sordid and degrading. Whenever they met he would find some pretext to criticise her and complain. He was careful to keep Alice in the dark about Jenny, so the change in him remained unexplained. After a couple of months she had to conclude they were no good any more together. So they went their separate ways.

Almost immediately after parting with Michael, Alice became enmeshed in an intensely physical relationship with one of her housemates, an architecture student. From her first encounter with Justin, she was drawn into a vortex of enchantment from which there was no escape, not that there existed the remotest will to escape. Up until then Alice's adventures had always been a terrible let-down. In almost every case pleasure was absent for her. She felt as if she were on the outside, a spectator to a faintly risible performance of convulsive jerks preceded by clumsy prods and strokings, all of which seemed ultimately a waste of time and energy. She felt she didn't fit into this ritual. She even got to wondering whether she might be frigid.

With Justin everything changed. She plunged with him into a pool of pleasure, through which they swam and floated like a couple of dolphins never tiring of play. Their hunger for one another was insatiable. They shared a continuum of delight, without gaps or troughs. Physical interaction was all they sought. Talk was unnecessary, a waste of time. They had no interest in one another's thoughts, ambitions or feelings. They had nothing in common beyond their mutual obsession with each other's bodies. They had neither the desire nor the need to share anything else.

But when they had been together for eight months, Justin went away. A thousand miles away to New Jersey to continue his studies. He went away, and everything got confusing and chaotic once more. Together there had been a classic simplicity, the physical pleasure was all-encompassing. If she had to put it into words, she would not have demeaned it by labelling it as 'love'. Absolutely not.

Love was for the mediocre, the middle of the road, the country-and-westerners. Love was for mainstreamers, compilation-lovers, semi-detached suburban types, nine-to-fivers. Love was for tennis clubbers. Love existed in two dimensions, in the space between reality and dreams, in pictures that moved or pictures that stayed still and voices that called every evening to girls who were told and believed that love was waiting for them. Somewhere. Some time. Love was for lovers who took sandwiches to the park and fed them to ducks. Love was for wives who bought curtains and kitchenware in John Lewis and took in a show. Love was for husbands who drove BMWs and screwed the temp in the lunch-hour. Love was for the Thomas Cookers, love was for Easter skiers and winter summers and those who travelled just-that-little-bit-further. Love was for pension planners and writers of wills and savers for a rainy day. Love was for those who sent Valentine's Day cards with plumped-up red satin hearts and for those who received them with a squeal and misty eyes. Love was for the mowers of lawns and the growers of patio plants. Love was for those who drank whisky at seven and waited for the cricket score. Love was for secretaries and for those who had secretaries. Love was for teachers and doctors and farmers and managers and manageresses and pillars of the community. Love was for the employed and the unemployed. Love was for those who pretended their hedges were walls of medieval fortresses, leafless and lifeless. Love was on the airwaves and spread all over the silver screen, love was in print, love was on cereal packets. Love was everywhere and nowhere.

For a long time Alice felt like a wounded animal. The absence of his body was like something wrenched out of her, leaving her bleeding. They wrote once or twice, but neither had anything to say. The thing they had shared could not survive physical separation.

In fury she threw herself into work. At first she tried with every piece she made to immortalise what they'd had, that was now lost for ever. But every attempt failed. In the end she had to concede that nothing could be salvaged or preserved. Nothing remained. There was nothing to do but move on.

It was then, as if fate had planned it, that Erasmus re-entered her life. Her desperate search for a new direction took her into a frenzy of visits to shows, sometimes three or four in a day. She devoured art journals and reviews and it was in one of these, buried in the back pages, that she read the letter. It was signed only *'Erasmus.'* Instantly she recalled when she had first seen him at a private view in a small gallery in Bruton Street about a year before. A short, wiry man in his seventies, bald, sun-tanned head, white beard and penetrating blue eyes. An aura of calm and wisdom floated about him. She watched him in fascination, but was too timid to approach. He moved from painting to painting, surrounded by a dozen or so adoring acolytes.

'Who is *that?*' she whispered to Jane, her tutor, who turned to her in surprise.

'That's Erasmus, of course.'

She told Alice he was a painter who had lived for thirty years or more on an obscure Greek island, too inaccessible to be of any interest to tourists or developers. He lived a monastically simple life on next to nothing, and, for the last ten years, every summer for five or six weeks, small groups of amateur as well as professional artists had been trekking off to his tiny island abode, braving the complicated and uncomfortable journey to reach him: two ferry trips island hopping from Piraeus, followed by an hour's hectic journey by road in rickety, twenty-year-old buses.

Each year the pilgrims returned, new as well as old. Erasmus never quite figured out why. Every summer he secretly hoped he would be left alone, but hadn't the heart to turn anyone away. It all started with an exhibition of his work at a gallery in the East End of London, near Whitechapel, ten years before. It attracted so much interest that it was extended for several weeks. Erasmus turned into a kind of icon for a short time. No-one was more surprised than he.

'His art was so different,' said Jane, 'nobody was doing that kind of thing. It was all mostly Pop Art then. His paintings were just full of ... I don't know... joy, beauty. Something very pure and true. They made you feel good. But I'm not surprised you've never heard of him. He's out on a limb. A one-off. What you'd call a niche public. Certainly no money to be made out of him. But he did touch a nerve with a lot of people.' Her included, she added. 'He became a sort of guru.'

One year Jane herself joined the pilgrimage to his island in the Aegean. No accommodation was provided. People either brought tents or slept in one of the derelict fisherman's huts to be found scattered here and there along the beach. Erasmus lived in a tiny whitewashed house that stood like a beacon on the crest of a hill that sloped down to the sea, carved into terraces of fig and olive trees.

There was no fee, but visitors contributed what Erasmus called a 'donation' – whatever they chose or could afford – for the privilege of sharing ten days or more of the artist's life, for as many hours as they wished. He worked constantly, breaking off only to eat and sleep. He was up at dawn and finished only when the light became too faint to distinguish the colours on his canvas. He talked while he worked, inviting debate on everything from styles of painting to aesthetics and the role of art in the world and people's lives.

He came of age artistically in a time when it was taken for granted that art and politics existed in separate spheres, each having its own system of reference, its own criteria, its own values, but he had the breadth of vision to accept that art could serve a multitude of purposes.

As soon as anyone started banging on about art having to be *this* and not *that*, Erasmus would cut them off roughly, reducing them instantly to silence, with no room for argument.

'No! There are no *oughts* in art. Except for one: honesty. Everything else is crap. Art can be whatever you want it to be, as long as it comes from *here*.' He banged his chest with his fist. 'You may think you can change the world through art. That's OK. You may be looking for another world that has nothing to do with this one. Art as a universe apart, with its own reality. That's OK too. Who's to say what art should or shouldn't be? Music, poetry, it's all the same. Art that's not from the heart ain't art.'

Jane told her of one guy who tried to get clever and challenge Erasmus. He had positioned himself a little apart from the group that was sitting in a semi-circle round the painter on the beach. He called out:

'So that's all it takes then, is it? Just being honest? That's great! So we can all go home now then. We're all artists already! We *are* all honest here aren't we?'

He twisted his head from right to left, mockingly addressing the question to the rest, who remained silent and immobile, their embarrassment palpable.

'That's right, John,' Erasmus replied quietly. 'You've got it in one. That's the key. Absolutely! You've understood. Well done. All of us here are artists. Just like every human being on the planet. You've just got to see that art really is a state of mind, that's all.'

'But what about skill?' he persisted.

'What about it?'

That threw him at first. Then he said:

'Well… What are we all here for then?'

Erasmus carried on painting for a while, smiling as if at some secret thought. Then he replied:

'Anyone can learn to draw. It's just a matter of looking, really looking at things, the way they are, not the way you think they are. Anyone can learn to paint in the manner of Titian, or Cezanne or Warhol, for that matter. Whoever takes your fancy. That's not what you're here for. Anyone can learn that kind of thing. Technique is unimportant.'

'The guy was staring at him wide-eyed and open-mouthed. He looked as if he couldn't believe what he was hearing.' Jane chuckled at the memory.

Then Erasmus said if there was just one thing they should take away with them when they left, it was this:

'Art means different things to different people. What you've got to do first and foremost is answer this one question: why am I, or do I want to be, an artist? Or a writer, poet, cinematographer, playwright, composer ... it's all the same. What is my true motivation? Is it fame? Do I want my name to resonate through the centuries, like Shakespeare or Michelangelo? Is that what it's for? Am I looking for immortality? Do I simply long for the world's adulation: there he goes, that brilliant, original genius, Joseph Bloggs! Or is it money I'm after? Do I crave vast riches or perhaps, more prosaically, just a comfortable, decent life for myself and my family? After all, there are worse ways of making a living... Or, when all's said and done, is it just that I'm in love with the romantic idea of being an artist, writer or whatever? If you say yes to any of these, well, I'm sorry my friend, but what you're doing isn't art. Not art that's worthy of the name. Forget skill. Forget technique. That's not what true art's about. It could be an irresistible longing to celebrate life or the world or nature or love. A spontaneous outpouring. A need to communicate, to share, something deep that you've felt, experienced. It could be fired by the desire to right wrongs, to show people how they could make the world better and to really want to do that. It could be simply a way of saying: listen to me or look at me: this is what's inside me. Is it that way with you too? Whatever it is you're communicating to others through art, that *is* art. When it's just a code for some kind of self-aggrandisement, or just a means to an end, whatever that end might be, that ain't art, believe you me.'

Alice never met Erasmus, never had any personal contact with him at all. In fact, he didn't even know of her existence. And yet for years she kept track of wherever he was in the world, and what he was up to. She read every piece he wrote, visited exhibitions where his work was displayed and listened avidly to snippets of information about him from people who knew him or about him.

He sat like a leprechaun or a little Buddha at the back of her mind, a mentor she had never consulted, who knew nothing about her, yet his presence was like a pure mountain stream to which she returned whenever she lost her way.

She penned innumerable letters to him, but in the end, sent not a single one. They never sounded right. Either over-effusive or inadequate or insufficiently profound or overburdened with platitudes. Something was always wrong. When Erasmus died, she grieved as much for his departure from the world as for the fact that she never got to tell him how important he had been in her life.

'Art is not art if words would do just as well. Art is like music: by its nature inarticulable.'

It was thanks to Erasmus that she found the confidence to follow the route that felt right for her, in defiance of Miriam and her ideas about art as an instrument of revolution. Her friend's response to Alice's new work in progress was brutally uncompromising.

'My God! What the hell's this? A heap of shit. It's useless. It's pointless. It's like porridge. You can't fight battles with mush!'

'I don't want to fight battles,' Alice said. 'I want to be true to myself. I want to be honest.'

Miriam shrugged, regarding her ruefully, as if she were a lost cause.

'It's a great shame. But inevitable, I suppose. You've reverted to type, haven't you? Of course you have! The little bourgeois through and through. Just can't help yourself, can you?'

Alice built up a portfolio of paintings, drawings and mixed media pieces in preparation for her degree show, making up for the months of neglect when she had produced virtually nothing. She found herself moving further and further away from Miriam's concept of art as a political tool. She turned inwards and was irresistibly drawn to the exploration of her own identity. Who was she? This in turn led her to the idea of freedom, the power we have to change ourselves, to be anything. She wanted the things she made somehow to illuminate minds, to show people what they were capable of, to stretch boundaries. The power of choice.

The challenge was to create something that would reflect hardness, the unchanging resistance to erosion, the immutable force of circumstance, and at the same time, the lightness of air, constricted by nothing, the freedom to move and change form at will, not being at the mercy of any force but your own. The very opposite of a leaf blown hither and thither, at the mercy of the wind. She had to produce a structure where change was displayed as self-controlled and self-defining. A perpetual process of self-definition.

She felt herself growing in strength, tough enough to stand up to Miriam's derision, to defend her project robustly and with conviction.

'I may not be able to change society, but I can at least change my own life.' Miriam remained mute. No further comment.

She made flowers from pieces of flexible wire. The shapes and sizes ranged widely. The tallest, four or five feet tall, with spreading tendrils and leaves, the smallest, tiny and compact, just a few inches from the ground. She squeezed, bent and wound the pieces of wire with her bare hands, which became covered in small scratches and cuts, till she achieved the simplicity of form she sought. There were different flower-head shapes, some interwoven to make layered forms that folded around and into one another, like roses, tulips or poppies. Others opened upwards and outwards, offering themselves, mirroring the forms of daisies, primroses or lilies. Still others were moulded into tightly packed masses of tiny circles like the patterns of alyssum and lobelia.

The shapes were open graphic forms set into plain wooden supports, drawings in space without volume or colour. Above the structure was a screen which showed a continuously repeated film of a butterfly in vivid colours, flitting backwards and forwards, then briefly alighting on a flower, before resuming its perpetual flight. Alice called the piece '*Aeolus*' after the Greek god of the winds.

Though Miriam never criticised Alice in the presence of others, when the two were alone she made no secret of her disappointment.

'But it's about freedom,' Alice protested. 'The freedom to act. To change things…'

But as far as Miriam was concerned, Alice had turned away from the cause to follow a path of her own – the wrong one.

'I've got to do what feels right for me,' Alice said, regretfully but insistently.

'OK. You do as you like then.'

CHAPTER THIRTEEN

When her degree course came to an end, Alice continued to exhibit regularly in group shows that took place mainly in rented warehouses in the East End. The income she gained from her art was negligible, barely covering the rent of her Battersea flat, so she had to take teaching jobs to make ends meet. Those led eventually to the setting up of her own tutorial agency that provided her with a modest, fairly reliable income.

She lurched through a succession of short, grubby liaisons and nameless one-night stands, looking in vain for another Justin, but only ending up sinking further and further into despondency. The creative impetus faded. She found herself producing work just for the sake of it, work that felt stale even as she was doing it, work that lacked inspiration.

One evening as she stood in the rain waiting for a 49 bus in the Fulham Road, cold, wet and dispirited, suddenly, unbelievably, there was Michael. He sat her in a taxi and took her back with him to his flat. The same place as before. Michael, too, was exactly as she remembered him. Familiar, warm, reassuring. It was like coming home.

Her overwhelming emotion was relief. Gratitude for his calm, positive strength. His uncomplicated perspective on life. The certainties that defined his existence. Relief from the directionless chaos her own life had become.

When Miriam heard that Alice was going to marry Michael, she inquired 'so when's it due?'

'What? *No!*' Alice laughed.

So there was no room for forgiveness then. No baby? No excuse! No reason to get hitched. Why the hell was she doing it?

Miriam knew all about that. At eighteen, seduced by romantic illusions of a rosy bower for two, she had moved out of her bedsit in Hackney into the bottom half of a maisonette in Balham with Andrew, a bespectacled physics teacher, recently qualified, in his first job at a local comprehensive.

She was fairly rapidly un-seduced. Till she started living with Andrew she still believed in the illusion of Woman as Offering. As a woman you *gave yourself* to a man, you perceived yourself to be something precious, and in return for the gift of yourself, the man shall revere and adore you. The primary purpose of Woman's existence was the delectation of Man, to pleasure his senses and surround him with peace and wellbeing. Woman as Offering, then morphing later, seamlessly, into Woman as Nurturer.

At eighteen Miriam had existed unknowingly at the bottom of a deep ravine. Green mountain ranges covered with flowers blocked out the sun. Her female mind and senses were bewitched by iconic images of Womanhood that were locked inside a sphere of eternal, rock-solid, unchanging and unchangeable values.

At eighteen, she was still raw, a casualty of a lonely and loveless childhood. A father who drank himself to death when she was too young to remember him, a mother who, when he died, went on to have baby after baby, all with different fathers.

'Five in all,' Miriam said lightly, 'counting me. Then, when I was ten, they put me into what's laughingly known as "care". The others, they stayed with her in the end. Don't know why really. The powers that be must have felt sorry for her. But they just forgot about me.'

Miriam worked her way through a series of well-meaning but hapless foster families, none of whom understood her nor managed to tame her wild nature.

Andrew made her actually feel cared for.

'For the first time in my life. So no surprise the way it turned out,' she said. 'It felt so good. I was grateful. Consumed with it. I adored him.'

At eighteen, whilst she and Andrew coalesced into a couple, she had the sense that their coupledom had about it an aura of sanctity, which made doubts about its absolute rightness inconceivable. Not until much later did the idea enter her head that the heavenly picture might be a fake.

It was a vision of Woman, the source of light, rising heavenwards in all her seductive guises. Woman, the perfumed garden, generator of sensual pleasures, repository of delight for the delectation of Man.

As the song goes: '*...thy temples are like a piece of a pomegranate within thy locks... Thy two breasts are like two young roes that are twins, which feed among the lilies...Thou art all fair, my love; there is no spot in thee... A garden enclosed... thy plants are an orchard of pomegranates, with pleasant fruits; camphire, with spikenard. Spikenard and saffron; calamus and cinnamon, with all trees of frankincense; myrrh and aloes, with all the chief spices. A fountain of gardens, a well of living waters, and streams from Lebanon.*'

At eighteen, she aspired to be the woman adored and worshipped in the *Song of Solomon*. And like the woman in the *Song* she saw Andrew as the north wind. In her imagination she called to him to '*blow upon my garden, that the spices thereof may flow out. Let my beloved come into his garden, and eat his pleasant fruits*'.

'And strangely enough, I look back on that time with great fondness. I can even say it was the only time I've ever felt truly happy. Never mind the crassness, the absurdity, the self-delusion. Of course I was deluding myself. We both were. But for a short blissful time it was living inside a poem.'

The beginning of the end of the poem was when the picture began to shift imperceptibly away from Woman as the object of adoration to Woman the Nurturer.

'You change for them eventually. You turn into a well. Somewhere they can come to slake their thirst, after a hard day's work toiling in the fields, or in the office, or the school – whatever. From mistress to housekeeper. That's when the rot set in for me. That's when the truth started to dawn, at least.'

She had lived with him for eighteen months when she realised her identity was being drowned in his. She was no-one – nothing but a projection of his desires and fantasies.

Ironically, both of them believed everything was reducible to politics and once you had the right system in place, everything good would follow from that. They were both wholeheartedly in agreement on that point. Not a question of a doubt divided them.

But in the end, what was happening between them, it wasn't a matter of politics. Nothing to do with it. It was something else entirely. Andrew and Miriam were as one in their reviling of the capitalist order. They were united in their determination to transform a price-based society into one that rested on human values. But that common aim had no influence on how they perceived each other's role. Andrew, for all his radical words and philosophies, in reality was no different from the two thousand-year-old lover in the *Song of Solomon*.

For a while, it never occurred to Miriam to question what was happening. Each remained victims of a temporary amnesia. In their enthusiasm to create their lives in the time-honoured image of the Couple – the only one they had ever known, they forgot what it was like before, when they were living apart: there had been no division of labour then, no prescriptive pattern, just a joyous freedom without rules or routines. Amnesia set in, and for a while helped to spread a comforting patina over the day-to-day existence of the fledgling couple.

Andrew was permanently exhausted by the rigors of his job, relieved to return to an environment which brought him contentment. He had neither the will nor the energy to explore moral dilemmas nor question the authenticity of their lifestyle. As far as he was concerned, Miriam was a perfectly agreeable companion, attractive, generous, compliant. He felt himself fortunate to have found such a girl. It was obviously not the same as before. But there were compensations for the loss of that sweet madness. You couldn't stay mad for ever, could you?

Miriam, on the other hand, began to experience an increasing sense of unease. At first she was happy to be in control of Andrew's well-being. It gave her a sense of fulfilment, even power. She desired so strongly to find ways of pleasing him that she began to fall behind in her studies, skipping lectures, missing deadlines, leaving abandoned essays to languish in disorderly heaps around the house. But euphoria rapidly grew tainted by doubt. Odd remarks, thrown at her half-jestingly, unveiled underlying assumptions.

'Hey! No dinner yet?'

'That can wait, Miriam. This can't.'

'Leave it. You can't do that. Leave it to me.'

'That's your job, not mine.'

She didn't put her doubts into words. Yet the signs were inescapable. The fluidity that once had informed their union was calcifying into a structure with fixed boundaries. She closed her eyes to the truth, pretending she couldn't see it. But finally it became impossible to deny that what they once had shared with joyous abandon was congealing into a contractual partnership governed by the principle of mutual exchange.

Almost nothing was left that was not conditional on something else. She wrote in the private journal she kept intermittently:

'Your tender acts of concern are wrapped around an arc that points back to you. My loving gifts and words are payment for services rendered. The linking of our lives is becoming denatured. Our love will soon have sunk into the mud, like all the others. At low tide, you can see them, millions of them at different stages of fossilisation, all of them in pairs, each pair exuding a glutinous plasma which binds them inescapably together and to their hole in the mud.'

The day after she wrote that entry, she packed up her belongings and went back to Hackney for good.

So it was inevitable that when Alice told Miriam of her decision to marry Michael, she responded with:

'So you're pregnant then.' It was not a question.

Alice's denial provoked incredulity.

'What? Then why? Why on earth...?'

Alice had no answer, except:

'He makes me feel... peaceful. Happy.'

'Peaceful? Happy?' Her voice was filled with disgust.

'Miriam, I'm weary. I need to rest...'

Which only made things worse.

She pressed Alice to re-consider, accused her of copping out, amongst other, even worse, crimes. Told her it was like signing the death-warrant to her freedom: her life would never again be her own. Decisions would be made for her. And if she disagreed, she'd have to battle and struggle.

'And you know he'll always have the upper hand. Is that what you want? There'll be nothing you can do about it. You'll be a kept woman!'

Alice couldn't help laughing at that.

'Hold on! This is the nineteen seventies. We're not living in the fifties any more!'

Miriam moved her head slowly from side to side.

'Nothing's changed,' she muttered. 'Only on the surface.' There was a pause. Then Miriam, in a voice no louder than a whisper, said: 'I expected better from you.'

'For God's sake! I'm only getting married, not selling my soul. Why are you looking at me like that?'

Miriam glared at her with ferocity.

'Anyway,' Alice went on, ignoring the look, 'I haven't changed my views. Michael and I want to carry on leading independent lives, our own space, you know…'

'Huh!' Miriam scoffed. 'Then why not just carry on as you are?'

Alice felt she was being squeezed into a corner. It annoyed her, because she had no answer. On one level, Miriam was right. She couldn't deny it. Of course she was.

It was Miriam who broke the silence:

'So you're selling out then. Bloody shame. You're a fool.'

'It's not what you think. I'm not opting out for the sake of an easy life…'

'Aren't you?'

For several years after her marriage, Alice was obscurely aware of a room in her mind that she kept firmly under lock and key. A space which, when she was still single, had been crowded with colours, with noise, with questions. Insatiable longings to find out about the mysteries of life, the world, herself.

With Justin, everything was imbued with a classic simplicity. She shelved everything that had formerly caused her disquiet. Mutual pleasure was all-encompassing. It was not just an element of their lives, but a universe beyond which everything else ceased to have any importance. For Alice at least, when they were apart, whatever she did was informed by the memory of their last encounter and the anticipation of the next. He was never for a single instant absent from her existence.

With Michael it was another thing altogether. Then Florence was born and the sealing off of that part of Alice, once shimmering, now dreamless and obscure, turned into a permanent fixture. Somewhere out there, in the universal scheme into which she had been placed, approval had been granted to what had until then been hedged around with uncertainty. The birth of Florence transformed the fluid, blurry outlines of an inner landscape which had fallen out of sync with itself into something sharp-edged, mercilessly brilliant, something that left no room for question or doubt.

When the baby was just a few hours old, Alice lifted her gently out of the cot that stood next to her bed. Tiny wisp of humanity, almost weightless, helpless and unknowing, yet her small body hummed and zinged with life. Her head rested in the palm of Alice's hand, like a round exotic fruit, rare and remarkable.

The baby sucked at her breast; she could feel the hardness of the child's spine under the thin cotton nightshirt, resting lightly in the crook of her arm. The baby's mouth pulling at her nipple sent waves of languorous pleasure through Alice's body. Eyes, violet blue, wandered open, resting for an instant on Alice's face, then swam away, then floated back again, like water hyacinths in the eddies of a pool.

A year later Chloe was born. But with her coming, welcome though it was, nothing actually changed. The pattern of Alice's life had already been set. She had no particular reason to fret or complain. Busy, busy, busy. She needed the busy-ness. Needed to be too busy to think.

The tutoring agency she had started up years before, she kept going. She had created it, built it up, was reluctant to let it go.

'What's the point?' Michael said. 'You don't *need* to do it.'

She did, though. She did need it. Something of her own. Something to hang onto.

She located tutors. Turnover was high. Mostly they were people in transit. Students on vacation, graduates marking time, artists, writers, actors between jobs. She was never short of people. Over the years she had also built up a pool of 'reliables' who could step in at the drop of a hat, to fill in for those that let her down. And there were many of those.

Despite the problems, it suited Alice. No office, no rigid hours. Plenty of space left for creative things. In the beginning, before she married Michael, she was able to subsist on what the agency brought in and still have time to continue her search for solutions, for pathways through art. Every painting she did was a web, which was both a visual language and something that went beyond language. She thought of it as music for the eyes.

It had nothing to do with fashion. Or money. She observed her contemporaries' manic hunt for weirdness and originality from the perspective of an interested spectator. She had no desire to belong to any kind of movement, and as a result she found herself shunned by most other artists and her work was rarely shown. She beavered on alone, doing her own thing. She had no choice. She had also the satisfaction of being true to herself.

Before that, long before, when she was still a student, there had been a period when she stopped making marks with paint on two-dimensional surfaces and began making objects which, in the vernacular of the time, would *'signify, but not represent'*.

Meaning was all. Meaning was of the essence. Miriam was consumed with a passion for this all-embracing principle that was transferred to and captivated Alice for a time, devout and unquestioning disciple as she then was.

'Doesn't matter what you end up with or how you do it, as long as you know what you want to say and that comes across crystal clear,' Miriam would say, her eyes wide and glistening.

This was the New Revolution, the beginning of a new way of looking at art and thinking about what art was for. It was the death knell for the art object as icon or symbol or talisman, or...

'whichever label you want to choose, makes no difference' Miriam remarked, with a dismissive shrug.

The absolutely once-and-for-all final curtain to the notion of the art work as a non-referential object for people to stand in front of, open-mouthed, and contemplate in awe. No more art-for-art's-sake. All that was gone for good. Dead and buried. Nothing but an archaeological relic. Never to rise again. Fit only for museums. One of the quaint notions once held by a civilization that had long ago outgrown its usefulness.

'Art isn't art unless it has direct relevance to the modern world.'

People would no longer feel compelled to tiptoe through galleries as if in a place of worship, adopting attitudes of silent or whispered reverence. Their eyes, ears and minds would be assailed by shocks and surprise. They would see displayed before them objects, miscellanies of materials they would not expect to be described as Art. Literally anything would be used and in any combination: pieces of textile, piles of earth, industrial materials – glass, steel, plastic, mass-produced things chucked away and reclaimed from rubbish dumps or purchased from flea-markets, photographs, sound-recordings of anything, even portions of empty space ringed around with stones or bricks or bits of wire.

Anything could be art because anything could be made to have meaning.

Alice was eager to discard old habits. They belonged to a fossilized world. Superannuated, obsolete, sterile. Had to be superseded because they had nothing left to give.

But then Alice encountered Erasmus, and that changed everything.

CHAPTER FOURTEEN

Alice's visit to Jack's little house on the prairie was followed by others. At first, on the pretext of work. Dropping off details of new pupils 'just happened to be passing... Save you a journey...' Soon, however, any attempt to find pretexts was dropped.

What's the point? We both know why I've come.

But it's not for sex. That's the last thing... *Well, maybe not the last.* And yet, it seems vital, to her at least, that they should not allow themselves to descend to that.

'What we have. We mustn't trivialize it...'

He shakes his head. She leans forward. Takes one of his hands, clasping it within hers.

'It's so delicate. Could so easily be spoilt. Ruined, actually.'

Like a dandelion clock. So fragile. You only have to breathe on it.

'*Affair!* I hate that word. So commonplace. Tawdry. Yuk!'

He smiles. Maybe sleeping with her is what he wants. Probably. But she doesn't want even to contemplate that.

To Alice, this would signal a fall from grace. A cheapening of something unique and special. The act of sex itself: so ordinary, so unexceptional. There is only one way to go after that, only one direction and that is down. Down, down, down. Downward to nothing.

'I guess you're right,' he says finally. He shrugs. She gets the feeling he doesn't really care either way. No matter. It's what she feels and needs that counts.

Jack has girls, she knows that. How could he not? With his casual, artless charm, his honey-coloured skin, his thick dark hair that curls down the back of his neck, eyes like a stream catching glimpses of sun as it darts through the forest shadows.

He has told her how he needs the touch of women. Takes intense pleasure in the sight, feel and scent of their bodies. He likes to have a female presence around him sharing his space now and then. But not to live with. No way. No thanks.

She loves the sense that there subsists within him a central core that remains ultimately impregnable. He is from choice a lone spirit.

'I don't make promises I know I won't keep', he kisses her lightly beneath the hair that falls across her brow. 'You can't say *for ever*. Nothing is forever. There's only now. The here and now. That's the only truth.'

'Kids?'

'God, I don't know. There may be a few scattered around. That was up to the woman. It don't mean a thing...'

'Really?'

'Really.' He falls silent. His eyes unblinking and directed straight into hers pin her to the spot.

'Don't look surprised,' he begins. 'Listen. When I was fourteen – no – just two days before my fourteenth birthday, my mum died. It'd been going on for about a year. In and out of hospital. I watched her growing weaker and thinner. Me and her. It was just the two of us, for years. I never knew my dad. He buggered off somewhere, just after I was born. She didn't know where he was. Didn't try to look for him either. He never got in touch. Didn't care.'

Seeing her stir, about to speak, he stops her.

'And before you say what you were going to say, the difference between him and me – see, my mum, she trusted him. He told her she could count on him, made promises. He lied. Like I said, I don't lie. She thought he'd gone to fix up some deal. In Germany, or Austria, she said. She didn't know really. He told her he'd be back soon as it was done. But he never did. He never came back. Hell, she was only nineteen. Him – he was about forty. What chance did she have? You know the score. You told me the other day you choose the life you have. You make your own life, you said. Well, that's as may be, I suppose. Works for some. Not for others. My mother's life. You couldn't really say she *chose* her life. It's not that simple, is it? She was all set to be a singer.

She had a voice like an angel. Really did. And she was beautiful too... Look.'

He reaches into his jeans' pocket and pulls out a battered wallet. He takes out a black and white snapshot of a slim young woman, who smiles guardedly into the camera, her head held slightly to one side, the way he holds his. Black hair and deep-set dark eyes, exactly like his.

'No, she never married,' he says in answer to Alice's question. 'Guys would come round... I think she lost the ability to trust anyone again. And I guess she didn't want some guy coming in, getting in between us. Yeah, I think that was it. So that's why nothing's gonna happen to fuck up my life. I've chosen, see? That's my choice. Wife? Kids? No thanks!'

He tells her how, after she died, he went to live with his mother's sister. A much older woman. He moved in with her family in Surrey. His uncle, he says, 'something in the City'.

'I was a real sod,' he laughs drily. 'Full of anger. Full of hate. So they sent me away to boarding school pretty damn quick. Can't blame them wanting to be rid of me. I was fucking up their lives. And then I fucked up at this posh school. The only thing that stopped me getting chucked out was when I got into music in a big way. I can thank my mum for that too. She got me started. Thanks to her I could read music and play piano from when I was about four or five.

They had a bloody good music department at that school. Some great teachers. They put up with me, God knows how. They let me play around with different instruments. Gave me freedom to do what I wanted. This guy in particular. Jim Brenner. Fantastic teacher. He never talked about *music*. Only *the sound*. Didn't matter if it was Mozart, or Jimi Hendrix, or Charlie Parker. Whatever. It's the *sound* that counts. Nothin' else! He had this vast collection of jazz discs. When he played me Parker's *'Out of Nowhere'*, that did it for me. It was like switching on a light.'

Amazingly, so it was for Alice too. She a bit younger. Just fifteen when she first heard the recording.

He stands motionless in the doorway of her studio. For a long while he says nothing, but his eyes are darting everywhere, devouring the riotous colours, absorbing the energy that spins out from the paintings stacked up along the walls. In the centre is the large canvas she is working on right now. Its surface is plastered with free forms, thinly painted – *try this try that where will this take me?* The first exuberance is the most exquisite. Now exploration has no bounds. Anything can happen. Nothing to cage her in. The evanescence of this moment in the painting's evolution, when every form, every wisp of colour hangs on the edge of becoming something else, *eternal flux, I wish it were really eternal, process without end.*

'Like the song, I'm just watching what happens. Nothing more, nothing less.'

'God, I love this smell!' He gulps it in as if starved of oxygen. 'Wow!'

She loves it too. When she opens the door at the top of the stairs, the heady mixture of paint, linseed oil and turpentine beckons her into the private domain of her workplace. When she closes the door, she switches off the outside world. The person known by the outside world as Alice is also switched off. There is no self here, no identity. She is at once plenitude and nothingness. The only reality is the process, the colours and forms that move and change in response to something beyond herself, beyond reason.

'Like the sounds,' he says. 'When everything works right. Something happens. You don't know why or where it's come from. Somewhere outside you. And you yourself, you're gone somehow…'

Like children, she thinks. Pure exuberance untrammelled by reason or doubt. If you can recover that… But with most people it never happens. It stays locked away beneath its dark carapace, never to re-emerge. Unless you're really lucky. Lucky enough to spot it.

'Does this sound silly?'

He shook his head.

'Absolutely not. Spot on.'

When she tried once to express this to Michael, using similar words, his response was to assume his familiar look: a mix of condescension and pity. Telling her she was just an incurable romantic. Then adding in a resigned tone: 'well, we're all different...' The unspoken corollary being: 'Never mind. We can't all be sensible and logical like me, more's the pity!'

'Trouble is,' Jack continues, 'it's so short. You can't hold onto it. Before you know it, the other side of the old brain starts kicking in. The boring side. What is it - right or left? Can't remember which. The black and white side, anyway. Right, yeah, that's the one. Right for logic. No, hang on, it's the other way round. Left for logic. Right for all the rest. Everything that's really important in life. We're only human. We're not God...'

A taste of God. She never thought of it that way before.

He points to a section of the painting.

'I like that. I really like it! That's good.'

'It's really surreal,' he remarks after a moment. 'Stepping into here. In this house. A parallel universe up here.' Suddenly he laughs. 'Oh hell. Hah! That's rich! Alice! Jesus!' He bangs a fist into the palm of his other hand. 'Bloody hell! Alice!'

He laughs hysterically. The hilarity is irresistible. Both are now laughing at full throttle. 'Alice!' he shouts, 'Alice!

Alice!' over and over, with renewed bouts of laughter, each time more out of control.

His drift is plain. Her secret world at the top of the stairs. The dream that turns everything on its head.

'Nobody comes up here much, you know.'

Well they wouldn't would they? He guessed that. And if they do they never see anything that counts. But he has. He knows. The exhilaration, the pain, the silence, the noise. Lurching from heaven to hell and back. He knows. He shares similar battles day in day out. The sudden elation when magic suffuses the sounds. Everything coming together, when nothing could possibly be other than it is. Not a note, not a whisper.

When they leave the studio it is already dark. Almost midnight. He follows her down the two flights of stairs. Fingal miaows as they move past him, curled up on the first landing, a crescent of fur all black except for the white splashes on his throat and the ends of his paws. Jack bends to stroke him and he miaows again. Two tilted ovals of green illuminate the blackness for just a second, then disappear.

She opens the front door. She shivers in the cold air. He turns back for an instant.

'You're a lovely woman, Alice. You know that? A lovely person. Something else!'

She is barely able to sleep at all. At dawn she gets up and makes coffee. Mug in hand, she climbs the stairs. She selects a primed empty canvas and begins to paint. She searches for form. The feelings she must get down right now, urgently. It won't wait but it's a gigantic struggle. Getting it right, holding it just here. The moment. The complexity is like nothing she has encountered for a long, long time. Explosive. Celebratory. The colours – searching for the tones that exactly match what she feels. Luminous, ones that will shout, that ripple outwards like a never-ending echo.

Passion, white-hot, a burning core from which radiate beams of iridescent light, hues of fire that clash and merge. Ruby and vermilion, cadmium red and alizarin, ochre and cinnamon, greens and amethyst purple.

Crazy riotous music. Charlie Parker's *Crazeology*. Then the exquisite *Out of Nowhere*, its plangent, aching sweetness: alchemy wrought from a bare line of melody, a simple harmonic progression – a cascade of starlight streaming and gushing into pools of mercury. She and the sounds are enlaced. Everything fused. She is a butterfly drifting awhile, meandering, alighting randomly, letting waves of chance float her along and always upward. The blue beyond is the flame that draws her irresistibly on. The transient, contingent now grows ever smaller, ever more blurred, ever less real. It has almost disappeared. Almost completely. The music that surrounds her shapes the forms, the colours, the tones. Everything is here. She has to go on. No question of stopping. Hour after hour. Searching, experimenting, trying things out this way and that, scraping off whole sections, starting over. Over and over.

The door to the studio opens. She hears nothing.

'What are you doing up here so late?'

She jumps so violently, the brush flies from her hand, hitting the wall behind her.

Michael approaches her. He holds out a bunch of flowers for her, freesias and roses.

'How nice! Lovely!' She buries her nose in the fragrance.

His face looks drawn, weary. He smiles and kisses her cheek.

'So how're you doing?'

They go downstairs. She looks for a vase.

'You've got paint on your face. Just there.' He traces an arc with his finger, just above her left eyebrow.

'How was your trip?' She mixes him a drink.

'A bit stronger than that please. I need it!'

She pours more whisky into the glass, adds ice and hands it to him. He sinks into the armchair and takes a long draft, the ice clinks loudly against the glass.

'What about you? Don't you want one?'

She shakes her head.

'So how was it?' she says.

'Difficult.'

She sits down on the sofa opposite him.

'Did you sort out the new man?'

He frowns. ' 'Fraid not. He's not going to work out, unfortunately. He'll have to go. Wish I could avoid it. But…He's a nice chap, but…' he sighs. 'he's made too many mistakes.' He looks at her. 'Can't keep bailing him out.'

'Oh dear,' she says, not finding anything else to say. He drinks some more. Looks past her. Thinks for a bit. Then looks at her again.

'I might have to go over there for a few months. Sort things out. Hold the fort till we find someone else.' He pauses again. She waits for him to ask, knowing in advance.

'How would you like to spend five or six months in Brussels?' He half-smiles expectantly. *It's a treat isn't it? A gift he's offering. Isn't she lucky?*

'I can't.'

His lower lip juts forward. He frowns.

'Can't? Why not?'

She feels suddenly overwhelmed with helplessness.

'I just can't.'

'Why the hell not?'

He puts his glass down on the table and stares at her. He looks vexed and at the same time puzzled. He's just offered her a jewel and she throws it back in his face?

'The kids could board,' he says. 'They wouldn't mind. Probably like it…'

'No. It's not the children.'

'What is it then?'

She feels pretty pathetic, she has to admit. Halting speech. Timid. Hesitant. And he, always so different. The complete reverse. Oozing confidence, articulate. Every word, every phrase, a perfectly formulated whole.

'It's my work. You know. I can't… just… go. Leave everything.'

He grimaces impatiently.

'Your *work?*' His eyes widen in fake surprise. 'I suppose you mean your *art*', this last accompanied by an almost imperceptible wrinkling of the nose. Before she can answer, he goes on: 'Well, that's no problem. We can surely find you a studio in Brussels.' He smiles with satisfaction, as if to say: '*that's* sorted then!'

She looks at him without comment.

He gets up. Yawns.

'Well, give it some thought. It won't be right away. Wouldn't want to *force* you into anything… My God look at the time!'

She hears him calling out as he disappears up the stairs:

'Quick shower and bed. I'm knackered!'

CHAPTER FIFTEEN

Since the closing of the *'Inspiration and Belief'* exhibition, Alice and Josie have met a few times, either at William's gallery, or various shows. They have forged an incongruous alliance. Though work-wise at opposite ends of the spectrum, they share an equal distaste for the *pseudo* and a desire to expose phoney-ness of whatever shape or form.

Josie is at her best when surrounded by people, with herself at the centre. She adores an audience. She loves, above all, to Have Fun. Most nights she goes clubbing and drinking, rarely getting to bed before five or six in the morning. When not Having Fun, Josie works.

Hardly ever surfacing before two or three in the afternoon, she gets her head down and slogs on for the rest of the day, with barely a break. Her love of attention has made her the darling of the media. She delights in feeding them snippets of gossip, the more exaggerated and outrageous the better, 'all absolute rubbish, but so what?'

Alice feels a kinship with Josie because, for all her posturing and partying, she can smell humbug a mile away. She never bullshits except if it's a ploy to ridicule an opponent and her sights are set squarely on those who do. She's on a permanent mission to expose them and, ultimately, to subject them to public humiliation whenever possible. In each of Alice's two habitats – the wife-of-Michael world and the art world – they, the bullshitters, are not hard to find. You don't even have to search around. You virtually trip over them.

Some days ago Josie invited Alice to visit her studio in East London.

'I'm kinda stuck. Need to sort things out. Somethin' ... Can't get me 'ead round. You know? Well, you don't 'ave to...'

It was the first time Alice had been to Josie's place. A tall end-of-terrace house in a quiet back street of Walthamstow. It backed onto an area of allotments, mostly overgrown with weeds, dead or dying bushes and exhausted trees. Josie lived in the bottom half of the house and worked at the top. The whole of the top floor was her studio. In practice the two halves of the house merged and overlapped. Bits of whatever she happened to be working on at the time – pieces of MDF board, scraps of metal, rolls of linen or calico, odd pieces of bric-a-brac she'd found in rubbish skips or flea markets, had filtered down into the rooms that made up her living area. Conversely, there was an ancient futon in the corner of the top-floor studio, onto which she often collapsed at the end of a session of intensive work, too exhausted even to move down to the bedroom. There were also a microwave, electric kettle and miniature fridge that she used for quick drinks or snacks when she was so absorbed in work she hadn't the patience to walk down to the kitchen.

Alice stood at the front door. She rang, but no-one came. She rang again. Still nothing. The front door was ajar, so she pushed it open and went in. She could hear heavy metal music pounding from the top of the house. She called 'Josie! Josie?' The music stopped.

'Come on up, Al!'

She climbed the two flights of stairs. The faded green carpet was mostly threadbare. In some places the fabric had disintegrated completely, exposing the wood beneath. The walls, once ivory, were now a muddy cream and the paint was peeling in some places. Josie had painted graffiti over them, permanent memorials to adventures and people that mattered to her. As she walked, Alice read 'Sheena', 'Bo', 'Jo the Dark One', 'Fuckin on beach Bali 82'... There were small drawings surrounding the names and messages, some indecipherable, others organic shapes of flowers, trees or shells, mingling with explicit semi-pornographic images.

When she reached the top landing, she gasped, almost overcome by the chemical stench of solvents and metallic paint. She rushed past Josie who was kneeling next to a construction of canvas, metal and wire, to fling open the big sash windows.

'My God, Josie! Are you mad? You'll suffocate in this!'

Josie looked up, unperturbed.

'Yeah. Don't feel so good…You're right! Saved from the jaws of death. Just in the nick o' time!'

She snorted with laughter, then came over to Alice and put an arm round her shoulders.

'Take a seat, love. Anywhere…' She waved vaguely in the direction of bean bags and a faded paisley-covered futon in the corner.

'Wanna drink?'

Alice said coffee would be fine.

'OK! Comin' up!'

She grabbed the grimy kettle and took it over to a large, deep sink at the far end of the room. It was encrusted with layers of dried oil paint and filled with muddy glass jars and tins which served to hold turpentine and oil and an array of different-sized brushes. She pushed them out of the way wedging the kettle under the tap. When it was full, she placed it on the floor in a corner and plugged it into the wall.

'So what d'yer think then?'

Alice got up from her bean-bag to contemplate Josie's work in progress.

It was very large, almost filling the studio – its shape reminded Alice of an igloo. It was round, hollow, empty, dark. At its centre flickered a bluish-white light, very small and circular, hardly bigger than a coin. From a foot away it appeared no more than a pin-prick of light.

'I don't wanna say anythin'. No clues. No titles. Just give me a word. The first thing that comes into your 'ead.'

Alice stared at it for a while longer.

'Survival...'

'Yeah. Well, I guess... Anythin' else?' Josie's eyes narrowed, her body tense and immobilised as she waited for Alice to speak. It seemed that so much was hanging on her reply, a weight of expectation Alice was not prepared for.

'It's not finished, though, is it?' she said finally, evasively. 'You told me that. So... what else are you going to do to it?'

'Yeah true. Not much really. So... whadya think of it so far then?' She assumed a theatrical pose, hand on hip, the other stretched out palm upwards as if to say 'well, we both know it's nothing but a big joke, don't we?'.

Alice said nothing. Josie moved across the room, then bent down, crawling round behind the igloo.

'Look! See this!' she peered round the side, holding something up for Alice to look at. It was a cheap photograph frame, not very big, made of white and gold-painted plastic. It was empty. Alice nodded.

'This is gonna be fixed to the outside. Like this.' She held the frame up to one of the walls so that it hung deliberately askew. 'And prob'ly one or two more the same.' She paused, waiting for Alice to react, then went on: 'And there's gonna be this music playin'. Over and over. The same thing. Over and over. D'you get it now?'

Yes, she got it. Understood in a flash what Josie wanted people to see. Instantly, brutally, without words. The loneliness at the core. The isolation that is kept so flawlessly concealed.

'So what about the block? You said you had a block...'

'Yeah...' answered Josie, lighting a cigarette. 'But more... kinda... I dunno.' She inhaled the smoke and blew it out again rapidly. 'Yeah. It's ... more... bein' scared. Yer know? People not givin' a shit.'

But that was always the issue, Alice said, really, wasn't it? Not getting through to people... Josie cut in, agitated, her hands moving up and down in a frenzied way.

'No no no! Not that! What's really scary... Like...It's when you get to sayin' to yerself what the fuck am I doin' this for, yer know? What the fuck does it matter? In the end, you've sweated over it. Hours and weeks. Workin' away. And in the end, it's like, so what? That's the really scary thing. And why? 'Cause nobody cares a shit about it. And that's 'cos it's NOT FUCKIN' INTERESTING!'

Her voice rose steadily in pitch, ending in a yell that made the room shake with anger and pain.

On the face of it, Josie was no different from the vacuous crowd she mixed with and, on one level, identified with. She was pulled in different directions at once. She could hoot with laughter at the sacred cows, the old masters, the artists revered by older generations. She could sneer at virtually the entire twentieth century canon – from Cezanne right up to Pollock, Judd and Serra, the only exception being Duchamp. Anything that referenced higher dimensions, unrelated to everyday life, was held to be hopelessly un-cool, deserving of scorn and ridicule.

'What's the use of art' she would say, 'that sits there lookin'at yer, sayin' bow down you dick'eads and worship at my shrine? What the 'ell use is it if it don't change anythin'?'

On the other hand, like the rest of her crowd, she had no qualms about using to her own advantage the gullibility of *fashionistas* and sycophants, consumed with lust for the sublime joy of being able to announce to the world:

' Hey! I just bought one of X's latest pieces!' or

'Hey! I'm getting Y to do a wall-painting for my new restaurant in Chelsea!' or 'Hey! W came to dinner with us last night!' and to await with bated breath the longed-for response:

'Wow! How exciting! What a coup! I'm so jealous!'

Just like the rest, Josie was able to knock things up with the minimum of effort, stick things together with cynical indifference – casual assemblages, installations, sometimes with the addition of random bits of video – attaching to them titles that derived from whatever happened to be passing through her head at the time, words or phrases that bore little or no relation to the object she was creating, nothing more than the product of a whim, or because it struck her as funny or mad or the best way to cock a snook at those she dismissed as 'dick-'eads full o' shit'.

She found it so easy and it always ended up sounding impressive, the more cryptic and eccentric the title, the more profound the work would appear and the more gleeful she became.

'What the 'ell? If it makes 'em feel good buyin' it, that can't be bad, can it, eh? I'm 'appy, dealer's appy, public's 'appy – everyone's 'appy!'.

Not long ago William bought two of Josie's pieces to put on display in his gallery. They were constructed from some items of junk she had fished out of a council skip at the end of her road. As she was rummaging through the discarded furniture and builder's refuse, her eye was caught by a piece of bright yellow-painted metal, once belonging perhaps to a children's toy truck or tricycle. She loaded it onto the back of her pick-up together with the ten or so other things of varying sizes and materials that interested her. When she got them home, making several trips up and down the stairs to transfer the objects to the studio, she laid them all out on the floor and contemplated them for a long while, turning them over or moving them round into different positions, walking around to view them from a variety of positions or picking them up, looking to see how they appeared at different levels.

By the time she'd finished her study, every object had begun to take on a new identity. The green of the chipped jug which at first had appeared disagreeably acidulated and tawdry, on closer inspection revealed unexpected subtleties. Enlivened by the vagaries of the glaze, it displayed a surprisingly beautiful surface, composed of a myriad of greens, blues and yellows melding into ripples and streaks which spiralled around its belly.

The broken sections of plasterboard, covered with white dust, each retained marks that recounted their own unique story : the natural history of a former life, smudges of soil, paint and dust collected in the course of their journey from manufacturing plant to builder's yard and thence to their ultimate purpose as frontiers dividing one living space from another.

The idea came to her of making something that would symbolize conflict and unity. It was a theme she was continually returning to, in particular the intimate interconnection between the two. The mystery of how they subsisted together in equal measure bemused and fascinated her. Why was it that the closer you got to someone, the more clearly you could see the distance between? How could it be that people who displayed unconditional love and care for others could at the same time be consumed with hatred and cruelty towards people who belonged to another group?

The herd instinct drew us together but also divided us. That was obvious enough. But what bothered Josie was the apparent impossibility of ever achieving real unity. The pity of it was that when you tried to get down to basics – to pin down the quintessential *human-being-ness* of us – it always eluded you: like a dream that begins to fade the moment you wake up, the faster you chase it, the more distant it grows. All the things that ought to draw everybody together kept getting sidelined. It was almost as if the qualities that made you into a person at all were the very things that divided you from others.

'If you hive off sex, country, language, religion: what's left is what makes you human. The family of mankind and all that... So what I can't get my head round is this: why does everyone forget the most important thing? Can someone explain that? Why are we so dead keen on hating each other?'

Josie, unlike her frivolous, hedonistic pals, was unable to blank out thoughts like this: they persisted in troubling her. They returned time and time again to plague her, no matter how strenuously she struggled to escape from them, drown them in riotous, drug or alcohol-fuelled bouts of hell-raising, at the end of which she would crawl back home exhausted, collapsed semi-comatose for hours. If she attempted to share her malaise and confusion with her mates she would invariably be met with blank looks or wise-cracks like: 'So what's with the saviour act?' or 'a bit of hating does you good!'.

There was a sense of inner loneliness about Josie. Alice was acutely aware of it almost from the start. The persona she presented to the world was that of a precocious brat, loud-mouthed and super-confident, effortlessly successful and permanently surrounded by a retinue of admiring hangers-on, media people and agents, each in their own way trying to grab pieces of her for themselves. But at the end of long days or nights, when she crawled back to her place in the East End, she was always alone.

Alice heard from some acquaintance of William's that there had once been a girl called Naomi, a waitress, who also did occasional work as an artist's model, who had lived for a while with Josie. They were seen around together a lot for about two years. Josie brought her along to her shows, her favourite clubs and all the media events and they even went on several holidays together to different parts of the world, the Caribbean, Brazil, Thailand. Some exceptionally lyrical pieces emerged from this friendship, exceptional because Josie had never produced paintings like these before she met Naomi, nor did she ever again. Paintings tenderly executed in oils, with graceful lines and velvety, luscious tones of indigo, purple, rose madder and ivory, some were portraits or nudes inspired by Naomi, stylised in the manner of Modigliani, others were abstracts, revelling in the sensuous enjoyment of colour. People confronted by them now are incredulous when told they are works by Josie Wishart.

Then having become accustomed to seeing Naomi as Josie's permanent side-kick, people noticed that suddenly Josie was on her own again. Nobody asked questions and no explanations were given. That was that.

Alice, quite soon after meeting Josie, began to feel as if she were being eased into a role, not of her own making or volition – that of an elder sister perhaps? She couldn't quite put her finger on it. Josie's lament about the divisions and hatred between people evoked in Alice only the opinion that Josie was being curiously naïve, which was not the response Josie was hoping for, but she could offer her little comfort.

'That's just the way we are. Tribes, clubs, classes… You can't get away from it. To think of yourself as part of the "human family" – it's a lovely thought. But it's just an ideal. It's not reality. It'll never happen. Empathy, tolerance – that's the most we can hope for. Human nature being what it is, though, well…' *What more can you say?*

'Yeah, yeah…' Josie responded impatiently with a dismissive sweep of the arm.

It wasn't enough. She wanted more. There was something inside her, a voice that whispered 'No, no. I can't accept this. It's not good enough.'

As the piece she was working on progressed, she introduced sections of an old rabbit cage, white plastic covering thin metal bars and lengths of malleable wire. She used pliers and her bare hands to bend, stretch and squeeze them into the shapes she wanted. She fashioned the pieces of metal until she had constructed the skeleton of a pyramid with rounded edges.

The pyramid shape was made up of a series of tiers spiralling up to a small circular opening. The edges of the circle were jagged because the wire-ends had been left sticking out roughly and randomly at the top. It was an airy structure, reaching up and outward. A monument to longing.

Finally, when the frame was complete, Josie took a length of black rubber tubing and wove it several times around and through and in and out of the openings until it finally emerged through the jagged hole at the top. She roughly cut the end of the tube, leaving about four inches sticking out at an absurd, risible angle. The sight of this temporarily distracted her from the project. She cut off the ten or so inches that remained on the other end of the tube and burst out laughing uncontrollably as she held it up to her crotch. It formed an arc that sprang out from her body, ending in a sad earth-bound droop. She looked at herself in the mirror and laughed even harder.

She presented the two finished pieces to William, who manifested a degree of enthusiasm bordering on ecstasy. Josie gave Alice a vividly re-enacted, blow-by-blow account of the occasion.

'Wonderful, Josie!' William gasped rapturously. 'I particularly appreciate the wit of this one,' pointing to the smaller of the two: a piece of black rubber tubing about five inches in length, nailed to a flat rectangle of plain wood in the manner of a trophy. The droop of the rubber phallus was aided in its descent by the weight of a piece of pink satin ribbon tied in a neat bow around its tip.

'So what's the title, Josie?' he enquired.

'Dunno yet. Any ideas, Wills?'

He stood, frowning in concentration, his left thumb and forefinger squeezing into puckers the soft skin between his lower lip and the point of his chin.

'Hmmm...' his brow became more furrowed, the skin beneath his mouth more deeply puckered. Josie stifled a giggle.

'Well... perhaps we should leave it to the spectator to interpret...' he said at last.

'Oh NO, Wills!' Josie intervened angrily: 'Untitled? For Christ's sake! Such a cop-out. I *never* do that. You know what I think about *that*. Words are everythin'. Words, words... Wouldn't work without *words*!' She glared at him, shaking with fury.

'Listen!' she went on. 'I'll give you some titles. How about: "EH. EE. DEE. ESS"?'

He looked at her blankly.

' "A-E-D-S - Acquired Erectile Deficiency Syndrome". Ha ha! Good yeah? Oh well. Maybe not. What about: "the impossibility of gettin' it up in the presence of the divine Mother"? Not bad eh? Or – 'ang on – 'ow about…'

A voice piped up from a dark corner of the studio – Ken, one of the Group, who happened to be there when William called. 'How about this then…?' he pulled a thin roll of paper from his lips and slowly exhaled a cloud of smoke. '"Decline and Fall, Apple, the Sequel"'. An instant's silence, then Josie's cackling laugh.

'Yeah! 'she shrieked. ' Great! "Apple! The Sequel!" Wicked!'

Then Steve, yelling from the opposite side of the room: 'I've got one! How about…'

'Or this…?' before he could speak, blonde Kate, cutting in, bursting to add her contribution.

Phrases were lobbed back and forth across the room, each more ludicrous than the last, with William relegated to a bewildered and ineffectual piggy-in-the-middle. When finally the ideas ran out and everything went quiet, a diffident voice broke the silence.

'Suffocation?' William suggested hesitantly.

Not a sound was heard. Josie glanced round at her mates. A short snigger almost imperceptible, emanated from somewhere behind her and was hastily stifled.

'Nah,' said Josie. 'Don't think so, Wills.'

Alice stood before Josie's two latest pieces. They seemed dwarfed by the silent whiteness of the gallery. The tower with its snake now incorporated bright yellow sheets of metal that were positioned along the floor like a series of pathways leading to the tower's foot. The yellow roads were covered with black painted lines and curves of text – words from many different languages and scripts. Alice bent down to read them, twisting her head to and fro to follow the different directions of the lines.

She recognised some of the foreign scripts: Chinese, Hindi, Arabic, Hebrew, Greek, but many she could not identify. The phrases she was able to understand appeared at first sight randomly chosen. *'pravda...simulato...sanning...shinsei...hederlig...leal...sincere ...falsk... ryonshiuteki...verdade...wahrheit... mensonge...die ungeschminkte...la verita nuda e cruda...mentira....'*

But soon she detected a consistent thread and suddenly the work made sense and everything fell into place.

'For God's sake, Josie! How many languages have you got in there?'

'Dunno. Fifty mebbe? Took me fuckin' weeks!'

She called the work '*Speak*'.

The phallus with its satin bow was much admired. It was eventually entitled '*Eve's Revenge*' and was sold for a large sum to a New York collector.

Speak turned into a fixture at the gallery. The subject of a good deal of critical interest, both for and against, the two camps being about equally divided: 'bullshittin' progressives versus nostalgia-eaters,' as Josie described them.

Josie's reputation was growing in quantum leaps. She was William's star turn. He could not stop marvelling at his own perspicacity and commercial *nous* at having discovered her and taken her on when she was little more than a raw, irreverent rabble-rousing kid. Her meteoric rise to celebrity status was in truth as much of a surprise to him as it was to Josie.

Alice meanwhile continued to pursue her own personal odyssey, uncelebrated and mostly unnoticed. She had no memory of where or when her journey had begun. She had always pictured herself as a mountain spring turning itself into a stream that grew into a river that flowed through a succession of landscapes and climates, growing stronger and wider all the while as it forced its way onward to the sea. She had no choice but to keep moving but, in truth, she had no idea where the flow would lead her.

Jack found parallels to this in the mixture of compulsion and mystery that possessed him whenever he played.

'You start from a simple set of chords, an innocent little melody – almost nothing – and you're off! You never know where it's going to take you. A great leap into the unknown. It's crazy, it's awesome. It's the only thing that matters. Life. That's what it's for. That's what life's about.'

Alice whose musical training had followed rigidly traditional lines envied Jack his ability to invent spontaneous sound patterns that flowed straight from his heart and his gut. This composition on the hoof was a mirror image of the way she painted.

'I think in some ways it's a substitute. It makes up for what I always wanted to do on the piano, but never could,' she told him when he asked how come she chose art over music.

Of course, it was never enough. Never good enough. For Jack or for Alice. They agreed. Always falling short. Better next time. There's always a next time. Always another chance.

Michael couldn't understand that. Never in a million, trillion years. Whenever she showed him something she'd finished, he'd ask why, on the one hand, did she say it was finished because there was nothing more she could do to it, but, on the other, that it wasn't completely right. If it wasn't right, why not carry on until it was? It was pointless for her to say well it's as right as I can make it, but it's not *right*. For Michael, a thing was either right or it wasn't. It couldn't be both.

Jack knew exactly what she felt. She didn't even need to put it into words.

I suppose it comes down to this: a simple syllogism. If A is A, it cannot also be not A. OK on one level. But once you can see, really see, that A is also not A, that's when you understand the meaning of art.

Alice had come recently to picturing life in the form of a flower. We begin as a sealed calyx. We are shaped by our genes, but this is all there is, in the beginning. Inside the calyx lives a dream without a form. Nothing is fixed. Nothing exists apart from the will to life. And for years we live in the shadow of other people's choices. Whatever the cards you've been dealt, your life belongs to others. But then a point comes where your life changes hands. That moment when you make your first real choice. It's a bit frightening: like a book with all its pages blank. That's you. And there are a million ways to write it, but in the end it comes down to style. And style is something no-one can teach you. As Miles Davis once said: 'it's like your sweat'. But that book's got to be written one way or another. If you don't pick up the pen, someone else will.

And it seemed to Alice that the style of her book had been entirely hers – chaotic, crazy, incoherent maybe, but unmistakably hers – right up until the day she married Michael. Then she lost her style. For twenty years he wielded the pen. And all the fertile contradictory jumble that was Alice's own particular style got flattened out and painted over in geometrically perfect strips and arcs of white and pale umber and almond green, with nothing, absolutely nothing, left to chance.

But then something happened. Something out of the ordinary and unforeseen. Like the amaryllis that sits dolefully in its pot on the window-sill year after year. You wonder whether it's still alive and whether it really is worth watering it any more, or maybe you should just throw it onto the compost heap. But somehow you can't bring yourself to do that. And then one morning you walk into the kitchen and you witness a transfiguration.

From mute and invisible stirrings of life deep within its sleeping heart, an alchemy of juices, warmth and light radiating through the plant has triggered the upsurge of a three-foot-tall stem, rock-hard, ending in not just one, or two, but five huge flower-heads like giant lilies, raspberry red and veined with a single white stripe. Their fleshy petals thrust forward, then turn back upon themselves to expose the six male stamens and female stigma. Self-generating, consummate, magnificent in solitude, it soars beyond all that is commonplace and colourless. For one minuscule kernel of time, the contingent and the immutable coalesce into one seamless unity.

CHAPTER SIXTEEN

Gitte Blomberg begins to speak. And when Gitte speaks, everyone else shuts up. She and Lennart, her husband, are hosting the Annual Open Day at Hadworth Park in aid of The Endangered Languages Association. The six hundred acres of gardens and parkland, as well as the house itself, are offered up to the scrutiny of anyone willing to hand over the requisite fee of six pounds fifty (No Concessions) at the entrance gate. Nobody is barred, nobody questioned. Security cameras flash continuously, yet discreetly, from various strategic points around the estate. The massive steel gates, with jaws that unclench ponderously, like a yawning hippopotamus, to admit only those who pass the stringent CCTV inspection, have today been left wide open to welcome the public invasion.

It is one of the days of the year that Lennart Blomberg most dreads. There is no escape from the torture of standing by impotently to witness his sanctuary violated by hundreds of shambling feet and prying eyes. There is no escape because Gitte demands that Lennart, as co-host of the event, should be visibly in attendance throughout. Nothing barring serious injury or near-death will exempt him. Any meeting or appointment, no matter how vital, has to be cancelled or missed.

Gitte, unlike Lennart, is a fervent advocate of the Swedish credo that the earth belongs to the community. This entails the belief that any piece of land, whether forest, park, mountain or field, and regardless of its legal owners, must be made freely available to people to wander over at will, for the greater enrichment of their souls. If Gitte had her way, the rule would be extended to encompass even private gardens. Lennart, on the contrary, believes with equal fervour that privately-owned spaces ought to be kept private, which is why Hadworth Park opens its gates to the general public only one day in the year.

Lennart is a big man – far bigger than the average height for a man. Around six foot seven and powerfully built, his thick, steel-grey hair is slicked straight back and stuck as flat to his head as he can make it with brilliantine; his eyes hide behind thick pebble glasses. He is ill-equipped to escape notice.

Alice contemplates him from the edge of the lawn that fronts the house, as he stands on the sunlit terrace, his huge workman-like hands suspended awkwardly at his sides. His back is stooped, from years of bending his ear to humans of more regular proportions. He studiously directs his gaze away from any person who threatens to enter his immediate vicinity, with the intention of discouraging communication. But public curiosity is a formidable adversary and the strategy rarely succeeds. He reminds Alice of a caged bear in a zoo.

'We are so-o-o deli-i-ighted you can be with us today! As our guests!' Gitte screeches enthusiastically from her post at the front door, beaming rapturously as people stream through the hall and into the vast drawing-room. It sparkles with vases, bowls and glasses of Swedish crystal reflecting the brilliant sunlight from the gardens visible through the open French windows. The room is filled with a medley of furniture and art of wildly differing styles. Ornaments and sculptures ranging from Chinese antiquity to twentieth-century minimalism display themselves on glass tables or the polished wooden floor; furniture of wood, or steel or pale leather clutter the room; and countless pieces of original art – oils, water-colours and prints, of all sizes and many different periods and origins, adorn the plain white walls, demanding admiration.

Some of the visitors are visibly awe-struck, bewildered even by the extravagance of art on display in a private house. Others affect the ironic curl of the lip, the knowing *seen-it-all-before-oh-so-vulgar-typical-of-new-money-and-foreign-new-money-to-boot-no-taste-no-class* look.

'Welcome! Welcome! You are *all* so welcome!' shrills Gitte, stretching out her arms as if to embrace the world. 'And please *do not* miss the Orangery! The jasmine – so-o-o purr-fect now!' Her high-pitched exhortations follow them as they swarm out though the open patio doors onto the manicured lawns and weed-less flower-beds, shimmering with exuberant banks of reds, yellows and purples of every hue.

For the first hour, Gitte remains at her guest-welcoming post. After a while her enthusiasm begins to falter, her beam to lose its radiance. She tires of having to small talk endlessly with the benighted hordes, finally instructs Sigrid, her PA, to take over and sets off in search of Lennart. He is no longer to be seen on the terrace, no doubt attempting to hide somewhere in a remote corner of the gardens.

On her way she encounters Alice and Ben Grantley in conversation by the lily-pond at the lower east end of the gardens. They are contemplating a stone sculpture of a young woman sprawling face down in a Rodin-esque pose along the whole length of one side of the pond. The figure is one of Gitte's early acquisitions. The work of an obscure Swedish sculptor, now dead.

'I really cannot *stand* it!' she growls, 'It is Lennart – he will not let me get rid of it!' She shakes her head and sighs. 'Absolutely no understanding of art *at all* – but still he refuses to let this go! Can you understand this?'

Not waiting for a reply, she continues:

'Are you enjoying yourselves? I do hope so. Have you been in the Orangery? The jasmine! What a vision! And the scent! My Got...'

Alice says 'It's lovely, Gitte. And the gardens are perfect. I've never seen them looking so beautiful...'

'My dears,' Gitte interposes, putting an arm around each of them, in a warm, intimate manner, 'you know you are here for me. Mainly for me... I'm so selfish really...' Then, lowering her voice to a whisper, she glances briefly around, and adds: 'You know you are *absolutely* the *only civilized* human beings among this app*alli*ng crowd! The only people I can talk to about *any*thing worth talking about!'

Ben is looking down again at the naked stone girl.

'You know, Gitte, I know you don't like it but there is, nevertheless, a certain stillness about it. A kind of resonance of timelessness... In a way, that's what I try to capture in my own work.' He looks at Gitte, waiting to see the effect on her of his words.

Resonance of timelessness. The phrase sounds oddly familiar to Alice. Almost instantly she recalls where she last heard it. A recent review of Grantley's work by the critic John Fullerton.

Gitte pauses a moment before replying.

'Mmm... Yes, of course. I see what you mean. Probably the reason I bought it originally, all those years ago. But... oh dear... you have to admit. So... so nineteenth century, don't you think? So awfully, impossibly *life-like*. Not at *all* the thing today. Absolutely not. You look for so much *more*, don't you agree? Really, my dear,' she squeezes Ben's hand, 'you do flatter the thing when you compare it to *your marvellous* work!'

Grantley shakes his head in a token-ish way, to indicate unworthiness of the compliment, but without conviction.

'So what exactly do you mean, Ben, by wanting to *resonate timelessness?*' Alice inquires.

He glances with annoyance in her direction, impatient at having to provide a response. She smiles back innocently.

'Well! What a question!' he exclaims, his tone suggesting that the question is so breathtakingly naïve only the artistically illiterate could have uttered it. 'Well – you're familiar with my *Winged Creatures* series, I presume?'

Alice nods eagerly.

'So there you are!' He raises his eyebrows and in synchrony his hands, palms upwards. 'There's your answer: timeless resonances!'

He smiles with satisfaction and glances at Gitte. She returns his smile. Then, turning to Alice, she observes:

'I also see timelessness in *your wonderful* paintings, Alice my dear!'

Alice feels compelled at that point to launch into an exposition of her theory about art being necessarily *of* its time as well as *for* all time. She is conscious that all the time she is talking, Ben is looking over her head and fidgeting impatiently. She ends with the words: 'Art doesn't happen in a timeless void'.

Grantley nods distractedly. 'Absolutely! We're all a product of our times, and so on… But isn't art about going beyond that kind of – you know – trivial stuff? I mean, what we do, how can I put it? We strive to go beyond the particular into the universal dimension, if you see what I mean…'

Alice can't quite put her finger on why she so harbours so profound a dislike of Grantley. Sensing her antipathy, he takes up the offensive.

'How would you say *your* work reflects its time, Alice?'

'That's not for me to say,' she retorts rapidly. 'I'm an artist. Not a critic – or a sociologist.'

'Hmm… Good. But you must have some kind of opinion. Think about Josie's work for example. That type of thing – it's everywhere nowadays. The purpose seems to be to represent the Now, warts and all. And in fact, to be honest, mainly the warts. I mean, talk about art being *of its time*! Wouldn't you agree? But as they say: is that all there is? And where do *you* stand in relation to that?'

Without flinching she throws it back at him:

'Where do you?'

'I? Where do I stand? Well, I think the best way to answer that is to say that I don't stand anywhere in relation to it. I'm completely outside it. As I said before, art for me is to do with transcendence – transcending the particular. I'm looking for eternal truths. I'm not interested in the transient or the contingent.' Then, as an afterthought:

'Being, I suppose, basically a Platonist, I have to say I see no point – no point at all in most of the stuff William's so dead keen on right now.'

Gitte, bursting to speak during Ben's monologue, jumps in:

'But Ben – you know you are being a little... how to say... *blinkered*, are you not? You really can't – shouldn't just turn your back on what the young, new artists are doing now. It is really the vital centre – the *nerves*! Whether we like it or not, we have to be aware – at least interested in what these young people are saying. Don't you think?'

'Yes Gitte. Absolutely. But...'

Alice waits for him to say: 'But is it art?' But he seems weary of the discussion and impatient to end it. He says only:

'But each to his own. In the end, it's just a matter of taste.'

This inconclusive tailing off annoys Alice. She wants to push him further, force him into a corner. He is being let off too lightly. But the source of her disquiet lies somewhere else. She tries to ignore it, to focus on Grantley's unctuous pomposity, but she is unavoidably confronted with the unpalatable truth that this man whom she finds so deeply objectionable harbours an approach to art not a million miles away from hers.

Gitte suddenly catches sight of Lennart in the distance, skulking along the path that leads towards the herb garden. He is half-concealed by thick shrubbery, hoping to slink into invisibility, but he cannot escape her gimlet eye and she dashes off in pursuit before he once again disappears. The repeated calls of 'Lennart! Lennart! Come here!' echo peremptorily through the gardens, growing gradually fainter as she descends into the shadows of what she has named 'The Wilderness', an area of deliberately tangled shrubs and trees whose wild aspect is carefully preserved by Hadworth's experienced team of gardeners.

Left alone, Alice and Grantley contemplate one another in silence, each waiting for the other to speak. The time for argument having passed, they begin to talk of trivialities. The weather – 'so warm for the time of year'; traffic hold-ups on the motorway that morning – 'so tedious'; the large number of visitors – 'how extraordinary'... Then Grantley notices his young companion, Enrico, who is preening himself on the terrace surrounded by a group of giggling young girls dressed in tee-shirts and shorts. The tall, dark-haired Italian seems perfectly at ease, but Grantley shows alarm, makes his excuses and departs rapidly to join him. Alice watches as they exchange a few words, Grantley frowning, Enrico shrugging and smiling, then the two of them make their way towards the exit. Enrico turns back, grinning and waving energetically at the girls, who dissolve into giggles once again.

Alice wanders in the direction of the conservatory. Her thoughts drift back to a conversation with Josie a couple of weeks ago. They were drinking coffee in Alice's studio, Josie deciding to bring up the subject of 'her kind of art'.

'Your kinda' stuff – it just ain't relevant. Know what I mean?'

'Relevant?' Alice repeated.

'Yeah. You know. It don't *say nothin'*. 'Bout the world. No connection…'

'The world?' Alice said. Then, after a pause: 'But which world?'

Josie laughed. 'How many worlds is there? Only one, s'far as we're concerned.'

Alice said no, she didn't agree. Categorically not. There were other worlds. Personal worlds. Places you go to in your imagination. Dreams… Different kinds of reality.

But Josie was unimpressed. She scoffed:

'Oh yeah? Bullshit! There ain't nothin' else. This pile o' shit: it's all there is. You gotta face facts. The way I see it: you got two choices. You do what you can to make things better. Or you take what you can get and to 'ell with the rest. Me? I guess it's a bit o' both. Like most of us, I s'pose. But art? What the 'ell's the point if it don't change anythin'?'

'Like what?'

'Shit, I dunno. Like... You can make people see things. New things. Make them think different. You want art that's in yer face. Anythin's art. You know that. Don't matter what you use or how you do it. It's the message. Nothin' else matters.'

'So there's no point to art if there's no actual message?'

Josie lit a cigarette. 'Damn right. You got it!' She raised her head and directed a cloud of smoke to the ceiling.

Alice shook her head.

'But that means... It's got to mean ... Well, you might as well not do art at all. You might as well just use words. If the message is the only thing that counts. Just an idea...'

'No. Wrong! Art's got power. Always did. Right back to the time when people started making pictures on rocks. Art can shout. Much louder than words. Art can grab you by the throat and shake you. Words can't do that.'

'I know that. But I want to say...'

Josie raised her hand to stop her in her tracks.

'Yeah! Don't tell me! I know already. You're just gonna spin me the usual crap about *aesthetic values*. Please... Spare me that!' She laughed drily. 'Listen. Don't take this personal. I like you Al, really I do. But hey! You're a classic case, ya know. Sorry to say this, but you – people like you – your sort – you're on the way out. What you're doin', it's finished, dying, passed its sell-by date fifty years ago or more … Like I said, it don't relate. Got nothin' to say. Let's face it, you're nothin' but a nice middle-class lady spinnin' out pretty pictures. Pretty colours, pretty shapes for people like you. You and them, all of you belong to that happy little circle. I'm for you and you're for me and ain't this little world of ours just fine and dandy! Let's keep it just the way it is. No changes required. And don't for fuck's sake let that mob in. Keep 'em out. You talk about worlds. Yeah! There's different worlds all right. Yours and theirs. Us and them.'

She stopped abruptly. She lit another cigarette and stared out of the window. Alice felt punch-drunk. Her ears were ringing. She said nothing.

Next day Josie sent her an email saying 'freaking out duz u good'. Her way of mending whatever might be chipped without having to say sorry. Because she wasn't, of course. She had spoken the truth as she saw it and the truth needs no apology.

Well, maybe, when I was her age… But that's too easy. To look as dispassionately as you can at your own past, the anger with the world of your parents, the elation of the marches and demos, the exhilarating sense of being right there at the birth of a 'new world order' (whatever that meant), all that yelling and chanting and banner waving, the belief that art can be used — should be used — as a means. And then to find that ultimately nothing changed. *Maybe we were not angry enough. Or for long enough.*

Josie is probably right. Is that all it is? *Pretty pictures for people like me?* When anger gives way to compromise and compromise to apathy, does art become mere self-indulgence? When art is an end in itself has it become a hopelessly impoverished version of itself, a mere by-product of lost idealism? Does one lead ineluctably to the other?

Yet on the other hand, things don't stay the same. Change happens. Josie is different. Josie is not Alice that was. Angry, yes, but angry in a different way. Not so much ideas as facts. And she has her feet firmly planted on the ground. Alice-that-was had impossible to realize dreams of revolutionising human consciousness itself. This was Miriam's aim and pretty well taken for granted by many of their generation at the time. Changing the way people thought. And actually believing this was feasible and would put an end to war, tribal conflict, racism, oppression, hatred, cruelty, poverty — all ills wiped out at one fell swoop.

Josie said 'Art changing human consciousness? You can't be serious!'

'Makin' people see different.' You can't expect any more, even from something that shouts louder than words.

But on the other hand again, art that isn't some kind of propaganda tool, that doesn't pretend to be out to change anything, only to express some inner truth – you can't, you shouldn't, dismiss it as just *making pretty pictures for people like you.*

Erasmus, as always, has the final word: *There are no oughts in art. Art can be whatever you want it to be as long as it comes from the heart.*

CHAPTER SEVENTEEN

Alice perches on the stone surround of the goldfish pond in the Blombergs' conservatory, which they call *The Orangery*, though there are no orange-trees. The floor, which extends to a good hundred feet, is paved entirely in black and white marble. A warm rainforest hush pervades the place. Mesmerised, her eyes trace the continuous arc of water that spurts from out of the curled lips of an angry, turquoise-painted dolphin. Astride it sits a fat, euphoric cherub. This bizarre water feature apparently cost thousands, according to Laszlo. When it was first installed, several years ago, Gitte was horrified to see water gushing out of the cherub's armpits, a source of much hilarity for every member of the garden staff.

She jumps, startled by the sound of Lennart's voice. He has crept up on her without a sound. It is early evening. Most of the visitors have drifted away. The walls of the long narrow conservatory are smothered in jasmine blossom. Dozens of terracotta pots containing gardenia plants with deep green foliage and waxy blooms line the wide sills which extend along the whole length and breadth of the room. The air is thick and humid with the flowers' mingled fragrance.

Alice looks up at Lennart who has installed himself opposite her in one of the white-painted wrought-iron chairs.

He is holding forth in a voice that seems to have sprung from the depths of a giant barrel.

'What a relief!' he booms, peering down at her through extra-thick glasses. The lenses are so thick she cannot tell exactly the colour of his eyes. They look blue, but she might be wrong. They might be grey, or even green.

'Thank God for peace once more! The retreat of the marauders!' He passes his hand across his wide brow and stretches out his legs to their full extent. Her eye is drawn to his brown leather-bound feet, which have come to rest just inches from hers. She is struck once again by the impressive scale on which he is built – six foot six at least, a fact which evidently causes him no pleasure, given his permanent stoop, a vain attempt to disguise his giant's proportions. Alice wonders what size shoe he takes. Must be about sixteen or seventeen, she reckons. His shoes would certainly have to be hand-made. No shop would ever stock items of such monumental proportions. But then, being Lennart Blomberg, he would have custom-made shoes anyway, wouldn't he? Even if he had normal-sized feet.

She forces her lips into a complicit smile.

'So, my dear,' he continues, 'what was so absorbing your thoughts just now? I am quite sure you were not lost in admiration of this magnificent fountain!'

Alice struggles to find a reply as flippant as the question. But she is taken unawares, and anyway smart repartee is not her style.

'Well, to be honest, I was thinking about how short life is. And how it's so important to do something lasting before it all slips away.'

'So solemn thoughts on such a beautiful day!' He flashes a twisted smile awkwardly in her direction. He has full, self-indulgent lips.

She looks at him in embarrassment, wondering what on earth made her say what she's just said. She feels uncomfortable in the company of Lennart. She dislikes the effusive, grandiloquent manner he always assumes when conversing with women. It does nothing to conceal his unease, which amounts almost to a terror of saying or doing anything which might lay him open to ridicule.

His nervousness in public has afflicted him all his life. He is a man of very great wealth. Always comes up close to the top in the various rich lists. He took the sensible step of moving to England from Sweden many years ago because he can legally get away with paying next to nothing in tax, which he can't do in Sweden. Yet the vast wealth he has accumulated thanks to his unswerving devotion to the principle of permanently expanding capital, the legions of fawning sycophants and misty-eyed worshippers at the altar of the Blomberg billions, the honours heaped upon him by learned establishments in pursuit of another million or two to fund some deeply important research project, the endless stream of willing, simpering women who hurl themselves at his feet, even the reverential deference of business colleagues and acquaintances, all this, while certainly gratifying to him, have not succeeded in removing the insecurity and self-doubt that lurk permanently on the underside of his life. Sometimes, in moments of solitude and silence, flashes of truth illuminate the people who surround him, revealing them for what they are. He despises them, but he despises himself more because of his slavish dependence on them.

He draws his legs back under his chair, twisting his massive torso round to pick a spray of jasmine from the wall behind him. He breathes deeply of the fragrant bloom.

'I believe that people should not worry themselves about doing the *Right Thing* with their lives. As you say, life is too short. We should, on the contrary, make *every* effort *not* to worry about *anything*! Live in the here and now, my dear!' He crosses his arms and looks down at Alice with a satisfied smile. She likes his sonorous voice, his Swedish sing-song accent with its ponderously-stressed vowels.

Moving his eyes towards the window behind the pond, he catches sight of his dog, a brown and white St Charles spaniel, feverishly digging a hole in the middle of one of Gitte's prize flower-beds.

'There! Look at Co-Co! Does she worry? Follow the example of the animals. They always know best!' His smile broadens and he moves his head from side to side with pleasure, softened by an unexpected, yet unmistakable look of affection for the dog.

Alice senses his expectation of a light-hearted riposte.

'But unfortunately since we're human, that's not so easy,' is all she can muster, adding lamely 'much as we'd like to!'

She thinks he has not heard her, for he continues to follow with delight the antics of his dog. But a few minutes later, his voice booms out again:

'Not at all! We must continue to pursue the illusion of happiness! Absolutely! Because, of course, happiness does not exist. There is no such thing as happiness. How could there be?'

He pauses for a moment for effect, awaiting her reaction. But Alice also waits.

'What do I mean?' he continues, enunciating the question she has failed to ask, 'well, it's obvious. Happiness is an idea. You can't hold it, you can't touch it, or smell it, or see it. You can only think it. It's a dream. Like the rabbit Co-Co is digging for. Always in her mind. Never found. Life is like...' he pauses again for a second.

a bowl of cherries?...

'Life is nothing but a succession of moments, some pleasant, some painful, some indifferent. How to spend your life, you ask? It's clear. It's mathematics. Everything can be reduced to mathematics! Simply strive to maximise the pleasant and eliminate the rest. What could be simpler? What could be more straightforward? No need to worry your head any more with these miserable thoughts, my dear.'

The pattern is always the same: platitude upon platitude bouncing back and forth like a shuttlecock, then moving in for the kill with a punch-line dressed to convey wit and intelligence. But Alice is a difficult audience and declines to applaud.

'But where does memory fit into all this, Lennart?' She pecks and pokes at the bark, like a woodpecker intent on grubs. He looks at her in astonishment.

'The past is real,' she continues. 'Memory persists. It sits there, doesn't it, at the back of your mind, like a block of stone. It's part of you. It's what makes you what you are. The experiences we have, our personal past, our family's past... It's something you can't ignore, even if you wanted to. It's always there, fixed and unchangeable. Immovable. You can't undo it or change or remove it. Finding the best way to live – you say it's simple. Just maximise the happy moments. Sounds easy. But it's not. Memory doesn't fit into it. It's the reason why we human beings – we can't ever be truly happy. Live in the here and now, you say. Not possible!'

He looks at her and laughs.

'So much gloom! Come on! So memory is always there... But there are happy memories are there not? Memories to bring a smile....'

'But No. It comes to the same thing. When you remember happy times, it makes you sad. Because they're past and gone for ever. When you remember sad times, the regret is always with you. You're always thinking: I could have done something. I could have prevented it. But it's too late. What's done is done.'

'Exactly! If it's done, it's done. You may as well forget it. You can't change it. You must move on, my dear Alice. Move on. Regret is of no use, to you or to anyone else.'

' No, no. Of course... You can't change what's done. But the point is... The past – it's like' she stretches out her hand to touch one of the gardenia plants, 'like the roots of this flower. Cut them off and the flower dies. It's part of you. As long as you live, it'll be there, hanging onto you, like an extra limb.'

He laughs again. 'Hmmm... So, my dear, if we follow your logic, we are inexorably drawn to the conclusion that should we be struck down by Alzheimer's disease –well – it may not be such a bad thing after all?'

Alice's silence prompts him to continue:

'Everything after all is reduced to mathematics. The answer to every problem is there. Simple addition and subtraction. It's a fact!'

'But people. Other people. You can't just say maximise the happy moments. What about everyone else?'

He lifts his hand as if to stop her right there.

'My dear, I long ago came to the conclusion that other people are there to be used. Whatever you might care to believe, it's the I that counts. Doesn't matter what you think about people. Just use them. Once you understand that, everything else falls into place. You will never find happiness otherwise.'

Gitte's head appears at one of the windows. She is gesticulating furiously at both Lennart and Co-Co, whom she has just chased off the flower-bed, now adorned with a huge hole encircled by a raised ring of soil and half a dozen uprooted plants.

'You see,' remarks Lennart to Alice, 'my moment of pleasure with you has now unfortunately been succeeded by its opposite. But such is life!' With a theatrical sigh, he shrugs and raises eyebrows and hands, palms turned upwards, resignedly.

Gitte now beckons to Alice, who gets to her feet and moves into the garden. The dog flies past Alice in the opposite direction to the safe haven of Lennart, and collapses, panting, at his feet.

'That horre*e*ble dog!' Gitte shrieks. 'It ruins my garden, my house, my furniture, *everything!*'

Her moon-shaped face is flushed with anger and several hours of hatless exposure to the sun. The deep sapphire-blue eyes, trapped between pink-rimmed lids and pale ivory lashes, appear even more iridescent than usual against the reddened skin.

'Come, Alice,' she is calm now, 'you have time for a tea or a coffee?'

'Well, I ought to be going really…'

'Just a few minutes… I need to talk to you.'

They walk back to the house across the now empty lawns. The sky is clouding over. A light breeze chills the air.

She leads Alice into a room lined from floor to ceiling with bookshelves packed with books. Lennart's personal library.

'Wait here for a moment. I go to find Laszlo to bring us tea. Please sit down. I won't be long.'

There are books in many different languages, which Alice can identify – English, Swedish, German, Russian. Lennart is fluent in all of them. There is nothing in French, though. Before leaving the room, Gitte tells Alice he has a hatred of all things French.

Equalled only perhaps by his loathing of the Swedish tax system?

There seem to be books on every subject under the sun. Everything except music. Music is conspicuous by its absence in this house. Alice is surprised that there are no musical instruments in evidence, although a Steinway, polished to the utmost degree of lustrous sheen, if positioned alongside one of the wall-sized windows, would have been the ideal missing complement to the drawing-room, set against the panoramic views of lawns, woodland and lake. She hasn't seen any sign of music players either, or even radios, at least in any of the main parts of the house. How did Shakespeare put it? Oh yes...

'The man that hath no music in himself,
Nor is mov'd with concord of sweet sounds,
Is fit for treasons, stratagems and spoils; ...
Let no such man be trusted'.

As Alice waits for Gitte's return, she cannot escape the sense that, although this house is surrounded by nature and beauty in abundance, it gives off a desolate feel, like a person who is both deaf and blind.

'I want to show you something.' Gitte tells her. 'I would very much value your opinion'.

She leads her to a black, highly varnished table by the window, on which stands a small glass sculpture. It is in the form of a plant and coloured in amethyst and the most tender green, fashioned in such a way that the colours seem continuously to mingle and separate like water flowing along a river-bed. The light shines through and around the stem, leaf and flower shapes in a way that draws and charms the eye.

'So what do you think?'

'It's exquisite.'

Gitte lifts it carefully from the table and holds it out to Alice.

'It's yours.'

'But... no... no... I couldn't take it...'

'Yes, yes. Please do. I saw it and I thought immediately of you, Alice. It has your spirit. Take it please. I will be offended if you refuse.'

'I don't know what to say...'

Gitte puts her finger to her lips: 'Sssh... Then say nothing, my dear.'

That evening Alice shows Michael the sculpture. He looks at it for a minute.

'It's nice,' he declares eventually. 'Very nice.' A few seconds later he asks:

'How much is it worth, do you think?'

'I've no idea,' she replies. 'Does it matter?'

'Well of course it matters. I mean, if it's something she just picked up in John Lewis or something, well – what does that make you?'

'What? I don't get you.'

'Reflects on you. What she thinks of you. Whether it's worth, say, fifteen quid, or thousands. Do you see?'

Alice smiles wryly. 'I should think it's somewhere in the middle. I don't really know. And to be frank, I don't care either. I think it's beautiful. That's all that matters. It was a lovely thing for Gitte to do, don't you think?'

'Yes of course.'

He pours himself a drink and asks her what's for dinner.

Alice on the spur of the moment blurts out suddenly:

'Michael. I think I need to go away for a while. On my own.'

He wheels round to face her, his expression a mixture of astonishment and annoyance.

'What? Are you mad? What's brought this on?' He holds the whisky glass suspended in mid-air. Then moves it to his lips, the ice clinking loudly.

Alice pours herself a whisky, her second that evening.

'I've been thinking. About going somewhere quiet. Don't know where exactly. Just – I don't know – to be by myself for a while. I need to think things out…'

'Things? What things? For Christ's sake, Alice! This is very sudden, isn't it? What's been going on?' He sits down in the armchair by the window. She sits too, on the sofa facing him.

'I just don't seem to understand you any more,' he says helplessly.

'Perhaps you never did.' Her reply is almost inaudible.

'Oh God, don't give me that! Making out you're so bloody deep. You know, you have this view of yourself – as if you're something special, superior to the rest of us ordinary mortals. Alice and her secret world. People think you're weird, did you know that?

'Yes, I did know, believe it or not. It doesn't bother me.'

'No, I guess it doesn't…' He shakes his head.

They drink for a moment in silence.

'Why are you so angry?' she asks quietly.

'Angry? I'm not angry. Just don't get you, that's all. It doesn't make sense. You have everything you want. A free hand. Things for the house, for the kids. Do I ever refuse you anything? Do I? Then you turn round and say you want to leave…'

'I didn't say that. I just want to think…'

'Think? Why the hell can't you think here?'

'I don't want to leave. Just go away for a *while*…'

'A *while*? What does that mean? How long? A week? A month? Three months?'

'I don't know.'

She doesn't know. She hasn't even thought it through. She didn't even know she was going to propose it. She is almost as surprised as he is.

They eat dinner in near silence. Afterwards Michael goes out to walk the dog for half an hour, as he always does. Alice clears the table and loads the dishwasher, as she always does. She is still engaged in this when Michael returns. He has been out for about ten minutes.

He starts to spill out words, continuing their discussion as if there had been no interruption. But he is calm now. He speaks in considered, rehearsed phrases, with no obvious emotion.

'I see what all this is about now, Alice. You need to be on your own. To *think*, as you put it. It's funny. Takes me back to when we were together the first time – all those years ago. Such a long time. Do you recall? I remember a conversation we had then. I never thought about it till now, just a minute ago. I can picture it, really vividly. We were sitting on the grass in Regent's Park. It was hot. You were wearing a white dress. With blue flowers. We were talking about the future. How we saw ourselves in ten years' time. I said I'd be slogging away, probably in a City firm, doing lots of boring stuff, working towards a partnership. I said: but anyway I'd have you with me, so that would make everything all right. And you...'

'And I said: don't look into the future. Because things are bound to turn out differently. And I said – I remember now – I said: don't rely on me being with you. And that I needed to follow my own path...'

He nods. ' "Your own path." Yes. That's right. "Like a cat," you said'.

Like a cat. Yes. Not a dog. A dog will never leave you. Once a dog moves in, that's it. It's there, with you, for life. But a cat always reserves the right to stay or go. At any time. And always at a time of its own choosing.

Alice had always adored cats. She loved their glorious infidelity. She loved the careless arrogance with which they turn up one day on your doorstep demanding food and attention. She loved their insolence, their languid self-confidence, their nonchalance, their manipulative guile. Indifferent to your wonderment, they glide effortlessly from earth to tree and tree to roof with spellbinding precision and grace. Soundless and invisible they stalk their prey, not a blade of grass displaced, then WHAM! Disdainful of your pusillanimous cries of pity, they tease and torment their hapless victim, parading their power to inflict suffering. Then, losing interest, they discard the mauled trophy and saunter on to the next kill. There is a magical quality about cats. An empty chair, a patch of sunlit grass. You turn round and suddenly a cat is sitting there, grooming itself and purring. It stays with you while you work, weeding or digging or hanging the clothes out to dry. Then turn round again and it's gone. A cat will stay or go as it wills. It might leave you for ever, never to return, if the grass looks greener and the food more delectable somewhere else. Cruel and egotistical, a cat belongs to no-one but itself.

Michael is still rambling on about the past. How can he remember it all in so much detail? Was it really a white dress with blue flowers? On and on he drones, his voice is thick and cloying, she does not recognise it. But all of a sudden he stares straight at her, blinking and wide-eyed as if emerging from a dream. He speaks and the tone of his voice has changed. With bleak and bitter irony he asks:

'Don't you find it a little odd that you should still have the mind-set of a nineteen-year-old at the age of forty-three?'

She shrugs lightly and does not reply. It doesn't matter how many years of life she has had or has left to live on this earth, she wants to say, she will always be that girl of nineteen. And no, she wants to say, she does not find it in the least odd or absurd, even if he does, that the purity and ecstasy some thought reserved for the after-life can be experienced in the here and now. She believed it at nineteen and believes it still.

Time and stillness, stillness and solitude. The essential conditions. But the tiresome minutiae of daily existence are always getting in the way. How enviable is the hermit's life! To live alone on the edge of the sea, or in the middle of a forest, or on the side of a mountain, without the sound of a human voice to be heard anywhere seems to Alice the most desirable form of existence imaginable.

She wants to say all this and more, but she says nothing, because she knows what his reaction will be. Logical and commonsensical he would set about demolishing her hopes and ideals one by one, demonstrating how impracticable and ultimately impossible each of them is.

'So what about food? Even Buddhist monks have to eat occasionally. And what about soap, running water, heating? You've never lit a fire in your life. You wouldn't know how. Not to mention your precious art materials, electricity, batteries. And do you really think you'd be happy living like a Trappist monk, never speaking to another soul for the rest of your life?'

She knows what he'd say because he's said it all before. *Bringing her to her senses.* No matter that *sense* has an altogether different meaning for Alice and in any case, she has always thought of *bringing someone to their senses* as a particularly stupid and sterile expression.

'If you had to describe what sort of a person I am, what would you say?'

Hesitating for an instant, he answers:

'If you'd asked me that a year ago, I'd have said – you're sensitive, caring, creative. The perfect wife...'

Noticing her cringe, he adds:

'I suppose I'm not allowed to say that any more...'

'A year ago? And now?'

'Now... It's not the same. You've changed. Is it me? Have I done something?'

She is suddenly weary. The prospect of having to explain, to justify. In a way, it would be so much simpler just to carry on accepting the lie, feigning, acting the part.

'I haven't changed,' she sighs. 'It's just that you never knew me, I think. You married someone you wanted me to be. But it wasn't really me...'

'What rubbish! What are you saying? And what about me? Are you saying..' he hesitates, swallows, 'are you saying you never... loved me?' The last two words come out in a choked whisper, dragged out against his will. Troubled by this hateful display of weakness, he bows his head.

Alice is temporarily unable to speak. Her silence agitates him. He exhorts her to answer:

'Well? Answer me! What are your...your... feelings for me?' He can't bring himself to say *love* again.

How do you choose between truth and pain? And in any case, what does "love" mean? So fraught with complication and contradiction, you can never grab hold of it. It slips away whenever you try and peg it down. All air and light, no substance, no fixed shape.

She looks helplessly at him. He grits his teeth, clenches his fists, like a parachutist about to throw himself out of a plane for the first time.

'Is there... someone else?' The words are exhaled through barely parted lips.

Agonising seconds pass.

'I... No... I don't know...'

'Dammit, Alice. What the hell do you mean? You don't know? Yes or no?'

'If you mean... am I sleeping with...' She sees him wince, 'No... I'm not.'

He looks relieved to an extent. His tension goes, his eyes soften.

'OK. You go away for a bit if you must. But don't stay away too long. We need you...'

His sad, tender smile has the effect of mitigating the agony. Everything will 'turn out OK in the end' it tells her. He has this gift, it surely must be a gift, of making every problem seem solvable. No crisis, no disaster even, nothing is ever wholly intractable. Everything subsumed beneath cushiony layers of moderation and common sense, that he makes into a wall to protect him from chaos, the uncontrollable, and, God help us, the sublime. If there is a simmering of emotion beneath the composed exterior, it is well hidden. Concealed even from Alice, who knows him better than most. But his abhorrence of the extreme is clear. And his terror of losing control makes him regard passion as a sign of despicable weakness. The idea of allowing your emotions to take control is for him like a fall from grace, a betrayal of the quintessentially human, which is spirit – almost a descent into the bestial.

When he witnesses musicians shutting their eyes or swaying their heads and bodies as they play, lost in the joy of the sounds, he cannot resist a contemptuous curl of the mouth, as he rubbishes their histrionics.

'*Why* can't they keep *still?*'

There is no place in Michael's life for the un-ticketed. Everything must be quantified, classified, recorded, accounted for. Any kind of ambiguity is to be swiftly either corrected or rejected. Every chance occurrence, every unforeseen event must be rescued from the viscous, turbulent flows which threaten to engulf and contaminate the orderly progress of existence, scooped up and rendered harmless, explained and thereby captured. When Alice took him by surprise, having suddenly turned strange and different from the person he thought he knew, he was briefly at a loss to know how to deal with it, momentarily fearful the disruption of the familiar order would defeat his need to absorb it, but he willed himself to stay calm and, as always, worked out a solution. She was tired, fatigued, suffering from some kind of mental crisis. This sometimes happened to women around Alice's age. Yes, of course. That was it. She needed a holiday, a change. Nothing odd about that. She'd get over it. Of course she would. Only a matter of time. She'd settle. Everything always settles in the end.

CHAPTER EIGHTEEN

Alice is asleep, outstretched on a grassy bank overlooking a harbour on the Adriatic coast. The early morning sun is already hot. Distant sounds of fishermen calling to one another from the tiny cove below mingle with the insistent cries of gulls.

Lennart Blomberg bought this stretch of land on the eastern coast between Ravenna and Rimini just before his marriage to Gitte thirty years ago. He presented it to her as his personal gift on the morning after the wedding. He named it *'Morghengifu'*, following the example, he said, of the medieval knights of England and their 'gift of the morrow from the groom to the bride'.

Gitte designed the house, which is now a landmark on the cliff-top, a convenient beacon for fishing boats that might stray too far out on a misty night or dawn. Inspired by her twin passions for oriental architecture and Byzantine art, she created a curious hybrid, somewhere between an indo-islamic temple and a small early byzantine church.

When Gitte offered Alice the house for the summer, she hadn't given her any clue of what to expect.

'Our little summer place on the Adriatic,' she told her sadly. 'We don't go there very often any more. It's yours! Stay as long as you like, my dear!'

Mostly it was used by different members of the Blombergs' extended family or those whom they considered 'close friends'. Alice was expecting a house like the country villas in the Emilia-Romagna style that abounded along the north-eastern coast. Instead, as she drove up the narrow road that led to the tiny fishing cove, then turned up a steep hill and round a bend, she was confronted by the spectacle of two minaret-like towers covered in cream stucco and culminating in rounded pinnacles, like miniature versions of the Taj Mahal minarets. She caught her breath both at the incongruity and also because of a simultaneous sensation of *déjà-vu*.

As soon as she walked through the arched doorway, she instantly recognised Gitte's hand, her quirky exuberance. The house is in many ways a distillation of the Blomberg mansion at Hadworth Park, but more intense and flashy, like a kitschified version of Byzantine art with admixtures of the worst excesses of Rococo architecture, all rolled into one bizarre fusion. The enthusiasm for brilliant colours and decorative ornamentation, diluted and just about controlled in the English house, is here allowed free rein and running wild.

The ceilings, some of which are domed, are decorated with gold, blue and green mosaics, displaying intricate plant and bird designs. Others reveal hand-painted, vividly-coloured abstract patterns in a convoluted art-nouveau style.

Abstract mosaic forms in black, white and muted browns and creams adorn the floors of many of the rooms. Others are inlaid with marble in delicate pinks, greys and pale umber. The house is constructed around a spacious courtyard with, at its centre, a small oblong pool surrounded by palms.

When Alice arrived she was greeted at the door by an old man, no more than five feet tall, with a wrinkled nut-brown skin and toothless smile. He lives with his wife in the village below and the couple have taken care of the house ever since the Blombergs built it. He does not speak any English and Alice knows barely any Italian. All she understood from his continuous babbling was that his name was Federico. He carried her suitcases through the house, depositing them in a bedroom shuttered in gloom.

She followed him from room to room as he pointed out nooks and crannies, opened and closed doors, turned switches and taps on and off, demonstrated how bolts and keys were to be operated, windows and shutters to be controlled, commentating all the while in an unintelligible stream of Italian, to which Alice responded with occasional nods and smiles at regular intervals. She allowed his words to drift over her; it was pointless to do otherwise. Since everything was so clear and obvious to him, he could not conceive that she understood nothing. When he had assured himself that there was nothing left to tell her, he made to leave. She held out a tentative hand to offer him a few coins, but instantly realised her mistake, because he evinced horror at the sight, rejecting her indelicacy with vigorous shaking of the head and disapproving words that needed no translation. He regarded himself as an old and faithful friend of the Blombergs and so, by extension, of all of their guests, who must be treated with precisely the same degree of courtesy and care.

She lies on the grassy bank, drained of energy after a sleepless night spent struggling with the new painting. Utter frustration at its refusal to work alternated with occasional moments of exhilaration, when a sudden glimpse of purity and light emerged for an instant, before vanishing once more.

    She stirs and raises her arm to shield her eyes and left cheek from the sun. The warmth floods through her body. She floats into a delicious half-sleep. A confusion of images plays out before her, half-remembered memories, visions of people, snapshots of events. Faces of children. Her children. Children running and shouting. A playing-field. Umbrellas. Mud. Chloe, racing along with the rest, with a twist of her head suddenly catches sight of Alice. She breaks away and dashes across to the edge of the field where Alice stands beneath her blue and red umbrella, stretching up her arms to hug her. Alice falling into sleep next to Michael, with no space between them, their bodies fused into the shape of a perfect S. Scents of pine trees at night wafting through an open window. Mountains. The smell and sound of rain falling in a forest. Skiing down an empty slope in Yugoslavia with Michael, the sun so hot they're wearing tee-shirts. Florence and Chloe leap up and down in a pool. Shrieking: 'Two-part bug! Two-part bug!' each time a giant wasp zooms into view, they plunge their heads simultaneously into the water like a pair of kittiwakes. A garden in high summer. Butterflies dart through purple flowers and bees are droning. Florence lies face down on the grass, observing a community of ants on the move. She and Chloe build a rabbit hutch, then cry and laugh as it falls to pieces around their rabbit's ears. Music. Silent sounds of a melody unfold. A pulsing rhythm. Phrases from a horn reprised. Familiar phrases. Something Jack played. She can't remember the title. Lines and colours spring from the music. They leap, dive, curve earthward then soar once again, arabesques of sound and light. Dancing. Dancing with Jack in a haze of blue and green. She hears whispering. She can't make it out at first. From deep inside her ear. 'Alice, Alice'. Her mother or maybe her father. Father's voice from a great distance. Doors slam shut. Train leaving. Too late too late. How to find them? Gone and her left standing alone. 'Alice, Alice'. Quick. Hurry. Too late. Too late. Where is my mother? I can't find my mother. People mill around, walk into me, don't see me. I am invisible but I can still feel. Where am I? Take me home. Let me touch your amber skin. Soft hairs pale gold. Justin naked. Honey and cinnamon in my mouth. We glide silently through waters iridescent with cobalt blue, sapphire, lavender and indigo. We sway with the waves forward and back, but always outward in ever-widening circles. Wider and further till the land fades away. We are born of rivers, lagoons, lakes and oceans. Borne away by currents beyond duality, beyond everything which is sundered, beyond difference. A saturation of yes. Plenitude without limit. 'Alice, Alice'.

'Alice. Alice! Alice? For God's sake!'

She opens her eyes. Jack's face close up to hers. His breath glances across her cheek. He peers into her face. Frowning, concerned.

'Are you OK? I've been trying to wake you up for bloody ages.'

Without moving, she looks at his blurred face, smiling, unbelieving.

'Are you on something?'

She sits up slowly. She feels damp, sweaty, groggy.

'Have you ever had a dream where everything seemed to be part of everything else? And you didn't exist any more, not part of the world, and yet somehow you *are* the world. As if the whole of being is you and not you at the same time...'

'I dream it. I live for it! It's where I want to be!'

She takes his hand. His being there seems natural, almost inevitable.

'Why are you here?'

She has not seen or heard from him since he started touring with his band. Once she called him, but there was just an answer-phone message.

'To see you. What d'you think? You knew I'd come didn't you?'

'But how did you know? How did you find out?'

'Easy. Just dropped by your place and they told me.'

'Told you? Who? Nobody's there.'

Then she remembers. Mary. Of course. She still comes in every day, to water the plants, feed the cat, keep the house clean.

'Mary! She's not supposed to give my address to anyone! She had strict instructions...'

He grins. 'My natural charm! What do you expect? No. I told her I was your dealer. About a painting someone wanted to buy. She's a bit gullible isn't she? You want to watch out!'

She leads him into the house. He glances up at the painted ceilings and byzantine pillars.

'Christ! Is this real? Some kind of kitsch joke, it must be. Or is it serious? Whose house is this anyway?'

She tells him it belongs to the Blombergs and Gitte designed it and he says:

'Oh well. I guess it must be serious then.'

A bit later, and further into the house:

'Hey I like this!' He caresses a small obsidian carving, an Indian figurine which stands on a black lacquered table in a corner of the main living room. He has his arms around her. Lifts her hair. His mouth damp on the nape of her neck. So... It's gone beyond thinking now.

Her hands explore planes and promontories, soft recesses, lines, curves, smooth and rough, the feel and topography many times imagined, now finally lived. Every shape, tone, texture, smell and taste of his body.

Dance of hands, mouths, touch. She traverses the curves and hollows of her body through his fingers. Desert springs fill parched throats with life-giving sweetness. Fountains spring into dazzling sun. She aches to enfold him. She is a cave of black water, debarred from light, which after centuries of somnolence erupts without warning, sending thousands of stones hurtling into the ocean. Broad shafts of light and heat penetrate the shattering walls of the cave.

Exquisite saturation. Absence of denial. Total immanence. Absolute thingness.

It turns out that he's in transit. En route to a venue in Grenoble. Had a week free between gigs so thought he'd drop by.

He wakes early, at first light, leaving her still dozing, to be gently nudged awake by the morning sun. The light filters insistently through half-open shutters.

She watches him from the doorway as he works his body by the pool. He is totally absorbed in his physicality. He is quite unaware of her. She watches him execute a series of movements. They follow a predetermined order and number of repetitions. She has never witnessed this performance, but he told her once about it, 'like servicing a car,' he said. 'So it runs smoothly. Run and run. Not seize up halfway through the race.'

She envies him his pleasure. Has always envied people like Jack who need and love to exercise their bodies.

She makes drawings of him as he moves, filling sheet after sheet with marks inspired by his fluency and grace. She is still drenched in the feel of him, his smell, his taste, but already it has started to fade. She struggles to keep a hold.

She watches him in the pool, floating on his back, head to the sky, eyes shut. His body sways with the gentle movement of the water. A sense of ebbing away. Water dripping through tightly-closed fingers. Visions from a lovely dream that dissolve into the fog of un-memory that feels but no longer sees. Transient bliss of the undivided cell. One becomes two and the sorrow begins.

From the rose-coloured terrace she stands and watches. A thin stream of fluid trickles warmly down the inside of her thighs. It leaves milky patches on the pink stones.

Jack has a fast-approaching gig to play in Grenoble. He has only a few days left. His mind is full of leaving. He busies himself washing clothes, collecting up belongings dispersed around the house, spends hours calling people on his mobile. Alice returns to her painting. They spend large sections of the days apart.

One evening they sit on the swinging chair in the garden sipping wine when the telephone rings. It is Michael calling from Berlin. The sound of his voice jolts her backwards as if into a discarded skin.

'How's it going? How are things down at the seaside?' His tone is strained, falsely cheerful and his voice sounds hoarse.

'Have you got a cold?' she asks.

'Bit of one. Been staying up too late. Too much work.'

A silence falls.

'So… I'm taking a few days off,' he resumes. 'Thought you might like to join me? You'd like Berlin. Buzzing place. Lots to see… And the kids'll be here next week. We could all be together…' He tails off.

She says no, not possible at the moment. Mutters something about her work. Involved. Can't break off right now.

He says OK. The cheeriness gone, his tone flat. His voice seems to be coming from a great distance. They talk briefly some more about the kids. The arrangements he's made for their trip to Berlin. Anneke, his PR in the German office, she will pick them up from the airport and take care of them. The call ends. She stares miserably at the telephone in her hand.

Jack walks in. He hasn't heard the conversation but her expression tells him everything.

'I feel hateful. Miserable.'

His hands on her shoulders, he tries to soothe her tension, working it with his fingers. He tells her about moving on, that you can't have change without pain, that you've got to face up to the truth.

'Don't let guilt drag you down, there's too much at stake. You'll regret it for ever if you let this chance go. You choose your life, you've always said that.'

But his words are of little consequence. Her mood remains dark.

Jack's last evening. They drink brandy on the terrace in the fading light, watching sea and sky merge into a mist of purple grey. When it is too dark to see anything, they stumble into the house. Alice falls over his saxophone case which stands by the bedroom door, ready for next morning's departure. By midnight they are asleep.

Alice wakes first. She is propelled into consciousness by a loud insistent knocking at the front door.

'What the hell?'

Then Jack sits up.

'What the fuck? What time is it?'

The knocking stops. Alice throws on a bath-towel and peers through the window that gives onto the entrance road clearly visible now in the moonlight. She sees nothing. Then looking through a window on the other side of the house, they both see a car parked just outside the main gate. A dark-coloured BMW.

'Oh God!' Alice says.

The knocking resumes. With sinking heart she switches on the light and moves towards the door. Jack stands behind her a few metres back. His brown hair tousled, his eyes blinking in the light.

The tall, straight figure of Michael framed in the doorway is the righteous prince, the noble knight of the fiery cross. She and Jack are the cringing sinners, mired in ignominy. Pushing past her he strides into the house. Alice is fleetingly aware of how much taller and bigger he is than Jack. A lion and a gazelle.

Surely this will not descend into farce, a fight even? That would be too absurd.

For an age, it seems, the three of them stand motionless and silent. Then Michael begins to speak. Ignoring Jack, in a voice heavy with irony, he says :

'I see. So this is what it was all about. Your little jaunt. *Getting away on your own*! *Time to think*!'

She tries to protest, but he doesn't let her speak.

'What a fool! What a fool I was! I actually believed you. *Needing space!* How could you do this, Alice? How could you lie to me?' He halts for a moment and swiftly she interposes:

'It wasn't like that, Michael. I had no idea he was coming...'

A short bitter laugh.

'Christ! What do you take me for? I'm not that much of a fool...'

Jack, trying desperately to save her says no, she didn't know anything, it wasn't planned...

'Look, can't we be civilised about this...' he goes on.

'Civilised?' Michael echoes, then loudly and with mounting anger: 'Civilised? That's rich! Has he been screwing you in a civilised fashion, Alice? Been doing a good job, has he?'

Turning towards Jack, he looks at him quizzically, frowning.

'I know you, don't I? I've seen you before...' he says, searching his memory. Then remembers.

'Yes, I know. I know now! You're the little music teacher. Christ! You've been to my house!' That fact seems to enrage him more than anything else. He strides close up to Jack and looks down at him, clenching his fists. Jack stands his ground, glares back, his jaws grinding.

Anger surges into Alice's throat.

'Stop!' she yells at the top of her voice. Both of them twist sharply round to look at her.

'Aren't you forgetting something? It's all about me, isn't it?' she carries on, her voice strident and trembly. 'Me!' She rams her finger into her chest several times. 'Me! Me! It's not about *you* at all. Either of you!'

For a few minutes there is silence. Jack decides this is an opportune time to leave and slips away behind one of the byzantine pillars. Michael glances up, noting his departure, but the spur of his anger has lost its edge.

'Why did you come?' Alice asks him softly.

He collapses wearily into a sofa.

' I thought, in my naïve way, to surprise you…' he laughs ruefully. 'Surprise? I certainly did that!'

Alice sits down opposite him.

'Listen, Michael. I want to set the record straight. Jack and I… We've been friends for a while…'

'Friends!'

'No, listen. I said *friends* and that's what it is – was. There were strong feelings. Difficult to describe. An attachment… But nothing ever happened. Nothing. Until a few days ago…'

His look says *do you expect me to believe that?*

'I've never lied to you. Don't accuse me of that. I honestly didn't know he was coming. I had no idea. He just… turned up.'

'There's just one thing I need to know, Alice,' he says haltingly, 'this bloke – whatever you've got going with him – does it mean… you and I… does it mean… it's all finished between us?'

His despairing, broken look. How can she deal with this? It's impossible.

'Whatever's happened or will happen between us. Just remember, it's got nothing to do with Jack. That's all I can say.'

CHAPTER NINETEEN

England. Early September. Alice rests her head against the back of the seat. The sky through the taxi windows is the colour of dirty bathwater. The taxi passes through the village, its houses and cottages, the small shop and post office, the green, the village hall which doubles as a nursery school, all the same as before. Nothing has changed, but why should it? It's been barely three months.

The driver, who has hardly uttered a word since they left the airport, turns right up the lane that leads to the house at the top of the hill. For the first time she has a whiff of strangeness. Nothing is different. Yet everything feels it.

As soon as she turns the key, she experiences the curious yet inescapable sensation of walking into someone else's house. The feeling persists and intensifies as she enters the hall, then the kitchen. Her footsteps echo eerily. The house seems too big and empty. She shivers. For the first time in three months she feels cold.

Unopened mail is stacked on the kitchen table. The phone tells her she has eight messages waiting. She puts the receiver down wearily. They can wait. She makes coffee and leafs through the pages of an old *Country Life* that lies underneath the pile of mail. She casts her eyes over articles and pictures, registering nothing.

Fingal appears from out of nowhere, startling her as he jumps onto her lap. She strokes his soft black fur and is comforted by his purring which sounds preternaturally loud in the silence. He and Mary have been the only living creatures in the house for the last three months. But ghosts may have been floating through the empty rooms, keeping them company. No doubt she will hear a blow by blow account of their doings in due course from Mary, who claims to have psychic powers.

As she turns the pages of the magazine, she thinks about Florence and Chloe. They were last together, all three of them, just a few days ago, at the house on the Adriatic. Their stay in Berlin over, they flew to Italy to spend time with her before returning to school. An awkwardness clouded their stay. Things left unsaid yet clearly sensed.

She took them on visits to local places of interest every day, they swam happily in the pool, spent hours on the beach, but their greatest enthusiasm was reserved for when they told her about the ten days they spent with Michael in Berlin.

It was '*Anneke took us here, Anneke took us there…*'

'So what was Anneke like?'

'She was *lovely*!' enthused Chloe.

'She was OK,' muttered Florence, with a shrug. Michael stole time away from the office to take them round the city. He showed them the Reichstag building, its heavy nineteenth century facade displaying the words 'DEM DEUTSCHE VOLKE' a reminder of the grim past, in contrast to its incongruously modernist glass dome.

'That top bit,' he told them, 'was designed by a famous English architect'.

They loved the way, when you were inside it, you got the impression of a gigantic fountain thrusting its jets up to the sky. And when walking around the circular route at the top, you could see great swathes of the urban landscape.

Chloe liked, even more than this, the Television Tower in Unter den Linden, with its fabulous revolving restaurant from which you could see every part of the city. They had lunch there one day and spent most of the time peering out of the windows trying to pick out landmarks from steadily changing vantage points as the tower moved slowly through 360 degrees. Anneke, a native of Berlin, came too that day and went out of her way to point out all the places and buildings visible from that bird's eye view.

A request from Florence to 'look round the old Jewish sectors' was greeted with surprise by Michael till she explained she was writing a school assignment on the background and history of the Holocaust. Florence had for some time felt a strong link to her Jewish heritage. Though only amounting to a quarter of her ancestry, technically speaking, that twenty-five percent had acquired a disproportionate importance for her emotionally. She didn't know why exactly, nor did she try to explain it. She just felt irresistibly drawn.

Over the years during their frequent visits to their grandfather, while Alice chatted to Sophie, and Chloe crept away to play with the children who lived next door, Florence would settle herself on the sofa next to Julius, listening with rapt attention as he recounted stories of the past. Sometimes he would bring out his box of ancient photographs, creased and faded images of a lost world, of people dressed in strange clothes that she would never meet but that she felt were still, somehow, part of her. At the age of thirteen she confided to Julius her intention of converting to Judaism when she grew up. Taken aback, he didn't know what to say at first. Of course he was touched, and naturally he couldn't help thinking how happy his mother, if she'd been alive, would have been to hear it, but he had no hesitation in advising Florence against it.

'Well, dear,' he said eventually, 'unless you really have an overwhelming need to follow every single thing Judaism teaches – and believe me, that's a lot to follow – I don't think it would be such a good idea. There's already, in my opinion, too much trouble in the world – most of it due to people deciding to be one thing and not another. Much better to keep away from labels. They just make people hate. Think about it!'

So that was what she did.

Michael took them to the old Jewish cemetery in Oranienburger. It had a feeling of abandonment, neglected and overgrown, and apparently holding little of interest to visitors, as they were the only ones wandering about amongst the remains of graves which had survived the Gestapo's attempts to destroy everything. A heavy stillness hung over the place, stifling speech. A stone sculpture in the form of people raising their hands in supplication stood as a reminder of past suffering and tragedy, but nobody else was there to see it.

He showed them a place in the centre of the city, in a square by Humboldt University. One of the wide paving stones had been removed and replaced by a sheet of glass. They looked through the glass and saw an illuminated room, completely empty.

'The library with no books,' he told them, 'to remind people of the time in 1933 when the Nazis burned hundreds of great writings just because they were written by Jews and other people whose ideas they opposed.'

This symbol of the wilful destruction of knowledge deeply affected Florence. She tried to hide her tears as she read the message on the plaque:

'Wherever books are burnt, men will eventually be burnt. Heinrich Heine.'

Then Chloe, on seeing Florence's distress, immediately followed suit, tears pouring down her cheeks.

Thinking that a change of mood was needed, Michael took Florence off to the New National Gallery to look at Munch and the early twentieth century Expressionists, in whom she had recently developed a passionate interest. Chloe, always bored by art galleries, was carted off by Anneke to the Zoo.

'Was Grandpa in Berlin ever?' they asked Alice.

'I don't know. Perhaps he went there as a child. But Great-Grandpa was – before and after the war.'

She told them the story of the departure from Prague, just before Hitler marched into Austria, how Josef had managed to get his family away just in time.

'Auntie Irma was just a baby then,' she said. 'And Grandpa was only about eight or nine.'

They listened to the reporting of these facts, with blank expressions, as if they concerned strangers, their minds blocked by the impossibility of imagining their grandfather and great-aunt as little children.

Josef had died before Florence and Chloe were born, but there was a large and impressive gold-framed photograph of him in the drawing-room and Julius had often spoken to them about him.

Florence pressed Alice for more information.

'And why was Great-Grandpa in Berlin again *after* the war?' she inquired. She was keen to trace a connection between her family and the fascinating city she had just left.

Alice said she was not sure. She had a vague recollection of him going to Germany and France from time to time during her childhood, when they all lived together in the Bayswater house. Berlin was often mentioned as a destination, but she never knew where exactly he went to, or why.

Their disappointed faces prompted her to dig further in her memory. She knew of his interest in all things Czech and his dismay when the communists took over, so she said, partly to re-ignite their enthusiasm, partly because she thought there was a remote possibility it might even have been true:

'Perhaps it was something to do with meeting contacts in Berlin. Secret assignments. Passing on sensitive information from London, maybe? That kind of thing…'

'Wow!' said Chloe. 'Assignments! Was Great-Grandpa a spy?'

Alice smiled mysteriously. 'Well, you never know.'

'Spy? Well, perhaps that's too strong a word…' Julius's tone surprised Alice by its seriousness. She had expected his rollicking belly-laugh to reverberate down the line when she rang him that evening. But he spoke quietly and, unusually for him, without a trace of humour.

'Well, I never told you. Of course, I couldn't tell you at first. But now it's all over. And he's gone. And the world has changed so much... Josef worked for years with the Czech Liberation movement. Independence is what he longed for. A great shame – a tragedy, really – that he never lived to see it. He really worked tirelessly against whoever happened to be the enemy at the time – fascists, then communists... But surely, Alice, you and David, you must have been aware of this? Didn't you suspect anything?'

But Alice had never guessed. Not even bothered to think about it, to be honest. Too self-obsessed to even care about what her grandfather did, his thoughts and dreams. Certainly she and David had never talked about it.

'I never did, Dad,' she replied, ashamed by her past indifference.

'Well, I suppose we did a good job of keeping it quiet. Certainly your mother had only the vaguest idea of what he was up to. And your grandmother – well, she knew, of course. But she was a wise woman. Never spoke a single word that didn't need to be said.'

He started to tell her that Josef had been one of the principal information sources linking the Movement in London with other members working in Germany, France and Central and Eastern Europe. Then abruptly he stopped.

'I have to go out now. But listen, come over and see me when you come back. I have something to give you.'

She stayed for a couple of days in London before returning to Sussex. She took the tube to Kensington High Street one afternoon and walked from the station to Julius' flat nearby. It had been some time since she last saw him. Perhaps six months or longer. When he opened the door, she noticed he was stooping a little, more than she remembered. His white hair looked too long, uncharacteristically unkempt. When he gave her a hug, she could feel his shoulder-blades protruding beneath the cotton shirt.

'Are you eating enough?' she inquired anxiously.

He chuckled. 'What a question! You should see how Sophie piles up my plate! I can't even finish it sometimes. Don't you see my pot belly?' pointing to his waistband. Alice shook her head, unconvinced.

'Listen,' he reassured her, 'I'm fine, I'm fine,' adding, as if to draw a line under the matter, 'Sophie's away at the moment. Staying with her daughter in Brighton. But she'll be back next week.'

After cups of tea and pieces of cinnamon cake made by Sophie, he said:

'Come with me. I've got something for you.'

He led her into his study, a small windowless room next to the living-room, which gave the impression of a store-cupboard for books, assorted files and disorderly piles of papers that covered the whole surface of his desk, the chair and even the floor beneath. He opened a drawer in the filing cabinet by the far wall and removed two lever-arch files, one blue, one red, each containing a bundle of typewritten pages. He held them out to her.

'Take them.'

'What's this?'

'What I laughingly call *my memoirs*. One for you. One for David.'

She was dumbstruck.

'I was planning for you to have this after I was gone. But – well … Now is as good a time as any. After all, you might have some questions I didn't answer already. Go on, take them. You look after David's one. Give it to him next time you see him, will you? I don't get to see him much these days. He's always so busy…'

CHAPTER TWENTY

After a couple of dilatory hours at the piano, starting with Chopin, followed by Debussy and ending with Satie's *Gymnopedies*, Alice finally, reluctantly, gets round to picking up the phone to listen to her messages. A miscellany of inconsequential ones, which she immediately deletes, calls advertising things, one from the vicar reminding her of the date of the church fete and her promise to help out with the teas, two months out of date (*good she got out of that one*), another from William, saying he'd call back later.

Then she recognises Josie's voice. She sounds drunk. The usual background of heavy metal music and an uproarious clamour of yelling and laughter almost drown out her message.

'Hey Al! Are you there? Pick up the phone! You in bed already? Got somethin' to ask ya. Call me…'

This is followed by another message from Josie three days later:

'Al? For chrissake, Al! Pick up the phone! It's me, OK? Call me when you get back…Don't forget.'

Her voice is kind of croaky. Not usual. She speaks haltingly. There's a pause, then the sound of loud sniffing.

'Give me a call will ya…Gotta speak to ya… Can't deal with this.' The last words spoken in barely more than a whisper. Then it cuts off.

The final message from Josie is timed at eleven-thirty-eight on the evening of the same day. Her words are slurred, her voice muffled.

'Al? listen, Al... It's too late... Too fuckin' late...' Alice immediately dials Josie's number. She lets it ring. No answer. Ten minutes later she tries again. Nothing. She waits for an hour and rings again. Still nothing.

She calls William.

'You haven't heard then?' he asks, sounding baffled.

'Heard?'

'Josie died. A week ago.'

Her heart gives a lurch. She can't speak.

How could she not have heard? But she never listened to the news. Never bothered with a paper in Italy. And naturally there was no television in the Blomberg house. And she'd left her mobile switched off almost all of the time. She might have been on another planet. Wanted to be, really. So preoccupied with her own stupid life.

'But how? Why?'

'Overdose, they presume. Accident maybe. They didn't find a note. There'll be a post-mortem of course...'

His voice is unendurably matter of fact. Her hands are trembling. She can barely keep hold of the telephone. She collapses onto the nearest chair. William is still talking. She is only half listening. She keeps asking him to repeat things.

'But why? Why?'

'I don't know. What I think... I think the trouble with Josie was – she wanted it all. She was that kind of a girl. Whatever she had, you know, it was never enough... ' In the background she hears another phone ringing in his office.

'Got to go now. Speak later.'

She sits motionless and numb. She is aware only of the sound of her own breathing and the relentless ticking of the kitchen clock.

Wanted it all? Wanted the impossible?

No. No. She had to speak to him. Right away. Right now, to correct him. No, it wasn't that. Absolutely not. Josie didn't want it all. Just the opposite, couldn't he see that? She was looking for something really quite small, something unremarkable that would have passed unnoticed by the world she inhabited. She just wanted to cut the crap. But for her that needed a certain kind of courage that she didn't have. And she knew it. In some ways she was fearless, but that – she wasn't strong enough, never would be. To put an end to the fooling – herself as well as the world. But she couldn't carry it through. So she drew the line.

Alice picked up the phone. Dialled the first couple of digits of William's number, then cancelled. It was pointless to even try. He wouldn't understand. He never understood Josie anyway. How could he? Poor William! If she told him how much Josie had despised him, he'd never believe it.

Visions of Josie, at different places and times, at parties, shows, in studios, their talks, arguments, shouting matches, her brain seethes with Josie. She hears them yelling at one another, each full of venom, hurling at the other accusations of bad faith.

That's how it always was between them. A kind of catharsis. Each acted as a key that opened up the other's guilt. Each was utterly exposed in the eyes of the other. Nothing was concealed. Anger and acrimony a necessary stage to the unveiling of truth. No escape route, no excuses.

Looking at Josie's latest work in progress, Alice would begin the attack:

'Are you happy with this? D'you think anyone with more than half a brain is going to be fooled by this? Come off it! Who are you kidding?'

If it had social reformist pretensions, she would tell her she hadn't an ounce of politics in her body. It was all a sham. If it was slanted towards humour and wit, she would accuse her of devaluing art to the level of trivial smut.

'It's all a game for you, isn't it? Completely shallow, aren't you, Josie, really? And the worst of it is, you're not just fooling the public, you're fooling yourself.'

Josie always gave as good as she got – and more. She ridiculed Alice for clinging doggedly to outmoded, fossilized notions like *Form with a capital F*. She would hurl tirades of abuse and ridicule at her, denouncing her for acting as if she was 'so bloody superior to the rest of us! You think you're somethin' special, don't you? Fact is – no-one gives a fuck about this ivory tower rubbish. It's over!' she would bawl, 'Over! Went out with the Ark! Who the hell cares if this shape fits with this other shape, or this colour is *absolutely right* here and these two tones are *just so so perfectly attuned...*' She began to mimic with remarkable accuracy William's effete accent and emphatic delivery, ' and *oh what a superb composition*! And how *absolutely* and *supremely perfect and right it all is! How expressive! How evocative!* Bullshit! Expressive of *what*? Evocative? My arse! The only reason for what you do, Al, is so as dick-'eads like William can carry on talkin' and writin' about lines and tones and compositions as if they was discussin' the meanin' of life, and God and the universe, or somethin'. S'pose it makes them feel important. Bet it makes William feel good when he thinks about all that dosh flowin' in. Just keep slappin' on the paint, Al! You're doin' a great job! Yes really! Helpin' people to believe there's somethin' worth livin' for after all… Trouble is, at the end of the day, people don't really care. Don't really matter what you do. My kinda stuff or your kinda stuff – Comes to the same thing in the end, don't it?'

Her and Alice's fury spent, the outbursts of vitriol subsided to be replaced by a feeling that could only be described as love. Weird but true.

The last time they met, at the end of another venomous slanging match, they embraced one another. Josie unexpectedly, and for the first time, kissed her on the mouth. Alice was uneasily conscious of Josie's small hard breasts pressing against hers. She felt Josie's delicate shoulders beneath the denim shirt and her thin waist pushing insistently into the palm of her hand. Sensing Alice's resistance, Josie drew swiftly back.

'You know what?' she said lightly. 'Sounds crazy, but – well, I gotta say it – you're my best mate!' They both laughed.

The post-mortem revealed nothing. Josie had been drinking heavily the night she died. She had taken a large quantity of barbiturates. There was insufficient evidence to prove anything one way or another. An open verdict was recorded.

Alice agonises endlessly. If only she'd returned from Italy a week earlier. If only she'd been at home to pick up the phone. If only her mobile hadn't been permanently switched off. If only, if only, if only... Too late. Right, Josie? Too fuckin' late.

CHAPTER TWENTY-ONE
Epilogue

Alice and William stand shoulder to shoulder at the door of the Du Pre Gallery, looking, it feels to her, pretty pathetic – parents bursting with pride at the christening of their first child. Her first one-woman show! An occasion to celebrate! Except that she feels no particular excitement. Not even a trace of nervousness. The event has been so long in the planning: paintings and drawings arranged and rearranged countless times, so that she can hardly be bothered to look at them any more. They have grown dull to her eyes, the sense of them as offshoots of her self, so intimately connected to her she cannot bear to part with them, has faded almost to extinction. Let them all go. So what?

Once they lived, they breathed, they were her pleasure, her agony. Now she hardly recognises them as generated from her. She looks at them without pride, without shame. They have become strangers. They have become things. Commodified. Objects for sale. Moments of her life frozen in time, their colours falsely gleaming, like a corpse embalmed and painted in a gaudy imitation of life. None of this counts for anything. It's done, finished, fossilized, dead. She has a longing to be out of here, to get back into life.

Glasses of wine, red, pink and white, glide about the room on silver trays balanced deftly by girls in burgundy dresses. She grabs a glass, drinks its contents then swiftly grabs another. The girls with their trays and fixed smiles appear and reappear, pouring, filling, re-filling.

She, for once the *Star*, dutifully strives to beam and glow. This is what stars do, don't they? For Alice this is a strain. Beam and glow, glow and beam.

Soon she escapes from the doorway and William. She wanders into the room and mingles with the exclusive invitees. Do they know her? Does it matter? She clutches her glass and hangs onto the smile for dear life. Says 'yes', 'yes please' and 'thank you so much'. What, this one over here? What do I think? Oh yes. I remember now. How I agonised over it. One winter's night. Through the window. Snow made the fields blue and the moon was orange. I worked through the silence of an icy blue and orange night.

And there – yes – that was my homage to Coltrane. Have you heard of him even? Do you know who I'm talking about? Have you ever felt that exquisite ache in your heart and mind, deep down in your guts? Did you ever hope that you would die by drowning in the sounds, that they should be the last sounds you ever heard before everything went black? Did music ever make you feel like a swallow in flight in pursuit of the sun?

Who are you? What have you to do with me? What are you doing here? Your carefully tailored voices that chirrup and drone in cultured cadences, do they ever speak of ecstasy, the kind that rips hearts into pieces? Do you know anything of that? Do you have even an inkling of what you're seeing as you drink your wine and flash quick glances at the segments of coloured canvas and boards that cover the walls?

Have any of you experienced the pain, the desperate hours, the force of trying, the disappointment, the endless new starts, the longing so bad you could explode with frustration, the craziness, the rare beauty of a moment that is like a line of stars streaking across an ink-black desert?

She drinks and drinks then drinks some more. She glances across the room, over the chattering heads and fulsome smiles and catches sight of Michael flanked by her daughters. They wave and smile. She wasn't expecting to see Michael. She tries to remember when it was they last met. When was it? Must have been the last speech day at the school, just before Florence left.

People approach her to tell her things or ply her with questions. They stand in patient deference, but she can no longer think straight enough to answer in more than a mumble. Still, what could they know? She's the star isn't she? She feels increasingly incoherent. Anything goes. She has an urge to escape, rush for the door, plunge into comforting anonymity. Not a chance.

William's voice, the familiar whining drone.

'Where the hell did you learn to speak like that?' she throws at him. She doesn't care any more. He looks dumbfounded. She catches his incredulous expression and laughs hysterically. She leaves him frowning and shaking his head. Linking arms with Florence and Chloe, she dismisses their worried 'Mum? Are you all right?' with a careless 'Me? I'm fine. Have some wine! Drink up, drink up! It's my party!'

Making a spectacle of herself, her mother would have said. But what the hell? Isn't that what being a star is all about?

Through a bleary fog she sees the room beginning to empty. People approach her again. They grab her hand, squeezing it, making her cheeks wet with kisses, shrilling 'Bye bye! Thank you *so* much! Wonderful show! Bye!' She feels like a child condemned to enduring unsolicited tickles, prods and pats from repellent relatives.

William hovers in her vicinity, his features imprinted with their familiar mild dismay, eyebrows quizzically raised.

'William! *Why* are you always *here?*'

"Off with her head!" the Queen shouted at the top of her voice. Nobody moved.

"*Who cares for you?*" said Alice (she had grown to her full size by this time). "*You're nothing but a pack of cards!*"

Then she sees Jack. Quietly unobtrusive, he stands in a corner, watching her. He smiles as their eyes meet. They raise their glasses in unison.

Julius is conspicuous by his absence today. Sadly he cannot be here to share her Big Day. Perhaps – more than perhaps – almost certainly, he is not even aware of it. That's the saddest thing of all. She tried as hard as she could to make him understand, so badly she wanted to let him know. He would have been tremendously proud. Though he never sought the world's recognition for his own talent and achievements, he would, she knew, have delighted in the chance to tell the world about her. *She's my daughter, you know!*

Estelle herself could not have gloried more, if she were still around. She'd have hot-footed it back right away, from wherever she was, even from the furthest reaches of the earth, to grasp this moment. Not a second's hesitation. But it wasn't to be. She would have relished this, the pinnacle she had been striving to reach almost from the day Alice was born, despite the series of bitter disappointments – her own failure to make it, Julius's indifference to success, Alice's stubborn refusal to fulfil even the most trifling of her hopes – today would have erased all that in one tidal wave of joy. But fate had snatched away her one final chance of glory – albeit reflected, a stupid, meaningless conjunction of events, two vehicles speeding in opposite directions along a motorway in central France, a split second of inattention, the end of a life.

And now – who would have believed it? – no Julius either – a double blow. Last time she visited him, just a couple of days ago, he had given up even attempting to sit up. He just lay there, virtually motionless, every ounce of will exhausted, all force relinquished. Whilst his eyes were closed, which was most of the time, she contemplated the hands and wrists she knew so well, musician's hands, that now were shrivelled, the skin wizened almost beyond recognition, the fingernails that had always been trimmed short and meticulously filed, were now overgrown, curling over, the fingertips outlined in black. For several minutes she had rummaged through her bag and searched in the drawer beside his bed, but could find nothing to clean away the dirt. She stood up and sought a nurse, requesting she attend to this immediately, but was met only with a haughty raising of the eyebrows. *Do you think I have time for that?*

His wrists were blotchy, blue, even, in some places, from unexplained bruises. His hands and arms seemed almost weightless, hardly making a dent in the neatly turned coverlet. Once or twice he lifted his eyelids and the dark globes beneath gazed vaguely in the direction of her smiling face, but he might just as well have been blind. He showed no sign of recognition, no awareness, even, of her presence. For the first time in her life her father neither smiled nor uttered a word.

She sees him now, floating between life and death, immobile beneath spotless white bedcovers with nothing left of him to see but head and hands, all but the lower half of his arms concealed within over-sized pyjama sleeves of cream cotton striped with sky-blue, the skin like a creased voile shroud carelessly wrapped around his limbs. The core of his body no longer adhered to its cover and, so it seemed to Alice, the essence of Julius, her father, the person she knew, had become detached from its physical moorings: there was no connection any more between the two.

She watches his frail figure stretched out beneath the covers, surrounded by white walls and white ghosts that come and go, exchanging whispers. She stands within a haze of drinking chattering humanity, but she inhabits a different space altogether, somewhere oceans away. She's listening to his full-throated laugh, sees him standing beside her, glass in hand, eyes crinkled up, his face broken into a myriad lines from every joyous joke he has ever told, every posturing parade he has ever ridiculed, every absurd human farce, every delicious debunking of pretentious tosh.

Music was his way of reaching out, his way of bridging chasms. He never lost his faith in the power of melody, harmony and rhythm to reach into people's hearts, to draw them together, somehow.

It shocks her that already she is thinking about him in the past tense. Already he is turning into nothing more than a memory. Even as he still lives and breathes. He never put his faith into words, but she knows what they would have been – something like: 'if music has the power to transport me to a higher dimension, if I can succeed in sharing this luminous experience with others, once they have tasted that, everything else will shrivel away to nothing.'

His words? Not really. It didn't sound like him. Too flowery. Her words then? Or a mixture of both perhaps?

Or maybe it wasn't that at all. Maybe it was just for him, exclusively. Because music was the one thing that gave shape and meaning to his life. She can only surmise. But she knows, without needing to be told, that making music was his refuge from chaos, the randomness of life. The act of reaching towards a world of perfect balance gave purpose to his life. Without that, disorder, unreason, unfathomable suffering would overwhelm him. Us. Everyone. The making of music, of art, is the key, not the end product, which itself always seems to fall short.

Depths of love infused his playing. People responded to it. It brought them pleasure, temporary, but intense. Even transports of joy sometimes. Well, perhaps. Who can ever know for sure?

Now she can hear his voice calling, calling out to anyone that cares to listen, trying with all his might to make them see that all that counts in life is to play from the heart. She grins broadly as she hears him sing out once again his joy at just being in the world, the way he does when he has a glass in his hand, the more he drinks, the more loudly his voice reverberates. '*L'chaym!*'

He's really belting it out now: she can hear him so clearly, repeating it over and over at the top of his voice. He's lifting his glass as high as his arm will stretch. 'To Life, to Life!' No more, no less.

Right now it is his voice and only his voice she can hear.

Printed in Great Britain
by Amazon